perfect VILLAIN

USA Today Bestselling Authors

J.L. BECK & S. RENA

EVERYONE HAS
AN ADDICTION.

Siân Giuliani
IS MINE.

VILLAIN

1

CHRISTIAN

Darkness is a constant that'll never die.

Many are afraid of it and the things that lurk within.

But then again, many aren't me.

I thrive on living in the shadows, the corruption, even the immortality of it all. I enjoy only two things more than the blackness: the fear I evoke in others and Siân Giuliani.

She's the product of my obsession, and her fear feeds my soul the most. It's a drug, an addiction I'll never shake. So, you'll understand why I watch her.

There she is, walking away from the campus with a friend in tow. She looks nothing like she did before, nothing like the first time I watched her. Her skin is still as smooth as silk and blemish-free, but she's a shade darker now, her olive complexion a gift from the Florida sun.

Her hair is different, longer, and dyed back to her natural brown. I like her with darker hair. It suits her better than the blond she previously wore.

From where I sit, parked in a Ferrari that's as black as my soul, I can see the shade of red that paints her lips, and I like that too. My dick twitches at the thought of her wrapping that pretty mouth around my shaft. It's a never-ending fantasy, really, one that's long past due to become a reality.

Usually, all I do is watch, but tonight, that changes.

Tonight, I'll make good on the promise I made to her all those years ago and let her know I'm back.

She belongs to me, was promised to me as a boy, and meant to be my wife the moment she came of age. The first time I saw her face, we were kids. She was ten, and I was fourteen. The sweet, innocent girl who had no idea about the life she was fated to live.

The Russos and the Giulianis are two of Italy's most ruthless families. We were born to hate each other, cursed by an age-old rivalry carried out by our fathers—a feud set to be squashed by the promise of an alliance. To put an end to the war between our families and strengthen their territories, Giuliani gifted me his only daughter with the promise of an heir. Together, we were supposed to reign over Italy, bringing the lifelong dispute to an end with our bond.

I knew then we were different. Unlike me, she was pure and oblivious to the world around her. I was raised to be my father's son, exposed to blood, carnage, and murder early on. By my fifteenth birthday, I'd already taken a life, and by the age of seventeen, I discovered my need to observe.

Before we had a chance to meet, at least the way we were supposed to, she was ripped away from me. Marco reneged on our deal, denying me what was mine. My father is a greedy man, and he doesn't take well to broken contracts. I learned another valuable lesson that night. Every alliance comes with secrets. And the skeletons buried beneath the pact our families made proved to be the worst of them all.

Marco never saw it coming, never smelled the deceit that brewed right under his nose. The saying goes, *keep your friends close and your enemies closer*. Well, what does one do when the friend is the enemy? Or when the woman you love sentences you to death and sells your daughter to the highest bidder?

He gave his last breath to save his precious daughter. For years, I searched until I found her—five years ago on her twentieth birthday. Far away from Italy in a small town in the northeast region of the United States is where I discovered her, protected and tucked away in one of the least likely of places.

For months, I surveyed her, and right when we were *getting* to know each other, my father called me home, dragging me away from her with his orders. Leaving was the last thing I wanted to do. After all, I'd spent time and many resources trying to find her. But if my father knew where I was and what I was doing, or that Siân Giuliani was indeed alive, shit would have turned south...quick.

I couldn't have that. My father couldn't know she was still alive because I led him to believe she perished in that fire with her family. I also get a thrill out of defying him every chance I get. She's mine, and I'll claim her on my own terms.

Yes, I could have taken her five years ago, and that was the initial plan, but where is the fun in ending the chase so soon? I like to hunt, to watch —and knowing I can turn her world upside down in the blink of an eye makes the wait all that more delicious. But she also mesmerized me, and the more I followed her, the more I learned about her. I quickly realized that to have her the way I wanted, I'd need to win her trust.

So even though I wanted to take her that very first time, I didn't. I returned to Italy as my father requested, but not before making a vow to her I intend to keep. She'll forever be my *topolina,* and we *will* meet again.

When I think back on it, my blood boils, but I push it away. It doesn't matter anymore because I'm here. That's the benefit of having connections all over the world. After I returned to Italy, I lost track of her for a while, but money goes a long way in getting what you want.

And for Siân, I'd pay any fucking price

When my guy found her, I smiled for the first time in my life. She'd moved and changed her name. Back then, she went by another moniker, something plain that blended in with the rest of the females in her town. But today, she's taken back her namesake, *Siân*, only now, she's chosen Danforth as her surname.

Siân and her friend draw closer, giving me a better view of her face. She's as fucking gorgeous as she was all that time ago. Not that I expected anything different. She's always been beautiful. I'm not the only one to notice it. My hands form into fists when a group of guys turns to watch her ass. Unlike her friend, who seems to enjoy the attention, Siân wraps her arms around herself and directs her focus into her phone.

A grin forms on my lips. "That's my girl," I mutter to myself.

It's clear to me from the slouch of her shoulders and the somber expression that she'd rather be anywhere but here. The two couldn't be any more different. Siân is more reserved and quiet. When I knew her last, she stayed to herself. Never in a million years would she be caught dead in a place like this.

But I guess when you start over and try to erase the life you've run from, you change everything about yourself. Except people like us, people born into a world of chaos, we eventually learn that it'll follow us everywhere. It's ingrained in our DNA, and the sooner one accepts that fate is inevitable, one will unlock their potential.

She disappears into the bar after her friend, and the doors muffle out the loud music when they close. There's a large window in the front, but soon, a line wraps around the building, blocking my view. I've gone too long without seeing her, and I'll be damned if I go a minute longer.

I exit the car, letting the door slam shut after securing my gun in my waistband under my shirt. I pull on my leather jacket as an extra precaution. The need to use my weapon will probably never arise tonight, but I don't go anywhere without it.

Crossing the street, I walk to the front of the line, ignoring all the pissed-off rants from those waiting to enter the bar. The bouncer doesn't hesitate to accept the hundred-dollar bill I hold out and moves aside to let me in. Immediately, I'm met with the stench of cigarettes and alcohol. It's loud on the other side of the threshold, the music drowning out the voices of everyone around me. A thick cloud of smoke sticks to the ceiling that's caked with tar from years of tobacco buildup. Cheap, backless stools line a single bar on the left side of the room just off the entryway. Old picture frames adorn the dark-colored walls along with beer posters and other dated marketing material.

It's a full house. The bar is jam-packed with swaying bodies as people dance, converse, and indulge in their drinks of choice. It's not a place I would have ever imagined Siân in. She's not the partying type, and in the past, she's stayed to herself.

I scan the room in search of her, finding her a moment later at the bar. She's ineffectively trying to wave over the bartender, her frustration growing with each passing second.

I trail my gaze down her frame, letting it linger on the curve of her ass. *Life has definitely treated her well.* Siân turns, and I catch a glimpse of her face. Just like back in the car, my dick stirs at the sight of her. Green eyes point in my direction, but it's more as if she's looking through me. Then she pouts and puts her attention back on the bar.

My spine tingles in anticipation, and my feet move toward her all on their own. And just like that, destiny has spoken, and for the very first time, my *topolina* will know my name, and by the end of this, she'll be screaming it.

VILLAIN

2

SIÂN

The smell of smoke, sweat, and liquor permeates the air, filling my nostrils and swirling deep in my lungs with each breath I take. Kyla stands beside me in the packed bar. It's the last place I'd prefer to be tonight, but Kyla insisted.

"When did Josh and Taj say they were coming again?" she yells into my ear, making my eardrum rattle. The music thunders all around us, making it impossible for me to hear myself think, let alone hear what someone else says.

I pull my phone from my jean pocket with a grunt. The denim clings to me like a second skin. I'd rather be at home in my comfy sweatpants reading a book and drinking a glass of wine, but… instead, I'm here. The screen of my phone lights up, and I check the time.

Late. He's fucking late. I wish I could say this isn't a recurring thing, but it's feeling that way.

"They're late. Ten minutes to be exact," I yell into her ear and shove my phone back into my pocket.

Kyla nods and wraps her pink-painted lips around the bottle of beer she ordered a couple of minutes ago. I'm drinking water because alcohol inhibits you, and I'm the least risky person I know for more than one reason.

"If Josh wasn't so hot, I'd ghost him and pick someone else out of the crowd. There are plenty of worthy candidates in this bar tonight."

That's Kyla. Fun, carefree, and always looking for her next hookup. The opposite of me in every single way.

"Easy for you to say. Josh isn't your boyfriend." I try not to sound as dissatisfied as I feel, but if I'm being honest, things haven't been looking good for a while now.

We've been having problems, and I don't think either of us wants to admit it, but we're growing apart. It started out merely as a physical thing. I never intended to let my feelings become involved, but I started to care for Taj. I gave him my virginity even when I knew I shouldn't. He was my professor, and I was working under him as his teacher's assistant.

Morally, we were crossing a line, but morals didn't mean shit to me. Life is too short to worry about what someone else thinks is right or wrong. I earned the grade I got, regardless of whether I sucked his dick.

That isn't my primary problem. No, my problem lies in the eerie feeling that follows me wherever I go. Ever since I came to America, I've been on the run, fleeing from an imaginary shadow I can never escape or see. All I know is, if I let that shadow catch me, everyone I love or care about will be killed.

It happened once, and I will not let it happen again.

Which was why I never let anything turn serious. Relationships are a no-go because eventually, people end up hurt because of me. Either that or I have to disappear into the darkness without a word said.

I would never want that to happen to me, so I choose not to do that to others. Taj isn't like all the others, though, which led me to my current predicament.

Leaning into Kyla's side, I say, "You know I can't break things off with Taj if you're trying to hook up with his best friend. It will make things messy."

"You're thinking too much about this. If you want to end things with him, tell him that. What's he going to say?"

"It's not what he's going to say. It's what happens after we've ended things and you're still hooking up with Josh that's the problem."

Kyla takes a long pull from her beer bottle. Her gray eyes meet mine, and my irritation toward her mounts. Maybe I'm jealous of how carefree she can be? Or maybe it's the fact that she isn't running for her life, watching over her shoulder for a sadistic stalker to find her.

The urge to tell her I'm leaving right this second sits on the edge of my tongue, but something stops me.

No, not something...

"We both know I don't stay with a guy long enough for it to become serious. We'll have sex a couple of times, and then, like two grown adults, we'll move on."

I shake my head. "You've completely disregarded the fact that—"

She interrupts me, pressing her finger to my lips.

"Excuse you," I grumble, ready to bat her hand away.

It's then that I notice she appears to have gone into a trance. Her gaze is wide, and there's this lustful shine to her eyes. It's a look I've never seen before. She reminds me of a bunny in a trap, waiting for her predator to pounce.

"Sweet mother-of-fucking-pearl. If the actual devil was a human, this man would look just like him."

I barely hear the words she's speaking from the loud thump of music.

Curious to see just who she's talking about, I turn on my ballet flats and look toward the entrance. It seems the entire room is looking in the same direction and at the same man as we are.

As soon as my gaze lands on him, I feel the intense urge to look away. The air in my lungs becomes heavy, and it feels like I'm breathing air through a straw. Who is this man, and why does he have such a strange effect on me?

A shiver ripples down my spine, and even as I feel the rush to look away, I can't. I physically can't stop myself from staring at this man. I swallow around the lump forming in my throat and try not to show interest. That's hard to do, though, when the man looks like he walked off the cover of a damn magazine.

Even in the dim lighting of the bar, I can see his piercing blue eyes. They home in on me, wrapping like a meaty fist around my throat. My eyes move over his unruly blond hair and down his body. His skin is the color of roasted almonds. His jeans are tight and tailored to his perfectly sculpted body.

His white T-shirt fits like a glove over his broad shoulders, and I can make out the lines of his muscles beneath the fabric. My mouth waters, and I lick my lips involuntarily. He's paired his entire ensemble with a leather jacket and a pair of black boots.

"He's not the devil. He's the villain in every single fairy tale ever told," I say more to myself than Kyla, who I find still at my back when I turn around to face her.

A smile breaks across her face. "Well, that villain is headed your way, baby. It's your time to shine."

I roll my eyes, trying to hide the turbulent waves of excitement sloshing around inside my belly. I'm still dating Taj, and Mr. Tall, Dark, and Handsome is the last thing I need in my life.

A second later, the air around me shifts. The tiny hairs at the back of my neck stand on end, and I force myself to breathe. *Oh, God.* I don't even know this man, so why does he have this strange effect on me? Better yet, why haven't I run into the women's bathroom to get away? This isn't me. I don't take risks. I don't talk to strange men I've only seen across the room.

I'm seconds away from running away, the panic finally reaching my brain when I feel the heat of his body brush against mine.

"Ladies." The mysterious man's deep voice reaches inside me and swirls around like smoke. My mouth has suddenly become dry, my tongue a useless organ.

"Hello, my name is Kyla, and this is Siân," Kyla, of course, introduces both of us with a dazzling smile.

I'm afraid to move, let alone draw a breath into my lungs, but somehow, I force my lips up into a smile.

I'm not sure there are words to describe how handsome this man is. His blond hair shines in the sparkling light. It's a little unkempt in a way that makes it seem like he just ran his fingers through it. The sides are cut a little shorter, and the strands on top are at a finger's length.

His features are hard and rough but manly, with an edge. His cheekbones are high, and his chin is angular and as sharp as a razor blade. Everything about him says *I'm bad, and I know it*. Usually, that is the first sign I need to turn and walk away, but I'll admit I'm intrigued by this man.

His full, very kissable lips curve up into a smile. It's the grin of a predator if I ever saw one. "It's a pleasure to meet you, ladies. I'm Christian."

I can see the wheels in Kyla's head spinning. She's going to try to set us up. *Shit.* I open my mouth to say something—what I'm not sure of yet—but she beats me to it.

"I apologize, Christian, but I need to use the ladies' room. Perhaps you can keep my best friend company while I'm gone?"

I don't even realize I'm snarling at her until I notice Christian looking at me. *Fuck.*

"I can come with you," I tell Kyla.

She smiles like the witch she is. "No, no. Keep our new friend company. I'll be right back."

Sure she will. The last time she did this, I had to search the entire bar to find her. I watch anxiously as she walks away, throwing daggers from my eyes. She'll pay for this.

"Why do I get the feeling you don't like being alone with anyone you don't know?" Christian's question draws my attention away from Kyla.

I turn to face him, doing my best not to appear intimidated by his presence. I shrug. "Isn't that any smart woman at a bar with her best friend?"

The smells of the bar linger around me, but Christian's intoxicating scent overpowers them. He smells of spicy, clove, danger, and sin. Stupidly, I want to lean in and take a deeper whiff, but that would be strange, right?

"Not a woman looking for someone to hook up with, which your friend is definitely looking for. You, however..."

His response has me on the defense. "Yeah, and what am I looking for?"

He shrugs without a response. The air sizzles around us, and I can feel the attraction growing. I tell myself it's all in his image, but even just having met him, it feels deeper than that. The bartender comes over, and he orders a bourbon. A moment later, a crystal glass with brown liquid is set in front of him. I watch as he swirls the bourbon around in the glass before taking a gulp of the alcohol. He doesn't even flinch, and I watch his throat as he swallows, his muscles flexing, drawing me in.

"I think you're looking for fun."

My brows pinch together in confusion. "Looking for fun? What do you mean? I'm already having fun."

He laughs, and it's the deep, throaty kind that makes you tingle in all the best places. "If this is your idea of fun, then I don't want to see what your idea of rest and relaxation is."

I wrinkle my nose at him. "Are you insinuating that I'm not fun?"

He takes another swig of his drink and places the now empty glass on the bar.

I will admit I'm a bit fired up by his assumption, but I don't show it, or at least I don't think I do. The space between us is nothing but a foot, yet somehow, he moves closer, his giant frame invading mine. He has to be six feet or taller, and compared to my height of five-three, I must look like a dwarf beneath him. I crane my neck back to continue looking up at him.

He takes mercy on me and leans down. The smell of cinnamon and sweet bourbon clings to his breath. My eyes linger on his lips for so long I can picture him kissing me. Would he kiss me hard, consuming me from the outside in, or would his kiss be gentle like a feather? My focus breaks when those lips of his start moving.

"I'm insinuating that... you're guarded. You don't look like the type who takes risks. You look..." His gaze roams over me, and I can feel it burning a road map across my skin. "Safe."

My cheeks heat. I'm flustered or maybe embarrassed. *Yes, the latter it is.* This man I've never met, that I know nothing about, has just insulted me.

"Safe?" The word comes out in a squeak.

Christian smiles, and I'd smack that smile off his face if I had enough balls. This man is intimidating, cocky, and honest, and I don't like it. Mostly because he can read me like no one else can, and that's terrifying when he's nothing more than a stranger.

His hand comes out of nowhere, and a small gasp escapes my lips when his fingertips contact my cheek as he brushes a couple of strands of hair from my face. His fingers are calloused, and I imagine them touching me in places I have no right thinking about a stranger touching me, especially one who could be dangerous.

"I don't mean that in an asshole way. I just mean you seem like the safe type. Never going anywhere alone, and definitely not talking to some stranger in a bar."

I lick my lips. "You're not wrong. I don't usually talk to strangers. In fact, I don't even like coming to bars, but my friend drags me along every time she goes. She's always blabbing about needing to get out of the house, be social, and meet people."

"She isn't wrong. It's good to get out, and it's even better to take risks. You never know when it could lead to something amazing."

I get the feeling he's reflecting on meeting him. "You mean meeting you?"

My eyes catch the way his tongue darts out over his bottom lip. My toes curl inside my flats. I can feel the air growing hotter around us.

"Well, of course, yes. Meeting me will be the height of your night. I promise."

His arrogant attitude makes me smile, and I roll my eyes.

"You're very arrogant."

"You're very beautiful. Has anyone ever told you that before?"

I can't believe I'm having a conversation with a complete stranger in the middle of a crowded bar, and he's calling me beautiful.

I'm reminded once again that this isn't me. I'm not this person.

"A time or two." I pause, and my anxiety sparks. "Tell me, what is it that brought you to this side of the bar? Surely, I'm not the only gorgeous woman here."

Something familiar flickers in his blue eyes, but I can't pinpoint the look in my mind. "I'm not sure. I just saw your face and felt drawn to you. Maybe it's fate?"

"I don't believe in fate," I tell him, the honesty bleeding out of me.

He raises a brow. "Really? What do you believe in?"

"I believe that if it's meant to be, then it will be. Everything finds a way in life."

"That sounds pretty close to fate to me." The sarcasm in his voice is unmistakable.

When I don't respond to him, he continues, "Well, I believe, Siân, that if you want something bad enough, you will do whatever is humanly possible to achieve it. Sometimes you might lie, barter, or even steal to get it. You might even just take it if it's something you want badly enough."

I can feel our conversation going in a different direction. The warning blinks bright in my mind. I shouldn't cross the line, shouldn't take a risk like this, not knowing this man, but maybe he's right. Maybe it's time to live a little. I've spent the past fifteen years trapped in a bubble of worry. What can a night of risk and fun hurt?

My gaze moves past him and to the entrance across the room. I realize then that Taj still isn't here. *Safe. You're safe.* A man who doesn't even know me can see how pitiful and inside my head I am. How worried and insecure I am.

What do I have to fear? It's been five years. I return my attention to Christian and he's staring at me. Wait, not at me, but right through me.

"What's something you want, Christian?" His name rolls off my tongue lustfully.

He leans into me, his lips almost touching mine. He's so close I swear I can feel his heartbeat beneath his shirt. He's inside me, in my head, under my skin, invading my senses.

His voice is a whisper when he speaks, so low I'm uncertain I hear him correctly. "You."

I swallow my tongue, and it's then that Kyla reappears, sauntering up to us with a grin on her face. Christian takes a step back at her reappearance, and I suck a ragged breath into my lungs, unaware I was holding my breath.

"Am I interrupting something?" she asks, grabbing her beer off the bar.

I wipe my now sweaty palms on the front of my jeans. "No, of course not. We were just talking." More like sharing an unexplainable moment. I don't know what it is about this guy, but I feel connected to him in a way I've never felt connected to anyone.

"Oh look, Taj and Josh finally showed up," Kyla announces, her eyes beaming, causing both Christian and me to turn our attention to the entrance.

I spot Taj and Josh easily. They're both standing there scanning the crowd, sticking out like a pair of sore thumbs. She must be excited to see Josh.

It's not a fancy bar, but Taj could've at least changed out of his professor getup. I swallow down my frustration when they start toward us. As I drag my attention away from them, I look back up at Christian. His gaze is trained on Taj. It's cold, and his features are twisted with disdain. He must sense my gaze on him because he snaps out of it and looks down at me, a grim smile appearing on his lips.

"I think it's time I go, but it was very nice to meet you, Siân. Maybe I'll see you around."

I nod, taken aback by his gruff departure.

He walks away and nearly bumps shoulders with Taj on the way out. This strange coldness fills the space around me where the mysterious man stood just moments ago. Taj approaches with a look of confusion on his handsome face.

"Was that guy giving you trouble?" His tone turns protective.

I shake my head. "No. I don't even know him." *Though it felt like he knew me.*

"Okay," he replies and engulfs me in a hug. His embrace is warm, and his clean cologne scent fills my nostrils, but it isn't what I want. It's safe. I'm safe, and for some reason, I know that stranger's words will stick with me for the rest of the night. "I apologize for being late. Some stuff at the university came up, and I had to stay late to finish grading papers."

"It's okay," I lie.

It's not okay. Nothing is okay. Everything about Taj is safe, from his russet brown hair to his pale green eyes. He's a professor with a good job and a heart of gold, but he's not who I want. None of this is what I want... he isn't what I want.

"Hey, are you with me?" Taj takes me by the cheeks, forcing my gaze to meet his.

I stare up into his green eyes. There's a smile on his face, a smile put there by me.

"I'm fine. Everything is fine. Let's get some drinks and enjoy the rest of the night together." I force myself to smile and move through the motions.

All I can think is *everything isn't fine, but it will be soon.*

VILLAIN

3

CHRISTIAN

Safe is the way I described her, but boring is more like it. It's been a week since I approached her at the bar, and something tells me that talking to me was the liveliest she's been. In fact, I'm pretty fucking sure of it.

After I left that night, I did what I do best—watched. I sat outside, waiting patiently for her to leave. To my surprise, she was alone. In my short time with her, she never mentioned having a man, but from the way she tensed up when Kyla informed her the guys they were waiting on had arrived, I put two and two together. That and the wide grin the one guy gave her told me that he is her boyfriend. Whether it was Josh or Taj, that's yet to be determined. I didn't stick around long enough to figure out who either of them was. But I'd bet any amount the one I bumped on the way out was him if the look of disgust on his face was any indication.

It was probably for the best that she left the bar alone, because had he been with her, I would have killed him in front of her. Then my plan would have unraveled before it ever started. And there's nothing I hate more than a ruined plan—that and knowing some other asshole is spending time with my woman. So, fate aligned, and I didn't have to murder anyone.

I trailed her closely that night, staying far enough away that she never noticed me on the opposite side of the street. The walk to the small house she shares with Kyla is only a few blocks from campus and the bar. And I know this because I've watched her long enough to observe Kyla entering the home with a key of her own.

Along the way, I couldn't help but notice how skittish Siân was, glancing over her shoulder every so often with her arms wrapped tightly around her frame.

She can thank me for that, too.

My poor topolina, so small and afraid in this big, bad world. The sadist in me loves it. The thought shouldn't bring a grin to my lips, but it does. The meekness, the constant fear and desire to flee—it's like music to my soul. If I didn't have plans for the two of us, I would have chased her down and reminded her of the little games we used to play before I had to leave her.

Instead, I waited until she disappeared into her home and watched for the light to flicker on upstairs. And every day since, I continued to observe. Her bedroom window is within a perfect view from the lamppost across the street. Unfortunately, only her silhouette is visible because she keeps her blinds closed. I wondered just how many neighborhood boys have gotten off to her naked shadow.

She tries to go unnoticed, except when you try that it makes you the most visible. Those who live their lives openly aren't who people want. It's the shy type that intrigues people the most. Their reserved personalities speak the loudest. Even if they tiptoed through life, they'd never be able to hide.

Siân's routine is the same: the coffee shop, school, home, and the occasional night out with Kyla. Rinse and repeat. Safe and boring.

I decided to give her more time and allow her to enjoy what's left of this pathetic existence she's chosen. Besides, it gave me the space I needed to figure out everything I could about this new version of her. That time is up now, and today, we start phase two of my plan.

Make her fall in love with me.

And that brings me here—the coffee shop. A place I'd never step foot in otherwise. The flood of voices, the loud buzzing of brewing equipment, people typing away on their computers, and the smells—bitter coffee grounds, spices, and steaming milk. I hate it all. But I'm here because of Siân. She's the reason for everything.

"What can I get you?" the petite barista asks.

She smiles and runs her gaze along the length of my frame. There's a gleam in her eyes, one I'm used to. The lust, the need—they're all the same, blinded by their libido and a handsome face.

"What's good here?" I question. Not that I care, but appearance is important if I want this to go off without a hitch.

"Well," she sing-songs, and from my peripheral, I notice her shifting from one foot to the other. "I guess that depends on what you want." She leans in and pokes her chest in my direction, drawing my attention to the extremely low neckline of her uniform shirt.

Here we are, another girl displaying all the signs that she's looking to get laid. It would be a lie if I said she didn't have a nice rack, but I remain unfazed by her blatant attempts. There's only one woman for me, and she is far from being her.

To move things along, I pick the first thing I see on the menu. "I'll take a cappuccino."

She rings up my order, and I pay her in cash, then step out of the way for the person behind me. I nestle into a booth in the far corner.

According to the clock on the wall behind the register, Siân will be here any minute now.

As if on cue, I see the top of her little brown head over the fence as she turns the corner. With her head down, she walks with her purse hanging from one shoulder, a backpack dangling from the other, and her attention on her phone.

A moment later, she enters the loud coffee shop and blends in with the other customers. Instead of standing in line like everyone else, she heads straight for the pick-up desk, and I soon realize her drink is already waiting for her.

I leave my seat and stroll across the room. The floor is sticky, music plays through the overhead speakers, and thankfully the shop is busy. Planting myself directly behind her, I run my fingers through my hair and pull the wax mold from my back pocket. Siân continues to converse with the barista, completely oblivious to my presence.

She flips her hair and offers the girl behind the counter a grim smile. "Thank you, Angela. It's a good thing I ordered ahead today." She makes small talk.

Thanks to her wide-open purse, I easily slip her keys from the bag. That's another thing I've noticed about her. As guarded as she seems to be with herself, she isn't the same way with her belongings. Every time I've watched her, she hasn't bothered to secure her bag. If someone wanted to mug her, they'd have no problem doing it.

Angela goes on about how busy they've been as Siân pretends to be interested. She goes with the flow to appear as normal as everyone around her. A part of me wants to feel a little sad that she hasn't yet figured out that people like us don't get to be normal. But I push the thoughts aside and steal an imprint of her house key with the mold. But Siân is on the move again before I put her key ring back where it belongs.

"Thank you, Angela. I'll let you get back to work and will see you tomorrow." Siân nods and raises her drink to the woman.

"Shit," I mutter to myself. If I don't act fast, she'll most likely figure out her keys aren't where they're supposed to be.

Thinking on my feet, I do the only thing I can do and bump into her, purposely knocking her cup out of her hand. The piping-hot liquid splatters across the floor and on the toes of my boots.

"Dammit," Siân curses.

She immediately snatches napkins from the dispenser on the counter, then squats to clean up the mess I made. She's so focused on the spill that she sets her bags down next to her.

"I'm so sorry," I admit. Gathering a handful of napkins, I join her on the floor, using my body to shield her view. "I shouldn't have been in such a rush."

Siân doesn't look up. Her only concern is her ruined drink. Keeping an eye on her, I use this moment to slip the keys back to where I got them. With my hand on my knees, I crane my neck, pretending that I'm recognizing who she is for the first time.

"Well, this is a nice surprise," I say playfully.

"Really? Nice surprise. Dude, you knocked my drink from my hand," she scorns me, yet still hasn't taken a moment to meet my gaze.

"And now I'm going to offer to buy you another."

As the words leave my mouth, the barista calls my name. "I have a cappuccino for Christian."

That gets Siân's attention because she snaps her head up, and a gasp escapes her the second she lays eyes on me. We stand simultaneously, with me taking the wet napkins from her. Our fingers touch, and she pulls back, then forces her spine straight. She's pretending again, attempting to make herself less small and flustered in my presence.

I dispose of the trash without taking my eyes off her. Her eyes follow me as I move to accept the drink I ordered and had honestly forgotten about. When I face her again, Siân's green eyes are slightly dilated, much like they were that night at the bar. She has a reaction to me, one that I sense makes her uncomfortable. Though not because she doesn't like it. No, that's not it at all.

Her breathing quickens, and her cheeks have turned a light shade of pink because she's captivated. I've wormed my way into her thoughts, the memory of our brief time together festering inside her. My words being the only thing she can think about.

One thing I'm good at is reading people, and Siân is no exception. It's clear in the way she moves—barely shying away so that she isn't so obvious. How her eyes land on everything but what's in front of her. The subtle hitch in her breaths when I'm nearby. It rang loud and clear in the way her body tensed at the mention of the two men who came to meet her and Kyla. And in the way she nearly came apart just from being next to me. This life she's chosen to live is smothering her, and deep down, she's been waiting for the likes of me.

That safety net she's built around herself crumbled the moment we breathed the same rancid, smoke-filled air.

"Christian," she mutters after a beat while I claim my drink from the counter.

I turn to see her gathering her bags from the floor. She drops her chin to her chest and tucks a strand of hair behind her ear.

Stepping close to her, I smirk. "So, I do have an effect on you. You know, remembering my name is the first sign that we're on the right track." I tighten my hold on the cappuccino and wet my lips, unable to keep my playful grin at bay.

Siân follows the path of my tongue, her breaths turning into short, shallow bursts of air. A smile teeters on her lips, but she wills it away and pulls her bottom lip between her teeth. I have half a mind to reach out and run the pad of my thumb over her plump lips.

I don't, though. It's a long game, and I'm already having too much fun. When I claim her, and I mean claim every single inch, she'll be begging for it.

"Really," she says after a beat. "And what track is that?"

I inch closer so she has no choice but to peer up at me. God, she looks so fucking sexy from this angle. She's petite, probably standing just a few inches above five feet—not quite average, but not so short that kissing her will be a problem.

Her light and natural makeup is perfect against her olive complexion. And her bright green eyes and very kissable lips are the highlight of her features. It would have been a shame had she covered them with loads of makeup.

"The one that puts us together," I tease and reach out to swipe her hair behind her ear, and like the other night, she blushes.

Siân nods and glances away before staring up at me again. It's a feeble attempt to disguise her reaction to me.

"Right. Fate, how could I have forgotten?" she adds sarcastically.

"Exactly." I pause for a beat, letting my gaze run along her frame, logging every inch of her to memory. "Let me buy you another coffee. I caused you to spill yours, and based on how frazzled you seem, I'd say you need it. Plus, it looks like I ruined your shirt, too."

"Frazzled? What's that supposed to mean?"

There, there, girl. She's easily tempered. Good to know.

"Just what it sounds like."

Siân rolls her eyes, then takes in the large stain along the hem of her blouse. Her shoulders slump, and a soft gasp slips past her lips. My cock twitches at the sound of her low, near moan.

"Dammit. I didn't even notice it at first. But—" She sighs. "It'll be fine. It's just a shirt."

"Oh, come on. Let me replace the drink and buy you a new shirt. There has to be a boutique around here, right?"

"No," she huffs out. "It's okay. I'm already late for class."

"Well then, here." I hold my cappuccino out to her. "Take mine. And I'll accept a rain check on treating you to another, or—something better."

Siân stares at the cup in my hand and shakes her head, despite obviously wanting to accept it. "I can't take your drink."

"I insist," I urge by grabbing her hand and forcing her to wrap her fingers around the cup.

A shock of electricity spreads from my fingers all the way up my arm, and the hairs in its path stand at attention. The rest of my body seems to come to life as well—my heart skips a beat, my breathing catches for a moment, and my manhood twitches, settling down the instant she pulls away. For years, I've wondered what it would feel like to touch her skin, and it's everything I imagined it to be. Supple, and way too delicate for me.

"Then what will you have?" I say after blinking to clear my thoughts.

"It's fine, really. I don't even like the stuff."

Her brows knit together, confusion building on her face. "Then why did you buy it?"

I shrug. "I guess I just felt like taking a risk."

She catches the reference to our conversation the other night and lets out a low laugh. "That's right, Mr. Risk Taker."

"And have you taken any lately?"

Siân doesn't answer, but her eyes and body language give it all away.

"Still holding on to those life vests, huh? You can let go, love. I won't let you drown."

"I-I take risks."

"Yeah?"

"Yes. I do," she states boldly, but the tremor in her voice tells another story.

"Name one." When she doesn't offer a response, I continue, "I'll wait." Crossing my arms over my chest, I lean in a little closer.

Her breathing changes again, but she doesn't shy away as I expect her to. "You're arrogant. You know that?"

"I actually do. It's one of my best traits, don't you think? And I'm still waiting to hear about these risks you've been taking. Tell me all about your daring side."

"Who said I had one?"

"You. Just now when you claimed you've taken a risk. Plus, we all have one."

She huffs and shuffles from one leg to the next. "Fine. I haven't. Happy now?" she feigns annoyance.

But I read right through her little show. She's more than intrigued, and soon enough, I'll take what's rightfully mine. *Her.*

"No," I say a second later.

"Then, Christian, I don't know what to tell you. But thank you for the coffee. I need to get going." Siân attempts to walk around me, her breath hitching when I wrap an arm around her waist to keep her from getting away.

We make eye contact, neither of us saying a word. Her face is close to mine. Her lips are parted and her eyes glazed over—all the signs of attraction rearing their pretty little heads. I could kiss her right now, and that daredevil side she's trying so hard to keep at bay will allow me.

But not now. She's not ready yet.

Siân breaks the moment and glances down at her hand, a frown forming on her face. She removes something from between the cup and the sleeve. It's a thin folded piece of paper, and when she opens it, a phone number is scribbled beneath the name Angela.

Her eyes widen, and I swear I notice a twinge of jealousy, but she pushes it away. "Looks like someone is interested in you," she deadpans.

I take the scrap of paper, ball it into a fist, and watch as a sigh of relief washes over her. "I'm good."

"You don't want to call her? She's pretty and really sweet."

I don't respond. Instead, I only stare at her, enjoying the way her cheeks heat from the conversation. She doesn't want me to call this woman any more than I want to myself. It's a charade and a pretty damn bad one.

"You know what I want," I whisper into her ear while digging my fingers into her side. She must have forgotten she was still in my arms because she flinches when I do.

Siân wets her lips but doesn't break our embrace. "Who said I was available?"

I smirk and mimic her, licking my bottom lip, then stroke her cheek. "And I told you that sometimes you just have to take what you want. No matter what."

She gulps so loud I hear it over the music and talking that surrounds us. Stepping back a little, I hold my hand out to her, and she peers down at it quizzically.

"Your phone," I answer before she can ask the question.

"Why?"

"Can't cash in on that rain check without your number?"

She doesn't move. "I don't know, Christian. I have—"

Already knowing what she's about to say next, I cut her off. Fuck her boyfriend. She belongs to me, and soon enough, she'll realize that.

I tilt my head a little and draw in a breath. "We're taking risks, remember?"

Siân's shoulders drop with her exhale. She's contemplating my request, her doubt and interest battling each other to take hold. As she thinks through all the consequences of accepting what I'm asking for, I take a moment to open the app I've used in the past. It's a cloning program that makes what I do easier. Knowing the ins and outs of potential victims' conversations keeps me one step ahead of them and any shit that may arise.

"Aw, come on, Siân. It's not like I'm some crazy stalker. Take the risk. You won't regret it."

She exhales and reaches into her bag. "One cup of coffee?" she asks for reassurance.

"I'll start with that." I grin.

Siân tips her head and places her phone in my outstretched hand.

"See. And no one died."

She cringes at my statement but pulls it together. With both phones in my grasp, I hold them side by side and press the button to start the cloning process. A moment later, the software completes, blinking green letters bouncing back at me: *CLONING SUCCESSFUL.* A sinister chuckle bubbles in my throat, and it takes sheer willpower to keep it down. Then I quickly program my number and call myself from her phone to keep up the ruse.

Siân offers me a soft smile. "Bye, Christian."

"I'll be seeing you around."

As she exits the store, I follow her, admiring the sway of her hips on the way to campus. My phone vibrates, breaking my concentration. My father's name shows on the caller ID, and I answer it without a greeting.

"Che cosa?" *What?*

His voice blares into my ear, his rant nearly inaudible. He's pissed. Though he always is. I came to America for one reason, and it didn't involve finding Siân. She is merely a non-sanctioned detour. This call, however unwanted it may be, reminds me of the job he sent me to manage.

"Va bene," I grunt. "Rilassare. Sara' gestito." *All right. Relax. It'll be handled.* I end the call, not evening giving him the chance to offer a retort.

For now, I'll do what he wants, and then I'll be back for that rain check.

VILLAIN

4

SIÂN

I can't stop checking my phone, hoping the time on the screen is lying. *Fuck!* I'm late. Not just a little late, but very late. I take pride in being on time. Punctuality is important to me, but I got caught up with the mysterious Christian at the coffee shop. My shirt is stained with coffee, and I'm stressed. I'm going to be a wreck all day.

My flats slap against the concrete as I run up the steps into the business building. Taj is going to be pissed. Hell, I bet there's a vein bulging in the side of his neck right now.

I know I should take it a little more seriously, but I've never been late. Unlike him, who has been running late and blowing me off every chance he gets. Rushing down the hall with my purse slung off my shoulder and holding the coffee I should've tossed on my way in, I nearly trip but somehow stay upright. *God, I'm a mess.*

When I reach the door to the classroom, I pause, my chest heaving. Taking a calming breath, I peer through the glass window in the door.

Dammit.

The class is full, and Taj has already started his lesson. While I'm standing here, Taj looks over, and our gazes collide. His pale green eyes are stormy, and even from this distance, I can see the irritation etched into his features.

Taj is serious about being on time for his students, so serious that he locks the door as soon as class starts. If you aren't inside the class on time, then you aren't getting in. What's funny, though, is that he doesn't have the same commitment for everything else in his life, like when he asks me out on a date—because he is late almost every single time.

I stand there wondering if I should knock. He's already seen me, but he's not heading toward the door yet. Another second passes, then another. His lips move as he speaks to the class, then he walks toward the door.

My heart is racing as he walks toward me, and for the first time in a very long time, I feel the rush of adrenaline in my veins. I haven't felt anything like this since...

He opens the door, wearing a scowl on his face. Peering over his shoulder, he closes the door behind him and steps out into the hall, forcing me to take a step back.

"I'm sorry I'm late. I had a minor issue at the coffee shop and then—"

"Those all sound like excuses to me, Siân. You're supposed to be setting an example. This is your damn job. Being late is inexcusable."

He's scolding me like I'm a child, and I don't like it, not one fucking bit.

I sigh. "I'm less than ten minutes late, Taj. Chill."

Taj's lip curls, and the gentleman I'm so used to melts away, revealing something cold and ugly. "You know what? Go home."

I blink, suddenly confused. "Look, I'm sorry. I didn't intentionally arrive late."

He shakes his head. "Go home, Siân." The coldness in his voice makes me shiver, and I stand there staring at him, wondering if I've heard him correctly.

"I..."

"Go. Home," he grits out and whirls around, giving me his back.

Before I can utter another word, he's walking back into the classroom, and the slamming of the door vibrates through me.

What the hell just happened?

An onslaught of anger and sadness encompasses me, but most of all, I realize how incompatible we are. If Taj loved me as much as he says he does, he wouldn't react in such an angry manner over something so small.

Maybe he's just stressed? No, that's not a good enough reason for him to treat me so poorly. I've noticed more and more each day that he becomes a man I no longer recognize.

I'm simply filling the place of his perfect girlfriend, who never steps out of line.

Angrily, I turn and walk down the hall. I exit the building and stand outside on the steps, staring out over the courtyard. When did I become such a pushover? No, not just a pushover... *Safe.* I'm safe. Christian's words—the man from the bar—resonate with me. I don't take risks, and I never step out of line. I'm the perfect doormat, and I'm tired of it.

Frustration pulses through me, and I walk across the courtyard and back to the house. I should return to the classroom and tell Taj off, but deep down, I know it wouldn't do me any good. We're both angry, and any words said at this point would do more harm than good. No matter what, I have to end this before it gets out of control. Taj is my boss, and at the end of the day, I'd still like to be friends, if that's possible. This has gone on much longer than it should've.

The walk is long enough that it takes the edge off my anger. When I reach the house, I find Kyla's car gone.

I climb into my vehicle and lean against the steering wheel. I was supposed to work all morning and into the afternoon before spending time with my caretaker, Cynthia. She's been in my life since the beginning and is the only family I have here in the United States—the only family I have left at all if I'm being honest. I do my best to have dinner with her twice a month, just to check in and catch up. She deserves more than I can give her for keeping me safe and caring for me all these years.

I start the car and pull out of the parking lot. I don't want to show up at Cynthia's in a shit mood, so I dial Kyla's number. It'll be easier to vent to her about Taj than Cynthia. She's like a mother to me, and on top of that, Cynthia doesn't trust anyone, so her opinion is skewed.

As I pull out onto the road, Kyla finally answers the phone.

"Hello," she pants like she's just finished running.

"Hey!" I sigh, trying to hide my anger. There's no point in trying, though. Kyla has been by my side for years. If anyone can tell when I'm upset, it's her.

"What's wrong?"

"Everything," I growl. "If I needed proof that Taj and I shouldn't be together anymore, I got it today."

"Oh God, what happened?"

I turn out onto the highway to head toward the suburbs where Cynthia lives. "I had a slight mishap at the coffee shop this morning, so I showed up ten minutes late for class. He flipped his shit on me and told me to leave."

There's a long pause, so long that I wonder if she hung up on me. Then she clears her throat and says, "Hmm, that doesn't sound like him. Do you want me to talk to him?"

Somewhere in my mind, a red flag goes off. I trust Kyla, but I don't want her to get involved in my relationship with Taj.

"No, he can think about what he did and how he treated me and then apologize for acting like a toddler. I did nothing to him, and he treated me like shit."

"Maybe he's stressed?" Kyla tries to interject, but it feels like she's sticking up for him, and that's irritating as hell.

Is she my friend or his?

"Stressed or not, he didn't have to tell me to leave. He didn't have to be an asshole. It was like he was a different person." I shake my head and focus on driving to avoid getting into a car accident. That's the last thing I need.

"Yeah, I agree... Maybe it's better to just end things before they get worse." Her response comes out of the blue, but it's not really shocking. I told her I wanted to break up with Taj before, but she never pushed me to leave. Now, it feels like she is.

"Even if he hurt my feelings, I still don't want to hurt him."

Taj was my first serious boyfriend and the man I gave my virginity to. He holds a lot of my firsts and letting him go feels like I am letting some of the best parts of me go, but I'm not stupid. We are past fixing.

It was only a matter of time before we started falling apart.

"I know you don't... but sometimes it's for the better." She pauses. "Look, I'll talk to you later. I have a lunch date with Josh."

"Lunch isn't for a while, but okay." I try not to sound irritated, but I can't help it. I need to vent to Kyla. Otherwise, I'll go back to the university, rip Taj out of class, and tell him to fuck off.

"Hey, I'm sorry, babe. I'll be home tonight, and you can vent until your heart's content."

"Okay." I sigh.

I hit the end key on the steering wheel and grit my teeth, stewing in my own thoughts until I pull into the suburbs. Usually, Cynthia and I have dinner, but I'm sure she'll enjoy spending the day together since we haven't been able to do that for a while. Between classes and my work as Taj's TA, not to mention all the extra nights Kyla's been forcing me to go out, I've inadvertently abandoned the deal Cynthia and I made. I pull the car to the curb, put it in park, and kill the engine.

I grab my purse and phone. I'm getting ready to step out of the car when the hairs on the back of my neck stand on end. My eyes scan the road in front of me and the houses lining the street, but I see nothing suspicious. Yet it feels like someone is watching me. *Am I being paranoid?* I push myself to get out of the car. I've lived my whole life in fear... when will it stop? When will I stop feeling these random spouts of paranoia? I just want to live a normal, happy life. Is that too much to ask?

I close the car door, and my phone vibrates in my hand. I startle and look down to see Christian's name flash across the screen, along with a text from him.

***Christian:** I just wanted you to know you looked beautiful this morning and not to forget that it's okay to take risks.*

Beautiful? My cheeks heat to the temperature of the sun. The mysterious Christian has weaseled his way into my subconscious. How is it a stranger can look at me and see that I'm drowning, but the people closest to me can't? I read the text back to myself again, and stupidly, I smile. It throws me off, but at the same time, it centers me.

It's what I need. I know if I don't take the risk, then I'll never see any reward. Still, I don't know how to do that. I don't know how to step outside of the fear I live in. Taj is my safety net and staying inside my bubble is what's kept me safe these past couple of years. What if I make a mistake and *he* finds me? I sigh so loud I'm sure the neighbors can hear me.

I straighten my spine and remember all I've endured and how far I've come. Everything is going to be okay. I need to be safe, at least for now.

Christian is right, but wrong at the same time. Safe keeps me alive. He could never know the danger taking a risk might bring to my door.

As soon as I reach the bottom step of the stoop, Cynthia opens the door. Her eyes are bright and joyous while a smile pulls onto her lips. There is never a moment when she isn't happy to see me. The love and compassion she's carried over the years makes her more than just my guardian. In my eyes, she's like a mother, always making sure I'm protected and loved.

"Siân, you're looking as beautiful as ever. It feels like forever since I saw you last," she whispers into the shell of my ear as she wraps her arms tightly around me. Her hugs are the best, like a toasty blanket and hot cocoa the moment you come inside from the cold.

Pulling away, I murmur, "It hasn't been that long. You look beautiful as well." And she does. She's practically glowing.

"Enough, you're going to make me blush. Let's get inside and have some soup. I even made bread to go with it."

My stomach, of course, chooses this moment to growl, and we burst into laughter. We enter the house together, and Cynthia closes the door behind us and heads straight for the kitchen. Her house has an open concept, with the living room and dining room blending into one another. Every time I step inside this house, I feel protected. I feel like nothing can touch me, probably because I know Cynthia would let nothing happen to me.

Not when all we have is each other.

"Is everything okay?" she asks, sensing the shift in my emotions while she readies herself to dish out soup.

"Yes. I'm fine. Just thinking of how grateful I am to have you. We've been through so much together. I always want you to know how much I appreciate you."

She stops mid ladle and looks up at me. "You mean the world to me, Siân. All we have is each other, and there is nothing I wouldn't do to help you. You know that."

With everything going on and the paranoia I've had, this is just the reminder I needed.

"I do, and I've never doubted that. I just miss spending time with you, is all. I've been so busy with school and work, and there aren't enough hours in the day." Now I sound like I'm complaining.

Cynthia only smiles. "Well, we've got right now, don't we? So let's eat, watch a movie, and enjoy one another's company." I can only smile and take the bowl of soup she offers me. She's so much more than my caretaker. She's my family.

VILLAIN

5

CHRISTIAN

The sound of my tires screech over the pavement as I whip my 458 Italia in front of the abandoned warehouse. A row of massive, dilapidated structures, wrapped in moss and vines, stare back at me. We're tucked away in a small town an hour outside of South Beach. What was once a thriving fishing port is now just a forgotten memory of aging buildings that serves as the camping grounds for the homeless, drug addicts, and—well, *us*. It's the perfect location for our type of work. It's quiet and off the beaten path, and when we are conducting business, the *regular* residents know to steer clear. Often, they are hired to keep an eye on the place.

I've only been here once, back before my guy found Siân in Florida. This place is in worse condition than it was back then. Trash and debris litter the grounds, and the smell of urine permeates the air. Even from where I sit in the driver's seat with the windows up, I can smell it.

Exiting the car, I grab the black leather gloves that match my signature jacket. Though today, I leave the jacket behind. With my hand wrapped around my Glock, I slam the door shut, tuck the pistol and gloves in my waistband, and inch forward. They've been waiting for me and based on the anger seeping from my father over the phone, things aren't adding up.

There was a plan, and someone fucked up *royally*. I keep my cool and take one wide step up the three stairs leading to the platform. The warehouse door is heavy and creaks when I open it. The silence on the other side is eerie. The air is stale, and in the middle of the open space is an old rusty metal table, a single chair, and a black cargo van.

Tony, my father's point man in South Beach, is next to the back of the vehicle, staring down at the dealer. Both men glance at me—Tony over his shoulder, and Armon cranes his neck to look around Tony.

The Russos dabble in a little of everything. But guns and girls are our specialties—well, guns are *my* specialty. My father can have what comes with running women. I'll pass on that. Violence is more my speed, and weapons are the best way to enforce that.

We supply the entire East Coast and most of Italy. Tony was tasked with closing the deal with our new contact, Armon Trentino, a low-level street thug who joined the military. Old habits die hard, and ole Armon here soon figured out that selling military-grade weapons paid handsomely—a shit ton better than the US government.

"Where in the hell have you been?" Tony barks at me.

I stare at him with my jaw clenched and my hands balled into fists. Tony straightens his spine and passes me a quick and apologetic wave. He knows my temper better than anyone, so he should have known better than to question me. He may work for my father, but I'm the one in charge. Shit happens on my word, and nobody wants to piss me off.

Things are better when I'm happy—or my rendition of it. Anger me, and people die, and I really don't feel like killing anyone today. It's messy, and the cleanup can be a pain.

"Armon."

"Christian, man, listen—"

I hold up a finger to silence him. "Shh." I continue, not stopping until I'm only a foot away from Tony. Armon stays quiet. *Smart*. Clearly, he knows enough not to push me. "What's this I hear about a problem with our shipment?" I ask, my tone even.

The farther I get into the room, the staler the surrounding air becomes. Dusk covers every inch of the place, and the walls are barren with chipped, dingy gray paint that was once a shade of white.

Pulling my gloves on one at a time, I stare both men down. Tony knows where this is going, and so does Armon. Sweat lines the dealer's face. He knows he fucked up, and his flight-or-fight instinct is taking over, but he's cornered. There is nowhere for him to go, and it's exactly how I like it.

"Speak," I say once I have my gloves on.

"Like I was telling Tony, there was a mix-up."

"Hm." I nod. "Go on."

Armon shrugs, his eyes filled with fear. "I don't have all the guns."

With my brows hiked up and my lips pursed together, I nod once more. "You see how this is a problem, right?'

"It was out of my control, Christian."

I glance over my shoulder at Tony, who gives me a disapproving shrug. "That doesn't work for me."

"There was nothing I could do," he protests.

"Sure, there was. We paid the deposit, and it's your job to deliver. Now, I was in the middle of something rather important, something I had to set aside to be here with the likes of you. And you're telling me there's nothing you can do?" I ask while circling him. Reaching for my gun, I release the safety and cock it.

"How about I drop the—"

Bang.

The sound of my gun rings against the walls, echoing around us.

"Argh," Armon yells, his cries coming out gargled and drenched in his pain.

"Fucking shit!" Tony yells, my actions catching him off guard as well.

Armon's body drops where he stands, and he grabs his knee, the color draining from him right along with the blood. Long ropes of red seep through his fingertips, and the sweat that lined his forehead is now a flowing stream down his face.

Now back in front of him, I hover over his weak excuse for a vessel. Surveying his features and the lines of agony written all over his mug, I grip my weapon tighter and kneel. With bated breaths, Armon scoots back but immediately collapses as all the energy he has leaves his body.

I watch the blood for a second, mentally following its path as it pools on the floor around him. His screams grow louder, his voice rattling my eardrums. When I look back at Tony, he shakes his head. He should be used to the way I work by now—a man like me thrives on the pain of others. What did he expect? If I must step in and handle something he should have, then blood will always spill.

"So, what do you say, Armon? Are we buddies or not?" I rest my elbows on my knees, letting the hand that holds my Glock hang loosely between my legs.

He glares at me, spit flying from his mouth when he speaks. "Are you fucking kidding me?" he growls.

I crane my neck to look at Tony. "Does it look like I'm kidding?" I point my attention back to Armon and use the barrel of the gun to scratch my temple.

"Not at all," Tony proclaims behind me.

I smirk and wave my pistol toward Armon. He flinches, and I let out a laugh. It's loud and vibrates through the space. Hell, it's even bone-chilling to me.

"How do you plan on fixing this?" I ask.

He groans. "I'll fix it, man, I swear. J-Just get me to a doctor," Armon pleads.

"Tony will see to it that you're treated."

Armon releases a sigh. "Thank you, Christian. I promise I'll—"

"After you remedy this problem."

His skin pales at my words. "Come on. I'm not going to make it. I think you hit an arter—"

Bang.

Another shot to his *good* knee. Because of the closeness, the blood splatters land on my cheek and the tips of my boots. Armon's cries continue to grow, drowning out any and everything around me. Adrenaline builds in my chest, much like it does every time my victims scream.

"Jesus fucking Christ. He's going to need to walk if you want the guns, Christian," Tony declares.

"His hands still work. Unless he doesn't tell me what I want to hear in the next five seconds. Then not walking will be the least of his worries."

Armon opens his mouth to speak, but all that comes out is heavy panting. The puddle around him is increasing, the blood congealing from the climate.

Hmm, maybe I did hit an artery.

Finally, he gets his words together despite how weak he's becoming. "O-Okay. I just... give me a little time."

I suck my teeth and tilt my head. "You had time, Armon. The deal was —" I stop short, distracted by the buzzing of my phone in my back pocket. I remove it but don't immediately recognize the number. It's not until I open the message that I realize it's the app and the context alone tells me who it is. *Taj*. The fucking prick—correction—the dead man Siân's currently seeing.

Taj: *Hey baby...*

I see red. Everything around me fades, replaced by crimson. Those two simple words bounce back at me, taunting me, fueling the part of me I work so hard to keep buried around her. But this, this bitch of a man calling my woman, *baby*. Who the fuck does he think he is? She belongs to me, and anyone who gets in my way will be dealt with.

"Christian," Tony calls out, but his voice is barely audible.

All I can focus on is my phone and the scent of blood and dirt in the air.

"Christian. Cosa stai facendo?" *What are you doing?* Tony yells.

Another text pops up on the screen, and my blood boils. I grip the device so tight my knuckles ache.

Taj: *Sorry I snapped at you. I shouldn't have yelled.*

Those three little dots dance along the bottom, showing that Siân is preparing to send him a response. As much as I want to know what she has to say, the only thing on my mind is his words. What the hell does he mean he shouldn't have yelled? Patience has never been a virtue of mine, and if the app were a two-way setup, I'd end this shit right now.

No one yells at the woman who belongs to me. I've let him be because it's all a part of my plan, but now, I want him dead. A growl bubbles in my throat, my anger spilling over into pure rage. Rage that continues to grow when another text comes through.

Siân: *You were an asshole today, and I didn't deserve that.*

If I had my way, this would be done tonight. But there's more at stake here, an empire and the heir her father promised me all those years ago. If I act now, she'll fear me, and while the thought of that fuels me just as much, I need more with her. And the only way to have it, to be with her the way I've wanted since I knew she was meant to be mine, is to be patient. She has to love me, which means I need to play it cool. The next step, get her the fuck away from him, even if that means making him disappear.

Taj: *I know, baby. I love you. Don't you love me too?*

"Motherfucker," I roar aloud. *You're smarter than that, Siân. Don't fall for it.* Early on, I mastered the art of manipulation, while even the subtlest forms go over others' heads. Like now, his message is steeped in it. There is more behind those words, there always is, and I would know that better than anyone.

"What the fuck?" Tony pries.

Armon, Tony, the guns, none of that matters at this moment. Tony's ranting and Armon's screams are all a distant memory now. My only concern is Siân's pending response hanging in the balance. More dots followed by what feels like the longest pause before she finally answers him.

Siân: *I do. But it doesn't excuse you.*

Taj: *You're right.*

Taj: *I'm sorry.*

Taj: *Forgive me?*

The messages come back-to-back, not even giving her the chance to answer him.

Siân: *I don't know. You were out of line.*

Taj: *Let me convince you. I promise I'll make it up to you. *wink face emoji**

Another pause.

Standing in the center of the room, I feel my nerves on edge, fists clenched tight around my gun and phone as anger consumes me. My vision blurs as her next text comes across the screen, and I can no longer think straight.

Rage becomes fury, and all I know is I want someone dead. And without a word or another thought, I spin on the heels of my boots and stalk toward Armon's now pale frame. His eyes grow wide at the lift of my gun, and he raises a hand in my direction.

"Christian. Wai—" His words die on his tongue the moment I pull the trigger, putting a bullet in his skull.

I turn and head for the door before his arm can fall back to his side, and the warmth leaves his lifeless body.

Tony gasps, and then a slew of profanities comes next. "You weren't supposed to kill him. You fucking psycho."

His words mean nothing to me. Tony has been around me long enough to know that I don't care who has to die. If someone is standing in my way, then they are dead, and since I can't get to Taj just yet, tonight that person was Armon.

I glare at him for a moment. Ignoring his comment, I reply. "Take the guns and clean this shit up."

VILLAIN

6

SIÂN

A person might think I enjoy going to bars as often as I frequent them, but that's not the case. After I came home from spending the day with Cynthia, I was exhausted. That, coupled with being angry at Taj's reaction earlier in the day, left me feeling even worse.

As soon as I walked through the door, Kyla bombarded me, begging me to go out with her to see Nova, a local band playing at one of the college bars down the street on Saturday. I was so mentally unprepared for her ambush that I agreed. Then I went and fell into bed.

Taj only made things worse when he texted me, claiming he wanted to "make it up to me." I understood full well what that meant, and I wasn't ready to see him yet. His apology via text didn't seem genuine, and I felt like forgiving him right now would make me a pushover.

So, it was good that Kyla invited me out.

However, right this second, I am regretting my choice to come here. The band has already played three songs and is getting ready to take a break. I am sipping a glass of whiskey. I don't really like the taste of it, but I enjoy the path of warmth it carves out in my body as I swallow the liquid down. With the whiskey settling in my stomach, I fish my phone out of my pocket.

There are no texts, and that only angers me more. She's ignoring me, and that's infuriating when she's the one who invited me. I type out a text and hit send before I can stop myself. It's the fourth one I've sent, but I don't feel guilty. I'm not a clingy friend. I just don't like being ghosted.

A server swings by the table. "Can I get you anything else?"

"I'll take another whiskey, please."

She nods and saunters away. My phone pings with an incoming text, and my stomach knots. Something bad better have happened for her not to be here.

My fingers hover over the screen of my phone when I see the text isn't from Kyla, but Christian.

Christian: *Got any plans tonight, beautiful?*

I lick my lips and look around the bar. This strange cross between guilt and excitement bubbles up inside me. I'm not really doing anything wrong if I message him back, right?

I stare at the text, contemplating my next move. He called me beautiful. There's a nagging at the back of my mind telling me I should be leery.

I text back.

Me: *Beautiful?*

His reply is almost instant.

Christian: *Would you prefer sexy? Stunning? Gorgeous? Since you're all those things and more.*

I can't stop the smile from appearing on my lips. Seconds tick by and then another text comes in.

Christian: *You never answered me. Do you have any plans for tonight?*

My cheeks heat. All he's done is call me beautiful. This is stupid to be reacting to his texts like I'm a teenage girl who has never been kissed.

Me: *Yes. *frowning emoji* I'm waiting for my friend to see the band Nova. She's running late.*

I don't know why I told him that, but I hit send on the text before I can stop myself.

The server returns with my whiskey, and as soon as she sets the drink down, I take a big gulp of it. The liquor burns a path of fire down my throat. What is wrong with me? I don't talk to random guys, much less flirt with them.

I'm with Taj. This is wrong, but if it's wrong, why does it feel so right?

My phone pings, and I look at the message.

Christian: *Fuck, you should never be left waiting... If I were there, I'd....*

He doesn't finish his text, and my mind's going a million miles a minute.

What did he mean to say? My heart pounds against my rib cage, and I see him in my mind as if he's standing in front of me. I think back to our almost kiss from the night I met him.

I bite my bottom lip and type out my response.

Me: *What would you do?*

He must be holding his phone in his hand because the bubbles from him typing out his response pop on the screen right away.

Christian: *Whatever you want me to do. *wink face**

My stomach tightens, and I can feel the butterflies inside, waiting to be unleashed. Do I want him to do things to me? I'm pretty sure I do, but I'm also confused over Taj. I take another drink and exit the message.

What do I say to that?

The band starts up again, and I shove the thoughts of Christian from my mind. I still haven't heard from Kyla, and I wonder what the hell is going on there? I'm nearly finished with my second drink when I'm startled by a deep voice.

"It's a pleasant surprise to see you, Siân," Christian's voice buzzes in my ears, and my entire body lights up. Suddenly, I'm hot all over.

My tongue is heavy in my mouth, but somehow, I manage to speak.

"I..." I stutter. "How did you find me? Are you stalking me?" The questions come out like word vomit.

He smiles this big, perfectly white, toothy grin. I'm taken back to the old fairy tale of the wolf who ate the granny with his wolfish teeth. This man oozes danger, and I'm deeply attracted to him. What the fuck is wrong with me?

He's looking devilishly handsome tonight, as he does every time I see him, and I can't seem to drag my gaze away from him. Tonight, he's wearing his usual dark blue jeans, but instead of his white T-shirt, he's wearing a dark green shirt that makes his blue eyes and blond hair pop. He's paired it with his black leather jacket and black boots. I force myself to swallow and look away.

"It wasn't hard to find you. I just searched for Nova's tour and found out what bar they were playing at. I was in the area anyway, and like I said, a woman like you should never be left alone. Any strange man could come along and hurt you. If you were mine, there wouldn't be a chance in hell you'd be alone in this bar." His eyes flash with something violent, and I shiver at the possessiveness in his tone.

I don't want to admit how much I like it, not out loud and definitely not to myself.

"But I'm not yours," I whisper.

He takes the seat across from me, his grin turning wolfish. "No, not yet, but never say never, baby. If I wanted you to be mine, make no mistake, you would be fucking mine."

My head is buzzing, and my palms are sweaty. I know nothing about this man, but I'm drawn to him like a moth to a flame. Maybe it's a trap? Maybe he is a bad man? My entire body tenses. We stare at each other for a moment, and then I take a drink, chugging the rest of the whiskey in the glass before setting it back down.

"A woman who drinks whiskey... it's like you were made to be mine?"

"Are you always this straightforward with women you meet?"

"Only ones I'm interested in." He winks.

I bite the inside of my cheek and change the subject. "What do you do for work?"

A muscle jumps in his perfectly sculpted jaw. "Sales. I do a lot of work for my father, so I'm always traveling. I'm in town on business right now."

I nod. Okay, so maybe he's not a crazy guy who's going to kidnap me and take me to an island in the middle of nowhere.

"If you're worried that I'm some crazy stalker, you have nothing to worry about. I'd never hurt you, Siân. I'd rather rip my heart out than hurt a single hair on your body."

The conviction in his voice says he's telling the truth, but still, it seems strange for him to say such a thing to me.

"Sorry, I'm a little paranoid sometimes. I wasn't thinking that. I'm just... my life hasn't been easy, and I'm leery of new people." I shake my head to ward off the strange feelings. I've never felt such an intense pull toward someone, so maybe that's what this is?

He reaches across the table. His hand cups my cheek, and sparks fly at the touch of his skin on mine. A soft gasp escapes my lips, and I peer into his eyes. "I understand what you mean, more than you'll ever know. When I lost my mother..." His voice turns hard, and I can feel his pain. The anguish seeps from him like a sponge. "Just know you have nothing to worry about with me. I will always put you first, *always*..." There's a finality to his words, and it confuses me. I feel closer to him, like he's shared a tiny sliver of who he is with me.

"Every time our paths cross, I'm reminded of the risks I don't take... I'm reminded of how *safe* I am. I don't want to be safe," I whisper the confession.

"Then don't be." He looks away for a moment, and the heat in his blue eyes burns me to the core. "I know you aren't happy with him, whoever he is. I can see it. I've only known you a short time, but I can see the happiness and life draining from you."

I look away. His words are like a slap to the face. I want to pull away, but he doesn't let me. His other hand grabs mine, and I see the contrast in our hands, how different we look. His hands are calloused and rough, with dark tattoos on them. Mine are tiny and clean.

He's different. This is wrong. *But is it?*

"I'm not saying this to upset you. I feel this intense pull toward you, Siân. I can't explain it, but when I'm in the same room as you, I'm burning up. Do you feel it too?"

Oh, God. This is too much. He is too much.

Nevertheless, I cannot lie to him. His gaze is piercing, and even if I said no, I know he would know I was lying.

"I feel it. Deep. Burning me alive."

I lick my lips, and I feel the need to nuzzle against his hand that's still cradling my cheek.

"See, we're the same," he whispers, and my eyes dart to his full lips.

I want to kiss him so badly it's almost consuming me. I dig my nails into the wood table to stop myself.

"I get the sense you're afraid to live, to be free. Probably because the people around you always leave. I was like that when I lost my mother. I felt so alone, like the world was against me."

"How...?" I fumble for the words to understand how he gets it, but that's all that comes out.

He grins. "I don't know how I know. I just get this sense about you. You're going through life, making accomplishments. Congratulations on the grad school program, but even with your achievements, something is missing, isn't it?"

Red flags go up in my mind, but I shove them away. He already said he wouldn't hurt me, and I know it's stupid, but I believe him.

"How do you know I'm a grad student?"

His gaze darkens. "I make a point to learn all the things possible about the person I'm interested in."

"So, you are a stalker?" I grin.

"If you consider doing a little social media search, then sure, I'm a stalker." He smiles once more, but the darkness in his eyes lingers.

I want to touch that darkness and wrap myself up inside it, even if it's only once. This man is like a virus to me, eating up my resolve, leaving me vulnerable and cracked wide open. I should hate it, be terrified of it, and what it might mean, but I'm not.

I like it. I like the thrill he gives me, the heat that spreads through my veins from his presence, and the way he breaks down walls without permission. He makes me feel, makes me see past my biggest fears. He has the power to consume me, and the scariest part of all is that I want him to. I want him to swallow me and spit me back out.

I'm just about to say something when Kyla's voice breaks through the radio silence in my brain. In an instant, Christian pulls away, leaving me cold where his hands touched me.

"Hello, am I interrupting something?" she questions, hands on her hips while she stands at the side of the table.

Christian's gaze darts to her and then back to me. I feel him pulling away from me, and I don't like it. A part of me wishes Kyla never showed up.

"Earth to Siân, are you still with me?" I don't like her tone, so I fire back with the same intense tone.

"Well, look who showed up, and well over an hour late. Thanks for letting me know," I retort.

"You don't seem to be bothered since Mr. Tall, Dark, and Handsome is here. I'm sure he kept you company."

I roll my eyes. "We didn't plan to meet here. He came to see the band play."

Kyla's gaze whips to Christian. "Oh, really? In that case, why don't you go get us a couple of drinks."

What the hell? That's rude as hell.

I pin Kyla with a scowl. "You don't have to do that, Christian. Kyla's joking."

"No, no." He pushes from the table, coming to a full stand. He's so tall I have to crane my neck back to look up at him. "I owe you a drink, remember?"

"Yes, but that was coffee, not a fifteen-dollar mixed drink."

I can feel Kyla staring a hole through me. I know she's wondering what the hell we're talking about and where I saw him last. She'll find out soon enough.

"It's fine. You can make it up to me by letting me collect on that rain check." His eyes glitter with amusement. "Now what should I order?"

"I'll take a Cosmopolitan," Kyla answers before I can.

"I'll have a beer." I really shouldn't have another drink, but the night is still young, and I want to enjoy myself. Christian walks over to the bar without another word.

With him out of earshot, Kyla leans into me. She's wearing a short little summer dress, denim jacket, and a pair of strappy heels. Beside me, she looks like a goddess. I'm skinny, but I'm short where she has legs for miles.

"What the hell was that about?"

"Long story short, we bumped into each other at the coffee shop the other day when Taj and I had the fight. He ended up spilling my drink on me by accident."

Kyla purses her lips. "Sure, he did."

"I'm serious. It was an accident."

"Maybe to you, but that man looks at you like you're a goddamn all-you-can-eat buffet."

I shake my head. Maybe he does, and I'm not ready to admit it. I'm still with Taj, and I'm many things, but I'm not a cheater. No matter how mad at him I am, I would never do something like that. Kyla seems distant tonight, and I'm not sure why. She doesn't say anything else, and things are a little awkward once Christian returns to the table with our drinks, but I ignore it mostly. Kyla's watching Christian like a hawk, and he, in turn, is staring at her.

It's like they're sizing each other up.

I sip my beer slowly, enjoying it and the band. Finally, a nice relaxing night. All that goes to shit when I spot Taj across the bar. He steps inside, a wide smile on his face as our gazes collide. He waves, and all I can think is... *What the fuck?*

My entire body tenses, becoming tight like a bow.

Christian senses the change in my demeanor right away and leans into my side. "What's wrong?"

I'm still staring at Taj as he makes his way across the room. Christian must piece the puzzle together in his mind because he doesn't press for me to reply. Kyla bounces on the balls of her feet with excitement. Anger ignites in my belly. I'm not ready to see him yet.

As soon as he's within arm's distance, he reaches out and hugs me. I'm stiff in his arms, unable to make myself return the hug.

"Oh, don't tell me you're still mad," he says, pulling back to look at my face.

I shove at him. "Still mad?" I'm ready to blow up at him. "How did you even know I was here?"

His eyes dart to Kyla and then back to me. "Uh, Kyla told me."

Crossing my arms over my chest, I ask, "Oh really, and when did you talk to Kyla about coming?" I still haven't talked to him about what happened. I'm not ready. Yet they did not give me the option of him coming tonight.

He scratches at the back of his head. "Oh, you know, school."

My anger only seems to rise at how nonchalantly he acts about the situation. He hurt me, and now suddenly he thinks he can decide when we see each other. I don't think so. The weight of my conversation with Christian just a bit ago settles on my shoulders.

Like he can tell what I'm thinking, Christian slips his hulking frame between Taj and me. His huge hands come into view, and he places them on my shoulders. I look up at him through my lashes. I feel both protected and vulnerable in his grasp.

"Dude, what the fuck? That's my girlfriend," Taj yells behind Christian.

It feels like we're in our own personal bubble, where no one else can reach us, but that's not the reality of the situation. The reality is that we aren't alone, and if I don't get Christian to leave, there is going to be a fight. I can sense it, smell it like rain.

Christian's gaze flicks over his shoulder to Taj and then back down to me. There is a maddening look in his baby blues, a raw rage waiting to be unleashed.

"Look, I'm okay, Christian. Thank you for keeping me company... but I think you should leave."

I half expect him to growl or tell me no, but he gives me one last piercing look before nodding his head. He steps away, and with every step he takes back, I feel a little more lost.

Taj takes his absence as an opportunity and slides into the spot beside me. He wraps his arm around me and holds me against his side possessively. He's never made such a daring move, but I assume he feels threatened by Christian.

"Yeah, I think it's time you leave," Taj instigates, and I shush him.

Christian is less than five feet away, but I can see the darkness and rage swimming just beneath the surface. As mysterious and beautiful of a man he is, something is incredibly dangerous about him, and I'm both afraid and intrigued.

Thankfully, he doesn't respond to Taj's stupid comment and turns and walks out of the bar without saying a single word. A part of me wishes he'd said goodbye, but from the look on his face I know goodbye would've involved fists, blood, and the police.

I let out a breath I didn't even know I was holding in and notice Taj is staring at me.

"You okay?" I ask, even though he should be the one asking me if I'm okay.

"I'm fine. I'm wondering if you're okay? That's the second time I've seen that guy with you at the bar. Is something going on?"

"You cannot possibly be serious right now, can you?" I'm flabbergasted.

Realizing he's made a mistake, he retracts his statement. "Look, I'm sorry. Things have been tense, and I don't like the way he stood between us, like he thought I was going to hurt you or something. The guy doesn't even know you."

That's the thing... I don't have the heart to tell him that a man who barely knows me sees more of me than the man I've been with for the past two years.

VILLAIN

7

CHRISTIAN

The neighborhood is dead. Or as dead as it can be for a college town on a Saturday night. It's perfect, really. While the rest of the town is out enjoying themselves, dancing, partying, or doing whatever makes their miserable existence worth living, I'm here, blending into the shadows and staying clear of any passing headlights.

It's wet out tonight, the sound of tires over the concrete serving as my soundtrack. I briskly cross the street, being careful to keep my head down, and when I'm sure no one is watching, I hop the fence to Siân's yard, making my way around the back of the house for safe measures. In all the surveying I've done, I've learned that the people on this block are entirely too trustworthy. No cameras, not even those new doorbell ones that most people rave about.

I guess when you live in a close-knit community where everyone knows everyone, one doesn't need to fear for their safety. People look out for each other, and if I was a normal person with normal feelings, I'd say how nice that must be. But I live in a world where white picket fences don't exist, and the monsters under the bed are real. And those monsters look a lot like me, and we don't hide.

The back of the house is a drastic difference from the front. It's unkempt, grass and weeds sitting high off the ground. The few stairs leading to the enclosed patio are worn, and the boards are lifting. When I attempt to open the door, I soon realize that it's stuck, and it takes a hard pull before it finally budges. Cobwebs and the smell of rotten wood tell the tale of just how unattended it is.

Thinking about Siân staying here in a place that lacks the appropriate upkeep angers me. Where we're from, she's royalty, and a queen should never lay her head somewhere like this. But when you've been on the run for as long as she has, you make do. It's smarter that way when you think about it. If you want to go unnoticed, then you hide in plain sight. You take residence in a place that looks to be inhabited by an old hermit.

I insert the copy of the key I had made into the lock and listen for it to click. It's pure luck that the key works back here, and considering how neglected this area is, I know it'll also fit the front door. Most people are smart enough to use different locks. It's dark when I enter through their kitchen, and to my surprise, there is a cat. It's parked near the foyer that leads into the dining area, with its back perched as it hisses at me.

I hate cats.

They're sneaky and smell worse than ass. Closing the door behind me, I use my phone for lighting. Unlike out back, the kitchen is clean—with everything in its place. As I make my way through the house, I take in my surroundings. The dining room is decked out with a table for four and peel and stick quotes on the wall. That is Kyla's doing, I'm sure.

In all the years I've known Siân, this isn't like her. Five years ago, when I watched her, she was a mess. Outwardly and in public, she appeared perfect—gorgeous in every way. But where she laid her head was just as unkempt as the backyard.

I saunter past the angry cat, ignoring the swat it makes at my boots. The girls are still out for the night, enjoying themselves at the club. I had to get out of there. Had I stayed and watched that Taj asshole fawn all over *my* woman, I would have done something I couldn't take back right in the middle of the dance floor. Not that I care, violence is my love language. But with Siân standing there, I had to walk away. And now I'm here, in the home she shares with her so-called friend.

Something about Kyla rubs me the wrong way. Her personality is that of a girl who has things to hide. The way she puts herself out there tells me she's compensating for something. What that is, I'm not sure yet, but I plan to figure it out. If she's going to be around Siân, then I need to know everything there is to know about her.

I step into the long hall that leads toward the front door. In the center of it is a table that houses several picture frames. Stopping for a moment, I observe them, my attention narrowing in on one of the girls. They appear younger and happy, and in the image, they're both holding boxes—move-in day, perhaps? Next to it is a picture of Siân and Taj. His arms are wrapped around her, but much like her everyday appearances, she's not happy.

I smile at the notion of that, knowing that she's not satisfied with him settles me, in a way. It makes me feel things I've never felt before. Jealousy because he touches her, pride for obvious reasons, and maybe even gratification. It proves that we're more alike than I thought. When the world smiles, we frown. Life is tragic, and the cards dealt to us solidify that logic.

I place the picture of her and Taj face down and make my way to the stairs. They are on the opposite side of the living room and creak as I climb them. At the top of the landing, I drag my gaze down both ends of the hall. Much like the rest of the house, it's pitch black except for the few rays that shine through the window from the lamppost outside.

On the left is a single room, and based on the position I normally take from across the street, Siân's room is at the other end of the hall. Curiosity takes hold, and I head to the left, staring out the window before pushing the door open. On the other side of the wooden frame, everything is in order. The bed is made, not a single litter of trash in sight.

The musky scent of cheap cologne hits me. It's familiar, but I can't quite put my finger on where I know it from. On the wall above the mattress is a framed image of Kyla. Just as I expected, she's self-centered. Staring back at me are brown eyes attached to the exposed body of Siân's friend. I crane my neck to further inspect the picture and shrug it off. The only naked woman I care about is Siân. Just the thought alone makes my cock twitch.

When I turn to exit the room, something shining next to the bed catches my eye. I pick it up and turn it around to inspect it. It's a gold cuff link and expensively made. At least whoever she's been fucking doesn't only own shitty cologne. With one final look around, I make a fist around the cuff link and step back into the hall while closing the door behind me.

Light flashes through the hall from a passing car, but I ignore it on my way to the other end of the hall. I pass the bathroom on my right and then a linen closet on my left before finally stopping at the end. With a deep breath, I push the door open, the hinges screaming loud as I do. In my mind, I'm drawing a map of their place, pinpointing every turn and creak in the floorboards.

Unlike the rest of the house, this room is a mess, and I know this is where Siân lives. Clothes are scattered on the floor, and her perfume permeates the air. Her dresser is cluttered, and there aren't any pictures on the wall. In one corner are totes, and aside from the bed in the center of the room, it looks like someone who never settled in stays here.

That doesn't surprise me. She's always on the run, though, based on what my guy found out about her, this is the longest she's stayed in one place. Not for long. Soon I'll have my way, and she'll return home with me to Italy.

I inch farther into the space and run my hands across the dresser, then stop in front of it and open a drawer. Reaching inside, I retrieve a pair of black laced panties and hold them up with my index fingers, the corners of my mouth lifting as I think of her wearing them. I set them back and close the drawer, then push off the surface on my way over to the totes. When I peek inside the top one, I find it's full of more clothes, and sticking out between a pair of jeans and the wall of the container is a plastic bag. Tugging it from its place, I soon realize it's all her important documents.

Several passports, fake IDs, and forged birth certificates are amongst a few of the items here. I tip my chin, impressed at how resourceful she has to be to have all this. She's gone by many names over the years, more than I ever thought. Fairchild, Myers, the moniker I knew her by, Maynard, and the current Danforth. Though, one passport stands out to me in particular. It dates back to when she was a girl, her family name etched into the pages: Siân Giuliani. I run my finger along the pages and notice something sticking between them.

I gently remove an image of a face I haven't seen in fifteen years. Marco Giuliani and next to him is his wife, and in his arms, tucked lovingly between them, is Siân. I see right away she's the spitting image of her mother. As I continue to survey the picture, a sense of deja vu hits me. I know when this was taken. This was the night her entire world changed, the eve she lost everyone she loved, the night she got away.

All of Italy thought she'd died along with her parents, but I knew differently, and I devoted years to finding her. And every time she gets away, we always meet again.

"Staremo insieme per sempre questa volta, topolina," I say to the empty room. *We'll be together forever this time, little mouse.*

With a deep breath in, I stuff everything back where it belongs and continue to glance around. Next to her bed on the end table is a black moleskin notebook. Intrigued, I pick it up and skim through it. It's a journal, and my name sketched in her handwriting grabs my attention. Based on the date, it's the night I approached her in the bar. I begin to read the passage, but the sound of a door closing downstairs distracts me.

"Shit," I mutter and calmly tiptoe toward the hall.

A light flickers on the shadow of two people against the wall near the stairs, and a moment later, a man's voice blares out.

"You look beautiful tonight, Siân."

Fucking Taj.

I grit my teeth and force my anger down. The only thing that matters right now is not getting caught. The top of her head is the first thing I see as she climbs the stairs with him in tow. Not to be seen, I duck back into her room, and just as they breach the doorway, I rush into the bathroom, hiding myself behind the door.

A second later, one of them turns on the lamp next to the bed. Through the crack between the hinges, I stare at them. They're in the middle of the room, and his hands roam every inch of her frame. My blood boils when he leans in to kiss her, but I keep it together.

"Thank you for forgiving me," he says, but Siân doesn't seem that interested.

Instead of a response, she stares up at him and aggressively shakes open his shirt, the buttons flying in every direction. I watch his breath hitch and lust build in his eyes. All the while I stand in her bathroom, with red hot frustration blurring my vision. But it's when she pushes him on the mattress, and the wind from his fall sends the scent of cologne across the room that the piece falls in place. Remembering the cuff link from Kyla's room, I dig into my pocket while narrowing my sights on his wrists, and sure enough, he's missing one of his own.

"I'll kill him," I promise in a whisper.

8

SIÂN

Taj falls back onto the bed, and I strip out of my clothes. I want things to be different tonight, for something to spark and remind me why we're still together. I peel the black jeans I'm wearing down my hips and legs, kicking them away once they reach my ankles. Next goes my shirt, and soon, I'm standing before him in nothing but my bra and panties.

He licks his lips seductively and smiles. My stomach tightens, and I make quick work of my panties and bra, tossing them to the floor with my other clothes. I'm ready for this to be over, and it hasn't even started yet.

Slowly, I crawl up onto the bed. Taj is leaning back on his arms, his eyes tracing a path over my skin like he's never seen something so beautiful.

"Fuck, you're gorgeous, Siân. I don't deserve you. I really don't."

I want to tell him that's the truth, but press my lips together instead. I stop once I reach him and press those same lips against his. As soon as our lips touch, my brain disconnects from my body.

Taj's tongue presses against the seam of my mouth, begging for entry, and I open for him. Our tongues collide and swirl together. I'm waiting for the spark, the warmth to overcome me. I should feel something, anything, but I don't.

I feel nothing. It's shocking and confusing.

Deepening the kiss, he tangles his hand in my hair, and our bodies collide. We roll, and he moves us, so I'm lying beneath him. He kisses me for a moment longer before he pulls away, his chest heaving. His pupils are dilated, and he presses his forehead against mine while staring into my eyes. I bite my bottom lip and watch as he moves off the bed and rips off his half-destroyed shirt. When he reaches for his belt, I move, slapping his hands away. I'm waiting for a zing of heat, a rush of excitement, but there's nothing but a dull ache resonating through my chest.

I undo his belt quickly and push his pants down his legs, along with his boxers. Taj isn't athletic or well built, but he goes jogging often, and it shows in the toned muscles of his legs. I drag my gaze up his body while he kicks his pants away. Like a lioness, I pounce on him and wrap my arms around his neck before slamming my mouth against his.

I kiss him with rage, with the need to feel more, so much more. We become a tangled web of limbs as we fall back against the mattress, and once more, I find myself beneath Taj's body. He blankets himself over me, his hard cock pressing against my thigh.

My heart thunders in my ears, and my breath quickens, but it's not because of Taj. It's because of *him. Christian*. I let my eyes fall closed, and I can see him as clear as day in my mind. I imagine it's him here with me and not Taj.

His fingers ghost between my thighs, parting my folds and sinking deep inside.

"You're so beautiful, Siân. I want to see if it's possible for you to look any prettier when you come on my hand and then cock."

"Oh, God." It's all I can get out in response.

He's everywhere. In the air I breathe, under my skin, and inside my mind. He's owning me like only he can, and I never want him to stop. I want to give him the keys to my heart and body and never get them back. His hot breath fans against my chest, and then I feel his lips on my skin like a fiery brand. I gasp, my hips lifting with pleasure that zings through me.

His woodsy scent surrounds me, filling my lungs with every breath I take. I can taste him on my lips and feel him beneath my skin.

I'm pulled from the fantasy when Taj wraps a hand around my throat and gently squeezes. He's never done something so erotic, and his touch grabs my attention.

My eyes flash to his, and he grabs me by the hip with his other hand before sinking deep inside me with one thrust. My core burns, and I barely bite back a wince from the intrusion.

"Fuck, you're so tight, Siân," Taj grits through his straight white teeth while peering down at me. He doesn't give me a moment to adjust to him and starts thrusting hard and fast. I'm not necessarily in pain, but I'm not nearly as aroused as I should be.

It's clear to me, even as I look up at him, watching his features twist with pure bliss as he selfishly takes from me, that this will not work anymore. I'm tired of not being satisfied, tired of not feeling the spark.

"Do you feel it? How good we are together? How perfect of a fit we are?" He grunts.

My mind reels, and I let myself sink into my mind. I become almost numb, letting him use my body, which he does. He fucks me, pressing me deep into the mattress with his body. His hold on me tightens. His movements become faster, jerky, and I know he's close to coming.

I force myself to moan his name, the single word coming out in a hoarse whisper. It's lifeless and quiet. He shudders against me, his hips pressed tight against mine as he empties himself inside me.

I let out a sigh, knowing that it's over.

Both physically and mentally. I thought maybe if we had sex, if he kissed me, if we connected intimately things would be different, but it's clear were past repair.

If I wanted Taj, I wouldn't have been envisioning Christian. Taj pulls away, his chest heaving. His lips graze my forehead, and it takes everything inside me not to pull away from him. I know I have to end it now, but I'm not sure how or when I'm going to do it.

Moving from between my legs, the connection between our bodies snaps.

All that can be heard are our harsh breaths filling the room. Even as I lie here on the mattress with my boyfriend in front of me, my thoughts are still on Christian.

In my mind, he is all I can feel, all I can see. I know it's wrong, and it makes no sense, but I'm drawn to him. I can't stop thinking about him. It's almost pathetic.

I wish it was Christian who brought me home tonight because even I know he wouldn't have left me so unsatisfied. Of course I didn't come, but that doesn't matter.

I'm not going to tell Taj. I'll wait until he leaves, and then I'll finish the job myself. Staring at the back of his head, I know that no matter what, I'm going to have to end this.

Neither of us deserves to carry on this way.

VILLAIN

9

CHRISTIAN

Is this what it's like for her, what she's settled for? A mediocre fuck from a mediocre guy in this ridiculous excuse of a life she's chosen. To be touched by a motherfucker without a clue on how to read her body. To give herself to a bitch made man, who's got more than Siân's sweet pussy on his mind.

I tighten my hand around the cuff link, my nails digging into my palms. Does she know? How long has he been fucking her best friend under her nose?

This is why I had to find her. This is why she needs me. To protect her and give her the attention she deserves. To make her see that fate is the only thing that matters. She was mine a long time ago, and to know, to see with my own eyes that someone else has touched her—*fucked* her—sets a fire ablaze deep inside me.

Taj climbs off her, a grin plastered on his pitiful face. As he scoots to the edge of the bed to dress, Siân lies lazily against her pillow, uncertainty and dissatisfaction written in the lines of her expression.

She didn't come. I knew that from the way she moaned his name, weak, unenthused, and lifeless. But watching the way she's staring at the back of his head, her face void of the bliss that usually follows a good lay, it's loud and clear.

And this sorry son of a bitch doesn't even notice. Yet he carries himself as if it's a job well done. He needs to go before I lose every ounce of composure and gut him like I've been dying to do from the moment I knew he existed.

But instead, he takes his time dragging his clothes back onto his body. "Wow." He holds his shirt out in front of him, inspecting it. "I've never seen you like that before." He fingers the spaces where his buttons used to be. "So aggressive. I liked it. Maybe we should fight more often," he says and glances at her over his shoulder.

Siân gives him a fake smile, and I realize she does that a lot. The first night at the bar and again tonight at the club. She doesn't love him, and it's clear to anyone with eyes that she's bored with him. Yet she hasn't ended things—why?

He playfully touches her outstretched leg, and her grin grows even faker. And again, this self-absorbed bastard misses the discomfort that's evident in her features. Her oppression reads loud and clear. Even I, a man with no feelings, can see it.

"You okay?" he asks when she doesn't respond.

She barely nods.

She's lying to you, dick.

"Good," he quips and pulls his damaged shirt up over his shoulders. "Walk me to the door?"

Siân sits up and grabs the T-shirt resting at the bottom of her mattress when I came in. The sheet she attempted to cover herself with falls around her waist, and she slips the oversized shirt over her head. I can't help but admire her naked torso, her full breasts on display for me.

She climbs from the bed, and the two disappear from view. A second later, I creep out of the bathroom, peeking around the corner to be sure I'm not caught. The coast is clear. I can hear the door open and Siân's voice carrying up the stairs.

"I'll call you later," Taj promises.

"Okay. Have a good night." The sound of the door hinges follows next.

"Wait," he interrupts. "You're not going to kiss me?"

"Yeah. Sorry," she mutters.

"Siân. You're not still mad after what we just did, are you? I thought we were good now."

Something crunches under my boot, distracting me from her response. I look down at a crumpled-up receipt. I pick it up and quickly snatch the pen that's next to her journal from the nightstand. With one last glance around the room, I quietly slip over to the exit to hide in the hall until I can sneak out the rear entrance of the house.

But when I reach the threshold, Siân is already at the top of the stairs and rounding the banister toward her room. Thankfully, her gaze is pointed at the floor. Otherwise, she'd see me.

"Shit," I mumble under my breath and run to her closet, closing it just as she enters the bedroom.

I peek through the slits, waiting as she steps into the master bathroom. My heart pounds in my ears, and adrenaline races through my veins. Siân flicks on the light and removes her oversized shirt simultaneously.

Smooth, blemish-free, ivory skin draws my attention, and I bite down on my bottom lip. My dick twitches at the sight of her small but round ass. *What a lousy fuck*, I think to myself. He doesn't know what to do to her, how to brand her body so that she'll feel him even when they're apart. That sweet ass of her would be marked with my palm prints, red and raw from a real good time.

I lick my lips as she reaches into the shower, and the water sputters to life. Siân steps into the tub, dragging the clear shower curtain closed. Steam builds, fogging the plastic. But I can see her anyway. I trace the trail the stream makes over her skin, down her breasts, and over her flat stomach.

She can't know how beautiful she is—how perfect. If she did, she'd demand better tonight. She'd taken her pleasure from him instead of letting him leave without finishing the job.

Siân dips her head under the water, and her head falls back. I can see her body relaxing and a sudden change in her breaths. It's not until I catch sight of her hands coming up to cup her breasts that it dawns on me she's turned on. By what, I'm not sure. It can't be because of that dumb asshole. No, that's not it. He doesn't deserve to be the subject of whatever fantasy is building in her mind.

She squeezes her tits together, putting extra focus on her nipples. My mouth waters with the wish that I could replace her hands with my tongue. I bet she tastes as sweet as she smells. The urge to touch her is strong, but I manage to keep from bursting in, yanking the curtains back, and taking her cunt with my mouth.

Instead, I lurk in the shadows of her closet, palming my dick through my jeans. And when she brings her face down to her chest, and I admire the way her tongue flicks across her pert nipples, I let out a hiss.

A smile tugs at my lips, a sense of intrigue taking over. She's different behind closed doors. The way she handled Taj and pushed him on the mattress and the way she's feasting on herself tells me so. In person, she's safe and boring, but when no one else is looking, when desire calls her name, she's wilder. She knows what it takes to get her over the edge, even if she's been too afraid to show the world.

But I see her, and I like this version of her.

She drags a hand down her front and between her legs. My back buckles, and my own hand moves of its own accord, rubbing my erection, then releasing my zipper. She moves her fingers over her sex while the other hand continues to massage her breast.

As her head falls back again, I pull my cock through my boxers and give it one long stroke. I'm as hard as a rock, pre-cum beading at the tip, the head angry and hungry for her. I can't even remember the last time I've gotten my dick wet. All I know is that if I don't get out of here, I'm bound to take her hard and fast. I don't move, though. I can't. Not even if I wanted to, because the sounds of her soft cries immobilize me, locking me in place.

Siân rests a foot on the edge of the tub and angles herself deeper into her pussy. I imagine what she looks like up close. I've already seen that she's bare, and I can only guess she's soaked and tight. I picture how hard and swollen her clit is and envision myself tasting her.

"Fuck," I growl low in my throat and grip my dick harder.

I stroke myself, slow at first, in tune with her rhythm, fucking myself as she finishes the job Taj wasn't man enough to handle. Heat floods my body, and all of a sudden, this small-ass closet is too small. It's suffocating, but I bear it if it means I get to come with her.

I want her so badly right now I can't think straight. My eyes close, but I force them open, not wanting to miss a moment of her show, one she isn't even aware she's putting on. That turns me on even more. Being here, jacking my dick to her without her knowing. The potential of getting caught by her is thrilling.

"Ahh," I mutter under my breath. "E vero topolina, fatti venire." *That's right, topolina, make yourself come.*

"Mm," she moans, her voice just a hair louder than the stream of water. "Christian."

I freeze a moment, unsure if I heard her correctly.

"Christ—mm," she starts to mutter my name again, but it's drowned out by another moan.

"Shit," I hiss and pump my fist over my shaft with a vengeance.

I visualize us together, losing myself as if it's real, as if I can feel her and she can feel me.

We're flesh to flesh surrounded by steam. Her bare breasts are soft against my hard chest, her ass plump and firm in my grasp. She releases a needy breath when my length presses along her thighs. With her eyes, she begs me to claim her. Her lips are soft when I kiss her. The remnants of the drinks she's had tonight are still on her tongue.

"I want you to fuck me, Christian."

"Piacere mio," I whisper against her lips. My pleasure.

Her breath hitches when I scoop her into my arms and dig my nails into her ass while I support her. I push her against the wall, and her back arches from the cold tile despite the heat around us. My dick nestles under her, the warmth of her valley all too inviting. She wraps her arms around me as I lift her, allowing my cock to find her entrance.

Siân gasps when I slip inside her, and my balls draw tight from the fit. So perfect, so hot, and all mine. Impatient and needy, she moves in my hold, taking what she craves. And I let her. For a moment, I stand still, balancing her with my palms to keep her in place and spread wide for me, allowing her to have her way with me. Water pours down over us, blurring my vision, adding to the experience. She's wet all over, and it's driving me crazy.

I feel her pussy clench around my dick, and I can't stop myself. I thrust upward, meeting her grind, and fucking her like both of our lives depend on it. With her mouth wide and her eyes closed, Siân's head falls back against the wall as I pound into her.

Her moans come out clipped around her heavy breaths, and her breasts jiggle with each thrust. I crane my neck to take her mound into my mouth, my motions increasing when she digs her nails into my shoulders.

"Oh, God. Christian," she whispers loud enough for me to hear.

The sound of my name on her lips again pulls me from my fantasy, forcing me back to reality, and it's just as hot. Just as real.

I focus on Siân, the ecstasy on her face calling to the beast in me. Her back is hunched, her mouth wide, and eyes closed as she rides her fingers. She's about to come. I know because I can already see her legs getting weak. A chill rips its way down my spine as my seed begs to be spilled.

Snatching a shirt from a hanger, I drop the pen and receipt I'd forgotten about and hold the shirt in place with one hand while continuing to beat my meat with the other. I grow harder, the tip of my dick throbbing for a release. But I can't let go yet, not until she does. Over and over, I fist my shaft, biting back a groan, nearly losing my balance, and just when I think I can't take any more, we come—*together*.

"Oh, oh, fuck," she cries out, her body bucking from her climax.

My shoulders slump from my bated breaths, and I stare at her through my lashes. Spent and sated, I clean myself up with her shirt and toss it to the floor. Remembering the pen and paper I dropped, I crack the door just a bit to use the lighting from the bathroom and the single lamp. I snatch them both up when I find them and slip from the closet.

Siân pulls herself together and is lathering up a loofah. I stick around for a second longer, making a silent promise to one day make her scream my name for real. As I step away, I glance down at the panties she wore right before giving herself to that worthless piece of shit. Quickly I grab them, bring them to my nose, and inhale her sweet scent. A scent wasted on the likes of a man who doesn't deserve her. I shove the underwear into my pocket and sneak out of her room and down the stairs.

Her cat is at the bottom, hissing at me as he did earlier, but when I get closer, it backs away. I round the corner, stopping in front of the console table that houses the pictures. I stare at the image of her and Kyla, my blood boiling again when I remember the deceit from the two people who are supposed to care for her. I guess I was right after all. A girl like Kyla always has something to hide.

A car door slams from outside, and it sounds close. A second later, Kyla's voice travels inside, and I decide to push it all away. The time will come when I deal with her, but for now, I'll let it be. I make haste and use the pen and receipt to scribble a note, tuck it under the picture frame, and bolt toward the back door. I make it out as Kyla swings open the front door and turns on the lights. I watch her remove her shoes and carry them into the kitchen. All it would take is a few measly seconds to end her right now and make her pay for ever betraying my topolina.

VILLAIN

10

SIÂN

Is it possible to be addicted to a person? I'm sitting at the kitchen nook, staring down at my phone with a stupid smile on my lips that won't go away.

I'm sure I look insane, smiling at nothing, but it's not *nothing*. It's someone. He messages me every morning and night. He takes the time to ask me how I'm doing throughout the day, and even though I know it's harmless and we're just friends, I also know it could be more. A part of me wishes for it to be more, but with Taj still in the picture, it can't happen.

The front door creaks as it opens, and I try to wipe the smile from my face before Kyla comes walking into the kitchen, but that's impossible when another text from Christian comes through a second later.

Christian: *We're going to cash in that rain check soon, so I can take you on a proper date.*

I smirk, the heavy feeling in my lungs lifts when I talk to him, and I can't help but type out a sassy reply. It's a feeble attempt at flirting, but I try.

Me: *Or what?*

I look up right as Kyla comes walking into the kitchen, heading straight for the fridge. Her chest is heaving, and beads of sweat trail down her face.

Christian: *You have no idea the lengths I'll go to get what I want, sweetheart. Don't tempt me.*

The mere idea of seeing him lose control… it makes me shiver. I feel that there is so much more to the mysterious Christian than what meets the eye, and I want to crack him open and discover all his secrets.

"Who's got you smiling?" Kyla interrupts my thoughts.

My cheeks heat, and I stumble over my words for a moment. "I'm… I'm not smiling."

Kyla rolls her eyes and twists the cap off the water, taking a couple of gulps from the bottle before wiping her mouth with the back of her hand. "You mean to tell me your lips being curved up at the sides isn't smiling? Next, you're going to tell me you aren't happy when anyone from a mile away could see the puppy dog look in your eyes."

Shit, do I really look that happy?

"Jeez, when did it become a crime to be happy?"

"It's not a crime, but then again, I've never seen you smile like you are right now."

I want to tell her it has everything to do with Christian but decide not to. Something tells me she wouldn't approve of us texting like we are.

"Well, nothing's going on. I'm just happy."

"Did you and Taj finally work things out?"

I nod, and my phone pings with an incoming text from Christian that I ignore. "Things are fine with us. I mean, they could be better, but we aren't fighting anymore, and he apologized." I shrug, and Kyla downs the rest of her water.

She leans against the counter. "So, he apologized and is off the hook? The way it sounded, you were really upset. Is something else going on? I'm your best friend. You can tell me anything, Siân."

I should lean on Kyla more and vent to her, but lately, I've felt like she doesn't hear me, no matter what I say to her. Then again, maybe I'm just projecting those thoughts on myself. She's my best friend, and she's always been here for me.

"Honestly, he's just been different, and we don't see eye to eye on things anymore. I feel us growing apart, and I'm not sure how to stop it." I frown.

"Well, there isn't anything you can do if you don't love each other anymore."

"Neither of us ever said we didn't love each other, just that..."

My phone pings again, and I get distracted by the sound, knowing it's a message from Christian. Damn, is that man insistent.

Christian: *You better think twice before you ignore me. I already told you not to tempt me.*

Christian: *Give me your address. I'll be there in five minutes, and I'll show you what happens when you play with fire. *wink face**

I can't help but giggle a little from that last message. Out of nowhere, Kyla swipes the phone from my hands. For a brief second, panic floods my veins, but I realize I have nothing to hide. She looks at the screen and grins.

"Who is this message from?" She tilts her head to the side, examining the screen further. "Christian? The guy from the bar? He's the one who's got you smiling?"

"Yes, he's the one who's got me smiling," I confess and swipe my phone back from her hands.

She takes a step back from the counter and places her hands on her hips. "I feel like you might be holding out on me. I didn't know you guys exchanged numbers? How long have you been talking, and better yet…" She wiggles her eyebrows at me. "What have you been talking about?"

I snicker. "That's for me to know and you to never find out."

"Oh, my God."

"What?" I ask, concerned by the seriousness in her voice. We were just joking and laughing, and now she's suddenly serious. Did I miss something?

A slow grin appears on her lips. "You like him, don't you?"

My face becomes a raging ball of fire. "No… I mean…" *Dammit.* Denying it isn't going to make things better. Kyla will push and dig until she gets the answer she wants.

Her grin becomes even bigger if that's even possible. Fuck, I can't lie, not when my face is already telling the truth.

"Fine, yes, I like him."

"I knew it!" she yells. "I knew you liked him. I can tell, and just so you know, I'm happy for you, and no matter what you do, I'll be here for you."

The meaning behind her words sends me crashing back into reality. I still have unfinished business with Taj. I shouldn't be getting close to Christian, but like a moth drawn to a flame, I can't help myself. The temptation is too great. He makes me feel things I've never felt.

As if she can sense the joy leaving me, Kyla interjects. "Don't feel bad for talking to another guy. You aren't doing anything wrong, Siân."

I nod in agreement, even if it doesn't feel that way to me.

"I'm going to go take a real quick shower, and then maybe we can grab some lunch together or something," she adds.

"Yeah, that would be great. I feel like it's been forever since we've had a girls' day."

"Gah, I know. Adult life, school, and boyfriend drama are ruining everything."

We break out into laughter, and Kyla exits the kitchen to take a shower. I pick up my phone and start to text Christian back, telling him he'll never be able to show me what happens when I play with fire when Kyla comes storming back into the kitchen, wearing a scowl on her face.

"Did you move the pictures in the foyer?" It's a random question, but the way Kyla's looking at me tells me she's asking a serious question.

"No, why would I?"

"I don't know, but the pictures are moved."

I shake my head. "Are you sure?"

Creases of frustration form on Kyla's forehead, and I can tell she's getting mad. "Yes, I'm sure. You know how anal I am about things being in their place. If you didn't move it and I didn't move it, then why is it moved?"

Her voice grows louder as she speaks, and I have to stop from rolling my eyes. Kyla can be, well, a little over the top sometimes.

"Look, maybe one of us bumped the table. It's not a big deal."

"Yeah, I'm not sure that's what moved the pictures, but I guess we'll go with it, since there isn't any other explanation." She turns and walks out of the kitchen before I can muster up a response to her outburst.

I'm still reeling from her verbal whiplash when she returns to the kitchen, a crinkled piece of white paper in her hand.

"What the hell is this?" she asks, shoving it at me.

I grab the piece of paper from her hand, bewildered by her attitude. "What the hell is going on with you?" I ask a moment before looking at it.

As soon as I see the words on it, my heart sinks into my stomach.

Sei Mio is scribbled in black ink on the paper, and my hands tremble while I stare at the words, reading them back to myself. *You're mine.*

Panic bubbles to the surface like a pan of water boiling over.

It wasn't me being paranoid the other night. I was really being watched. *Oh, God.*

"Where... Where did you find this?" I try to hide the fear I'm feeling, but the trembling of my voice gives me away.

"In the foyer on the table where the pictures are. I told you they were moved."

My brain short-circuits, and I know I have to leave. I need to go see Cynthia and tell her it's time to run again. I don't want to scare Kyla, but I can't tell her what's going on. I... I just need to leave, need to get out of here and devise a plan.

After all this time, he's after me again. What if he never left? What if he's been waiting for the perfect moment to show himself? The bad thoughts trickle in slowly, and I have to stop them before I drown in them. I shove away from the table and push past Kyla, who's standing in front of me like a statue.

"Where are you going? Is this some type of joke? You know how OCD I am. If you're trying to fuck with me, Siân, just say so now," she says, trailing me. I grab my purse and shove my hand inside to grab my keys.

My heart thunders in my chest, and a wave of dizziness slams into me. Everything I did was for nothing. *Everything.* All the moving, name changes, friends lost. All the years have been wasted, and for what? *Him* to find me all over again?

A hand lands on my shoulder, and I jump. A scream catches in my throat, and I whirl around, realizing it's only Kyla. *Shit.* I was so caught up in my thoughts, I forgot she was here. She's staring at me like I'm a wild animal ready to attack.

"I'm sorry I have to leave. I need to go see Cynthia," I stutter.

Kyla's nose wrinkles, and I can see her anger rising. "You can't just leave without telling me what the hell is going on."

I stare at her, pleading with her to understand. She's my best friend, and I haven't failed to realize that I've endangered her by association, but I need to figure things out before I tell her anything.

"I'll explain everything later. I'm sorry." I turn and walk out the door before she says anything else.

I can feel her eyes on me as I walk away, and I feel horrible because all over again, things are falling apart. He's found me, he's fucking found me, and while the last thing I want to do is run, what other option do I have? I climb into the car and shove the key into the ignition. The engine roars to life, and I pull away from the curb, racing down the street. My brain feels like it's been put in a blender. All I can think about is running, disappearing into the night before he gets ahold of me.

Cynthia is going to be devastated. *Ugh.* I grip the steering wheel a little tighter. Oh, God, Cynthia, she's given so much of her life to keep me safe. She's made sacrifice after sacrifice and lost years with her family just to be *my* family. We'd finally gotten some peace and have each built some semblance of a life here. She's bought a house, made friends with the woman down the street from her, and even joined a knitting club. And now—it's all been for nothing. We're going to have to move again, make name changes, and leave everything we have here behind, and I fucking hate it. She deserves so much better, but is there no other way around it?

I grit my teeth, trying to think if there could be another way, but the only other option is facing this man head-on. An image of Christian pops into my mind, and I see him telling me to take back control. I see him telling me to push back and not let my stalker dictate my life. Am I strong enough to do that?

I get on the interstate, the speed of the car climbing higher and higher. My heart is racing, and I'm paranoid all over again.

I continuously look over my shoulder and in the rearview mirror. Thankfully, nothing happens, and after a short drive, I exit and enter the suburbs on the outskirts of town.

By the time I pull up to Cynthia's house, I'm shaking. I park the car and force myself to walk up the front steps. Fear and anger cycle through me. This is all my fault. Had I been more careful or safer perhaps, maybe he wouldn't have found me again.

I pound against the heavy wood door, and a second later, it opens. Cynthia's eyes are big, and the look on her face tells me she knows something terrible has happened.

"What is it, sweetheart? You look like you've seen a ghost."

My heart sinks into my stomach. "He's found us. There was a note. At the house Kyla and I share. He's back. He's found us again." There is no hiding the devastation in my voice. I'm sinking deep inside myself.

Cynthia's forehead creases, and she grabs me by the arm, tugging me inside before slamming the door and locking it. I take a few wobbly steps toward the sofa. My entire world is being flipped upside down.

"Okay, first, you need to calm down."

"Calm down?" My voice cracks. "How can I calm down when I feel like I've screwed everything up? If not for me, this man wouldn't be after us. We wouldn't be skipping towns and changing names every few years."

Cynthia's the closest person I have to a mother, and I would never want to risk her getting hurt. She understands my fears and anger better than anyone because she's been with me through it all. She is the only constant in my life, and I can't let anything happen to her. I can't be selfish because it's not only my life at risk here.

Sensing how close to the edge I am, she takes the spot beside me on the sofa and places her hand on my knee. Her closeness brings me comfort, but it doesn't extinguish the fears playing on repeat in my mind.

"It was only a note, right?"

"Yes, a note that says *Sei Mio.* Why would he leave a note that says you're mine?"

Her green eyes, which mimic my own, turn soft.

"I'm not sure, but I think we should think this through before we make any rash decisions. Was there any suspicion of a break-in? Maybe it's an old note that fell out of one of your bags? We've worked hard to have the life we have now. I don't want to toss it away because of a miscommunication or something that might be taken out of context."

"I don't want that either. That's why you're going to stay, and I'm going to leave—*alone.*"

The likelihood of that is slim. It's a pipe dream. The man is relentless in making certain I see that he's after me. He wants my fear and my tears. He wants me scared and weak, but I'm not the little girl I was the last time he came into my life. I'm not the same at all, and maybe I need to realize that. Before, I needed Cynthia. She was—*is* all I have. But now it's time for me to think of her.

Cynthia stares at me a moment as the weight of my words settles around her. I see the change in her demeanor, the resistance to my suggestion written all over her face. She loves me and separating is not something she'll take lightly.

"Not happening, Siân. You can get that out of your head right damn now. If we need to leave, we'll go together. Same as always."

"Aren't you tired?" I ask, my shoulders slumping with my heavy exhale.

Cynthia stares at me, and I don't know if it's because she doesn't have an answer or because I'm right. She is tired. We both are. The difference here is that—whoever this stalker is—they don't want her.

She can finally be free. Cynthia has raised me, shown me what it means to be a woman, and taught me how to survive. Her sacrifice has been made. Now it's my turn to look out for her.

"You've said it yourself, Cyn. You have a life here. You've made friends and bought this beautiful house. Your sacrifice is over."

Cynthia turns away from me with her shoulders hiked around her ears. I inch closer and place a hand on her shoulder.

"Tell me you're not happy?"

She doesn't speak, barely even moves.

"You've taken care of me, taught me how to make it in this world, and given your all in the name of keeping me safe. It's my turn now. I couldn't live with myself if something happened to you."

"No." Cynthia shakes her head in rapid succession.

"I love you. And if you get hurt, I'll die. I need to do this. I need you to let me go." I suck a ragged breath into my lungs.

Cynthia faces me. "No, Siân. I won't have it."

"Do you want to leave?" I ask.

She drops her chin to her chest.

"Exactly. I know how much you care for me, Cynthia. You're the only mother I've ever had. You've given so much of your life and ran with me anytime we've sensed danger. You're the most selfless person I know. But he isn't after you. Please. I *need* to do this for *you*. Let me take care of this my way."

Cynthia throws her hand in the air, letting it rest at her side. "And what's that? Allow him to capture you. No, Siân. You can forget it."

"Cyn—"

"No," she deadpans. "Yes. I love you. I always will. But if you think I'm letting you go through any of this alone, you've got another thing coming."

"Cyn—"

"I'm talking."

I swallow a breath. There have only been two other times when she's put her foot down, and even then, I knew not to challenge her. When she means business—*she means business*.

"*If* we have to run, we will do so together. But right now, I think you need to contact the police. Only *then* will we decide. You're the most important thing to me, Siân. And while I appreciate where you were going with that little speech, it'll *never* happen."

I sigh, wanting to concede, but I know I don't have a choice.

"Okay," I say in defeat.

"This is what we are going to do. Call the police, make a report, and allow them to investigate. If we need to run, we will. You've been through a lot, Siân, but that doesn't mean he's found us. If he had, we would have known a long time ago."

"Maybe you're right. Maybe it's nothing. But I would much rather leave you out of it."

"I'm not saying if things become dangerous, we won't disappear, but I think we might be running before we're walking. You need to call the police and have them come to the house. They can check for fingerprints and see if anyone has broken into the house."

"Yes! As soon as I get home, I will call them." I jump from the sofa, ready to put this new idea into action. "I'm going to go now, and I'll call Taj on my way and have him meet me there."

"Good, and call me if there are any new developments."

I nod and wrap her up in a tight hug. She is getting older, and the thought of anything happening to her hurts my heart. In my eyes, she is my mother, and I will go to the ends of the earth to protect her, just as she has done for me.

"I'll let you know when I get home," I say, releasing her.

We stare at each other for a long moment, and then she's walking me to the door. She stands on the front steps, watching me until I reach the car. It s getting dark now, and I'm terrified of being alone, knowing this madman is after me once again. But I pick up the phone anyway and call Taj. The line rings and rings with no answer. I call four more times before I give up, my anger and pain directed at someone else entirely.

Why is it when I need him he is never there for me? I shouldn't be surprised. Even in this instance, Taj isn't the man I should turn to.

VILLAIN

11

CHRISTIAN

"Will it be just the two of you?" Jennifer, the leasing manager, asks as she escorts us through the penthouse loft.

"Who?" Tony blurts out and points his thumb between himself and me. "Me and this asshat?"

I scoff and glance back down at the phone in my hand. "No," I deadpan. "Just me."

From my peripheral, I notice Jennifer nod and continue walking us through the features of the living room. My subconscious is elsewhere, though. I open my messenger app. It's been hours since my last message to Siân, and she's yet to respond. After watching her bring herself to orgasm the other night, it's all I can think about. Her beautiful face and sweet cries continue to play on repeat in my mind. My dick is throbbing right now just picturing it.

"Perché siamo anche qui?" *Why are we even here?* Tony rushes over to me and whispers.

Still staring at my phone, my brows knit tight, and I release a breath, then let my shoulders fall as I switch to the cloning program. A bright light beams when the colorful app stirs to life, and her text thread loads on the screen. I swipe up, my attention being pulled away from Tony's persistence.

"Christian," he grits out and steps back a little when I drag my eyes to his face. "What the fuck is going on with you?"

"Nothing," I snip.

"Something's going on, and your father isn't going to like it. "

"Does it look like I give a shit about my father?" I bark.

My voice travels through the apartment, startling Jennifer, who gasps in the distance. I roll my shoulders back and peer over his head at Jennifer.

"All I'm saying is you're distracted," he groans through his teeth. "Taking out Armon when we still needed him. Got us looking at fucking lofts when we have a meeting in three hours. What the hell is up?"

"Is everything okay, boys?" Jennifer coos, but there's a slight tremor in her tone. I don't blame her at all for being cautious. She is a woman alone in a room with two suspicious men she doesn't know.

"I think you're forgetting who's in charge here." I stuff my phone into my back pocket, adjust my pants on my hips, and turn my gaze to him. "If my father has a problem, I'll handle it. Now, if it isn't clear to you, I'll be sticking around for a little while."

"This is about that Giuliani girl, isn't it?"

I stare at him, my jaw clenching tight at the mention of Siân. He's right. This—my staying in town, this apartment, even me being distracted—it's about Siân—*for* Siân. Tony wouldn't understand because this isn't how I usually operate. Typically, when I ask him to find someone, they're dead shortly after. Siân is different. Siân is my obsession, and like every other drug, she's addicting.

"Jennifer," I say sternly and walk around Tony, "thank you for meeting us. I know the office closes early on Sundays, but I just really had to see the place."

She smiles, her eyes lighting up the moment I'm close to her. And when I reach out to brush a strand of hair from her face, her breath hitches. "Of course. It's my pleasure." Her grin widens, and she shies away, turning to run her hand along the counter. "So, how do you like the space? This kitchen is to die for. Perfect for your lady friend to cook for you." And there it is, the inevitable flirting. "I'm sorry if I'm assuming. The paperwork you sent over before you arrived didn't list any other names."

But she asked if Tony would be here with me. She knows the answer and is just fishing for what she's truly curious about. The moment I stepped out of the Ferrari, I saw the lust build in her eyes from the entryway of this ridiculously expensive high-rise.

I let out a low smirk and walk farther into the kitchen. "Actually, I'm a much better cook than my girlfriend," I toss over my shoulder and catch the disappointment wash over her. I run my gaze along the length of the island. "Is this real marble?" I knock on the surface.

I lied—partially. Siân is mine, but she just doesn't know it yet.

"Yes. It is. Everything in this apartment is high-end, from the deep-set sink built into your island, the stove, fridge, and even a state-of-the-art shower. This is a loft, so the floor plan is open and leads out to the extended balcony. But the bedroom and office are closed to provide privacy."

Jennifer describes all the features while Tony talks on his phone, glancing between me and the view overlooking the city. But again, my mind wanders, and images of Siân's innocent face flood me. Everywhere

I look or move in this apartment, I picture her being here and me having my way with her. This countertop sits at the perfect height for me to splay her across it and fuck her senseless. In the center of the living room on the brand-new hardwood floors. Up against the built-in bookshelf that's right off the front door. *Everywhere.*

Blinking to clear my mind, I rejoin the others in the large, open living room. Jennifer is stationed back at the island with a stack of papers in front of her.

"So, you still want to call this place home?" she asks with a pleading smile.

I nod and give her the biggest and fakest grin I can muster. "It's perfect."

"Great. I'll tell you, Mr. Russo, this has been the easiest apartment booking ever. Thanks to your assistant sending over all your details earlier, I could get approval and do everything I needed on this end. So all I need from you is a cashier's check, money order, or card payment to handle the deposit and first and last month's rent, and you've got yourself a new home."

I clear my throat, and a second later, Tony saunters up next to me and holds out an envelope with the cashier's check I ordered him to get before we arrived. His grip is tight, forcing me to have to snatch it from him. Jennifer glances back and forth between us, the look of worry and curiosity building on her features again. But like most humans, her mood changes when she takes the check from my hand.

"The check is for the full six months. If you need any other verifying information, you can contact my assistant, and he'll get you what you need," I announce with a hard slap to Tony's back.

He flinches from the pain and glares at me, but keeps it together in front of Jennifer.

"Wow. I guess you weren't kidding when you said money was no object?"

I tip my head with a shrug. "And the furniture?"

"It'll be here and set up in three days, on Wednesday."

Jennifer smiles with her eyes when I offer her my hand. "Pleasure doing business with you, Mr. Russo."

"Please, call me Christian."

She nods. "Sure thing. Well, gentlemen, I've been here long enough on a Sunday. I have a five-year-old who's been texting me for the past hour to pick him up from his grandmother's. So, I'd say we're good here. I'll have your furniture set up and your keys ready for you midday on Wednesday, and if there is nothing else you need..." Jennifer waves toward the door, silently encouraging us to exit.

We step out into the brightly lit hall and wait for Jennifer to lock the door behind us. Usually, we don't stay in America long enough to rent property, but my father has a dummy corporation set up for occasions such as this. When you do the work we do, it's important to be prepared. You never know when shit will hit the fan, so we have a contingency plan for just about every scenario.

Jennifer leads the way back to the elevator when my phone buzzes in my pocket. I remove it to see a slew of messages bouncing across the screen. It's Siân, and if her text is any indication, I know she's found my note. A smile creeps on my lips as I read them.

Siân: *Where are you?*

Siân: *I've called you four times, Taj.*

Three dots pop up, showing that he's typing, but then they disappear.

Siân: *I need you to pick up the phone.*

Taj: *I can't right now...*

Siân: *Did you leave a note when you left last night?*

Taj: *What? Look, I'm really busy.*

Taj: *Can this wait?*

Siân: *Answer the phone.*

There's a brief pause, and my steps slow right along with it. It's not until Tony calls my name from a few feet away that I realize they have engrossed me in my phone for far too long.

Taj: *I told you, I can't talk right now.*

Siân: *I need to know if you left a note. If it wasn't you, then I think someone was in the house.*

Taj: *You were with me until I left. How could I have left a note? Who was in the house?*

Taj: *I'll call you when I'm done here. It's probably nothing.*

That's it?

This piece of shit never ceases to amaze me. This is who she's chosen to waste her time and energy on? Giving herself away to scum, a motherfucker who takes her safety as a joke. And yes, I get how ironic it is that I'm getting angry when I'm the one who's endangered her. But it's the principle. If he wears the title of being her man, then keeping her safe, even if he will fail, should be his priority.

Fire spreads through my veins as I realize that she even thought to call him. Everything about her changes the moment he walks into a room. He drains her, holds her down, and dulls her shine. She's not happy with him, so why hasn't she ended this? I realize now that if I want this to work, Taj has got to go.

We board the elevator on the lobby level and bid Jennifer another farewell. Once we're outside, I stop Tony with a grip on his bicep, waiting until Jennifer is out of earshot.

"What?" He frowns.

"I need to handle something. You're not riding." I step off the curb, back to my car.

"And how the hell am I supposed to get to the meeting? I rode here with you, remember?" he argues.

I shrug. "You're a smart man. Figure it out."

After dialing Siân's number, I unlock the Ferrari and put the speaker to my ear.

"Questa è una stronzata, Christian," Tony yells from across the street. *This is bullshit, Christian.*

She answers on the first ring. "Finally," she blurts without a greeting.

"You were waiting for me to call?" I tease, putting on my best show.

She sighs, and it takes her a second. "Oh, Christian. Sorry, I thought you were someone else."

"Ouch," I feign being offended.

She doesn't take the bait. "Christian. I—it's nice of you to call, but now isn't a good time." Her voice is strained, like she's afraid and trying desperately to keep it together.

"That doesn't sound too good." I hop behind the wheel and let the door slam shut. "What's going on?"

Siân sighs, followed by a brief pause. "Nothing," she pushes out, but by her tone, I know she doesn't believe what she's just said.

"Beautiful," I bite out.

She doesn't speak. The only sounds coming through the line are her heavy breaths and a low rumble from what I assume to be the radio.

"I can hear it in your voice. Why don't you tell me what's wrong? Maybe I can help," I promise.

Another deep breath. "I'm waiting for the cops to arrive."

Adjusting in my seat, I give my best fake expression of shock. "Did something happen?"

"I-I don't know. But... I think someone was in my house," she admits, her fear and frustration ringing loud and clear.

"Where are you?" I know the answer, but I just need her to tell me.

"I'm home. Me and Kyla, we're waiting for an officer to arrive."

I start the car. "I'm on my way," I exclaim, working extra hard to give her the impression that I'm concerned.

"No. No. Christian, you don't have to do that. I'm fine, or I will be when Taj gets here."

I grit my teeth at the mention of that asshole, but keep my anger from spilling out. "Siân. I'm here for you. I'll see you soon."

There's a rustling sound on the other end, and I imagine she's nodding. "Okay," she caves breathlessly.

Ending the call, I press the gas and peel out, heading past the campus, the coffee shop, and the bar where I first introduced myself. As I hang a left onto her block, my heart pumps loudly in my chest, so loud I can feel and hear it in my skull. Cop cars are parked awkwardly in the driveway and along the street, the flashing red and blue lights nearly obstructing my view. My tires screech when I slam the brakes into the space in front of her house.

I'm out of the car and onto her porch in a blink. The front door is open, and in the entryway is an officer, and when I glance past him, two more are surveying the house. Movement on my right alerts me to a fourth cop who's searching the grounds. I step inside but am immediately denied entry.

"Whoa, whoa. You can't just come in like that." The officer talking to Siân blocks me from entering. "Ma'am, do you know this man?"

I suck air into my lungs and will myself to relax. Authority issues aside, the last thing I need is to cause a scene. My *friend* might be in danger, and I'm the doting guy who only wants to make sure she's safe. That's the tale I want told—nothing more and nothing less.

Siân pokes her head around the door with her arms wrapped around herself—her usual form of defense, no matter how weak it is. Her features soften when we make eye contact, and it does something to me. My chest tightens at the look of relief on her face. No matter the thrill I get from being the reason for this fear, causing her relief feels just as fucking good. *I giveth and I taketh away.*

"Yes, Officer, he's my friend," she admits and rushes to me.

A groan of annoyance builds in my gut. *I'm more than your fucking friend, topolina.* I want to scream those words at her and punish her until she accepts it.

Siân throws her arms around my neck, pulling me in for a hug. I slowly wrap my arms around her waist. My body drums from the feel of her against me, my dick jolting to life just from one innocent embrace. Her scent tickles my nose, and I dig my nails into her hips.

She pulls back at that, and we stare at each other for a moment. She's been crying. Her eyes are red and puffy, and her cheeks are flushed. Then I glance down at her lips, spotting the evidence that she's been chewing on them. They're raw, and in the corner is a tiny drop of blood.

Fuck.

I want to devour her mouth and lick the blood clean off. I wet my own lips, a pitiful excuse of a surrogate for hers. This is the first I've touched her like this, the first time we've been this close, and dammit if she doesn't feel fucking amazing. So warm and soft in my hold, fragile and defenseless. She's tiny compared to me, and the realization shoots right to my balls as my mind thinks of all the ways I could break her. Even more so when I consider how ferocious she could be when she accepts who she is truly meant to be and joins me on the throne. Together in darkness is where we belong.

The heirs of two vicious dynasties.

"Thank you for coming." She pulls away, and I immediately tug her back to me.

Siân's eyes fly open, but she's something other than surprised by my actions. A response I can't quite pinpoint. One thing that is clear to me is that she wants me to touch her just as much as I do.

"Come in," she instructs after a beat.

I take a minute to let her words register before I release my grip on her waist and follow her inside. Every light in the house is on, even those upstairs. I glance at the officer over my shoulder, then focus my attention on the female a few feet away. She's hovering over the table in the hall that leads into the kitchen. The space where the pictures are. The cop dusts the frames for prints, and I have to hide the smile that threatens to break through.

Good luck, I mutter inwardly.

I've been at this game a long time. If they think I was stupid enough to leave prints, they have another thing coming. But as soon as the thought crosses my mind, my eyes shoot to the top of the stairs. The shirt I emptied my load in as I watched her finger herself.

Shit.

With an inhale, I turn to Siân and rub her arms. "Are you okay?"

She nods with her eyes closed. "Yes."

I crane my neck and hunch down to meet her gaze. "What are they saying?"

She shakes her head with her shoulders bunched up around her ears. “They don’t know. So far, there isn’t any sign of forced entry.”

“But you’re sure someone was here? How do you know?”

Siân nervously looks around, then pulls something from her back pocket. I peer at the note in her hand, my scribble scrabble staring back at me. She didn’t turn it in. What’s her game? I shake away my thoughts and rub her arms again before taking the scrap of paper from her.

“What’s this?” I ask while glaring between her and the page I now hold in my hand. “*Sei Mio.*” *You’re mine.* I recite the word on the page.

Siân frowns at me.

“Sorry. It’s Italian.”

Her brows furrow even harder.

“I studied abroad,” I lie to cover myself.

Siân blinks and shakes her head. “Right. They left this over next to a picture of Taj and me.”

“Okay?”

“The picture was faced down when Kyla found it.” She turns away.

“And that means...?” I shift to keep her eyes focused on me.

“We never touch those pictures. We’ve lived here for nearly three years, and this is the first time the picture was moved. There were even fingerprints.”

My spine tenses. “Can they pinpoint them?”

She shakes her head.

I yank her to me, nestling her head into the crook of my neck. “Can I use your bathroom?” I ask while leaning back only enough to read her expression.

Siân raises an arm to the staircase. "First door on your right."

"Okay." I swallow. "Look at me."

She does.

"I'm here, and I won't let anyone hurt you."

She nods.

The thing is, I mean it. Her safety, even down to her happiness, all matters to me. I back away, refusing to allow Tony's words to seep in. He's right. I'm distracted. Tonight, we're making a deal with a new connection, someone associated with Armon who promises to pick up the slack that ole boy left behind.

Instead, I'm hours away, working a long con to win over a woman who's been presumed dead for nearly sixteen years. Pushing my reality to the back of my mind, I jog up the steps two at a time, glancing behind me to be sure no one is watching me. The coast is clear, so I walk to the part of the house where Siân's room is.

With one more look behind me, I push past the threshold and tiptoe over to the closet. Using my phone for light, I search the pile on the floor for the shirt I blew my load in. When I locate it, I scoop it up and conceal it around the waistband of my gray slacks. I cross the floor and slip out into the hall, freezing when I run into Kyla.

Her brows pull together, and she fists the banister. "Can I help you?"

I run my palms over my pants. "I was using the bathroom."

Kyla crosses one arm over her shoulder, then pivots to point at the door three feet to my left.

I give her a pinched grin, deciding not to argue with her. Kyla stares me down as I saunter around her and make my way back down to the living room. Siân is sitting on the sofa, her sad green eyes meeting mine the second I come into view.

"Any updates yet?" I ask and take the seat next to her while letting my hand settle on her back.

It's subtle the way she reacts, so natural that I bet she doesn't even notice. She's comfortable with me. I noticed it the first time in the bar. She probably doesn't even realize how relaxed she is around me. Or notice how perfect we are together.

Not for long, though. This game has been fun, but I don't know how long I can go without claiming her.

"Nothing yet." She shrugs, and I squeeze her shoulder.

"I'll get you some water?" I stand and peer at Kyla, who is now standing at the bottom of the staircase, her gaze burning into me.

"What is he doing here?" I hear Kyla ask Siân.

Stepping into the kitchen, I open one set of cabinet doors before finding the cupboard on the other end. I can feel eyes on me, but I don't turn around to see who it is. My guess is it's the friend. It's no surprise she's suspicious of me when she's the one with something to hide.

I remove two glasses and fill them with water from the fridge. An officer enters through the back, the screen door slamming shut. I glance at the cop, but she barely notices me. She walks ahead of me, and I follow her into the living room. The officer moves out of my way as I step around her and pass the drinks off to both Kyla and Siân. Kyla keeps her gaze locked on me, then she leans in to whisper into Siân's ear. Except she's horrible at it, and I hear her anyway.

"How does he know where everything is?" Kyla accuses.

I pretend not to listen and settle in beside Siân.

"What are you talking about?" Siân mumbles.

"What's going on between you two?" Kyla tips her chin in my direction, and from the corner of my eye, I witness Siân glancing at me.

"Nothing," Siân claims.

We all know she's lying. Even this officer here can see it. He's watched us from the very second she hugged me.

"Ms. Danforth and Ms. Zimmerman. There is no sign of forced entry. None of your doors or windows have been tampered with. But when is the last time you've been in your backyard?" the lady officer asks.

Kyla and Siân frown at each other.

"Never. Not since we moved in."

"Hm." The officer scribbles on her notepad.

Siân scoots to the edge of her seat, and Kyla straightens her spine.

"No. What?" Siân quizzes.

"It's just that footprints are leading to and from the porch and back to the front yard."

A shiver runs the length of Siân's spine. "So, someone broke in?" She nods rapidly.

"That's the thing. We can't find a shred of evidence that someone broke into your home. All the locks are intact, and there isn't anything that tells us otherwise."

"Someone was here. I promise you," Siân cries out, her eyes blinking over and over.

Kyla leans in and whispers in Siân's ear. "Show them?"

I'm able to make out her words.

"What are you not telling us?" the first officer blurts.

Siân groans and digs the note she showed me from her pocket. The lady cop takes it, and the two of them examine it, frowns forming on their faces.

"What does this say?" the male cop questions.

"We don't know," Kyla interjects.

"You're mine," Siân translates, and everyone stares at the blankness in her expression. She drops her head and begins fiddling with her fingers. "I've been stalked before," she admits, jitters taking over her body.

Kyla glares at her as the cops wait for her to continue, and I pull her close to keep her from saying more than she wants to. No one seems to notice how fidgety she's become.

"Five years ago, when I lived in Philadelphia. Someone followed me around and left a note like that." Siân drops her head.

"Did they catch this person?"

She silently tells them no.

"Okay. We're going to take this in for processing, and if we need anything or have additional information, we'll contact you. Keep your phone on in case we have questions."

"Of course." Siân sits up and takes a sip of water.

"We're going to get out of here. We'll send an officer around every few hours until we sort this out." The male cop shakes all our hands.

I stand to meet his height. "Thank you, Officer." I hold out an arm, guiding them toward the front door.

From the corner of my eye, I see the girls stand as I bid the police good-bye. When I close the door and face the girls again, the tension is heavy in the room.

"Thank you for being here, Christian. You didn't have to come," Siân says.

I rush to her. "Are you kidding me?" My fingers pull at the fabric of her shirt, searching for the warmth of her body. I guide her close when my touch lands on her. “You never have to worry when you’re with me. I’m here,” I add and tighten my grip on her.

“Taj.” Kyla jumps to her feet.

Thankfully, Siân’s face is buried in the crook of my neck. Otherwise, she’d see the inappropriate plea of excitement on her best friend’s face when her boyfriend walks in.

“What’s going on here?” Taj asks, waving a hand at Siân’s and my embrace with a scowl upon his mug.

“Taj.” Siân pushes away from me and turns to her boyfriend. “You made it.”

He frowns, his arm still outstretched at me. “What’s all this?”

“Nothing. I’m glad you came.” Siân presses against him with a hand on his cheek to force his focus on her.

Taj sighs, though still visibly bothered. “What’s going on?”

“The police just left,” Kyla interjects.

Taj doesn’t look at her, and her shoulders slump.

“There was no forced entry. But they found footprints out back,” Siân fills him in.

“And?” Kyla snips.

Siân rolls her neck. “I’ve been stalked before and—”

Kyla cuts in. “And she never told me.”

“Kyla, I’m sorry. I just didn’t know how to tell you,” Siân defends.

“How about *hey, don’t move in with me because someone wants to kill me*?”

Everyone is talking over the other.

“Why would you say that?” Siân cries.

"What are you talking about?" Taj chimes in.

"I'm just saying." Kyla shrugs.

I grip Siân by the waist and spin her to face me. "Hey. Don't let her rile you—"

"Get your fucking hands off of her." Taj shoves me, and I stumble backward.

I lunge forward with my teeth clenched as I grab him by the collar and drag him across the room, then slam him into the wall nearest the door. Siân and Kyla are at my back, fighting to pull me off Taj. I sneer at him, daring him to even blink the wrong way. I've wanted to end his pitiful life since the moment I met him.

"Christian. Let him go. What are you doing?" Siân tugs on my shoulder.

Taj glares up at me with my forearm buried in his throat. "Get off me," he groans out.

"I'll fucking kill you," I whisper as we're being separated. "Fucking hear me?" I bark.

"Christian?" Siân yells.

Kyla rushes to Taj's side, checking to be sure he's not harmed. "Who the fuck is this guy, Siân?"

"I'm sorry." I blink and peer down at her.

She closes her eyes and nods. "I think you should leave."

I stare at her, searching her face to be sure she really wants me to. With her eyes, she pleads for me to go. I yank her to me and stare into her eyes.

"You'd never have to beg me to be here for you," I say, then storm away.

From the corner of my eye, I see Siân's face contort into an expression laced with confusion. I don't entertain it, though. Instead, I take the stairs three at a time and hurry to get behind the wheel of my car. I have to get out of here, or else the cops will return for a second time tonight, and this time, they'll be cleaning up a body.

I peel off into the night, hating that Siân has seen that part of me. Keeping up this charade is important. I need her to trust me if I want her to go with me willingly.

VILLAIN

12

SIÂN

Christian's parting words leave me confused, and I shove them to the back of my mind to digest later. I stand in the kitchen with Kyla and Taj, both wearing similar expressions of bewilderment. The tension is so thick you could cut it with a knife.

"Don't tell me you didn't just see that guy go batshit crazy on Taj?" Kyla questions, breaking the silence first.

I sigh. "I'm not saying his behavior is acceptable, but he was just trying to help."

"Trying to help or trying to fuck you?" Taj interjects.

"We're just friends, Taj, and he was concerned. Plus, you weren't here. He wanted to make sure I was okay. Is there really any harm in someone trying to be a friend?"

Taj's features twist, and his lips form into a snarl. "A concerned friend? He just cornered me and told me he would kill me. That's not a concerned friend. That's a psychopath."

Immediately, my defenses are up. Christian wouldn't say something like that. Taj is merely jealous that Christian was here before he was, making sure I was okay. I look over at Kyla, whose eyes are on Taj. She's watching him almost cautiously.

My chest heaves as I suck a ragged breath into my lungs. "I think you're jealous."

"Jealous?" Taj seethes, taking a step toward me. "What is there to be jealous of? I'm your boyfriend, and he's not, yet he walked in here like he was, and he treated me like I was intruding on something. So, tell me, Siân, was I interrupting something?"

My frustration toward him and the entire situation mounts tenfold, and the walls feel like they're closing in around me. I squeeze my eyes shut and tip my head back while leaning against the wall. The world is spinning, and I can't seem to make it stop.

Taj continues to spout off nonsense about Christian and me, but he's failing to realize the entire reason he was here at all, and that's what makes me snap.

Pushing off the wall, I walk right up to him and peer into his eyes. "Did you come here to fight with me, or did you come here as a concerned boyfriend who gives a shit? Because right now, all I'm hearing is how you're concerned that another man was here when what you should be worried about most is the fact that someone broke into our house."

The words come out in a rush, and I can feel my cheeks heating. I'm almost always the quiet, nonconfrontational type, but I'm tired of being a doormat to a man who clearly doesn't love me like I thought he did.

Silence fills the small space almost instantly, and I take a step back while watching his features fill with new emotions. Anger, sadness, and fear flicker in his eyes. Okay, so maybe he gives a shit, but obviously not enough to overshadow his own selfish needs.

Agony fills his features. "Look, I'm sorry, Siân. I didn't mean to lash out at you. It's just—"

I cut him off right there because I don't care to hear his excuses. "Just admit it, you don't give a shit about me. Admit it and save us both the trouble," I growl, my anger rising all over again. I need to walk away, but I'm so angry. Angry that he's reacting this way, angry that he's pointing fingers at me, and acting like I did something wrong when I didn't.

Can't he see he wasn't even here for me? An intruder was in the house, and someone tried to hurt me. *No, of course not.* All he sees is Christian replacing him, even though he isn't.

"Okay, let's not say things either of us are going to regret." Kyla steps between us, but her eyes linger on Taj for a moment too long before darting to me, and I wonder what the hell that's about. Before I can convince myself to look further into it, I shove the thought away.

"I regret nothing I've said. All of it is true. He cares more about Christian being here than about the fact someone broke into our apartment."

"The guy is a fucking lunatic, and I can't believe you don't see that. He threatened me."

I roll my eyes. "Whatever, Taj. I'm done fighting with you and done with this conversation."

I don't think any longer about the subject. I can't. I won't. Taj doesn't care about me, and that's a hard pill to swallow, but I'll be damned if I beg him to give a shit. Not today, not ever.

Without warning, I turn on my heels and rush to the stairs. I need time and space, neither of which I will get standing in the living room arguing with him.

"Come on, Siân... Look, I'm sorry. Let's talk about this," Taj yells from the kitchen.

His words meet my ears just as I reach the top of the landing. A part of me wants to turn around and go talk to him, but I know better. Taj doesn't care, not like he should.

"Stop, there's no point right now." I hear Kyla say, her voice quiet. Clearly, she doesn't want me to hear what she's saying. Otherwise, she would speak louder. "She's mad, and so are you. It's best if you guys give each other some space."

It's unlike Taj to listen to anyone. He's very much the type that makes his own choices, so I expect him to shove past her and come rushing up the steps, but as I hold my breath, anticipating his next move, I hear him say. "Yeah, you're right. We need some space and time to digest what just happened." It's completely unlike Taj to be so easily persuaded, but I ignore the warning sign blinking red in my mind.

I'm encompassed in my emotions and slowly drowning inside them. When I reach my bedroom, I close the door behind me and crash onto the bed. I can feel the tears forming behind my eyes, but crying is the last thing I want to do. An angry fire pumps through my veins. I want to make Taj see how wrong he was about tonight, but I can't make him see something he doesn't want to see. He doesn't see he should care more about me than Christian's presence. He doesn't see that the only important thing to him should be me.

Maybe my reaction would be different if this was the first time, but it's not. Taj has been showing me more and more that he doesn't give a shit about me. Tonight just proved that further. Taj doesn't love me. Taj wants to control me, and I refuse to be stuck under his thumb. I bury my face in the pillow and scream, unleashing all the pain. I'm nothing to him anymore, and that's okay because he's nothing to me either.

13

CHRISTIAN

I hate this fucking place but being here is a necessary evil.

Florida is nice when it's warm, but I've been here nearly a month, and I'm already over it. Three and a half weeks I've been in town, and it's rained or stormed fifty-five percent of the time. The only benefit to these dreary days is that it stays dark enough that I can go unnoticed.

After coming close to bashing Taj's head through the wall about a week ago and being asked to leave by Siân, I kept my distance. I read somewhere that the easiest way to make someone miss you is to be the last thing they think about. I knew after showing up and being there for her, Siân would connect with me on a deeper level. That she'd be unable to deny that nagging urge to take those risks we've talked about. Knowing me, truly learning who I am, and understanding what she means to me would be the biggest risk of all. And with the way I stormed out of there, she won't be able to get me off her mind.

Going so many days without talking to her only adds to that. *Who am I?* That is the question I'm sure she asks herself. I know because at least once a day she texts me, and I finally responded after ghosting her, as the kids would call it. Really, it's just a stage in the plan to get me what I want—*her,* and the legacy I was promised.

To say it's been hard would be an understatement. In the few short weeks that I've spent watching her, my obsession has grown. Tony was right, and I hate that shit. As much as we fight and talk shit to each other, he's the one person to get a handle on me. They sent me here to secure the guns, and we did just that. Being by Siân's side derailed the deal slightly, but I made up for it the following day. Father wasn't too happy with me for delaying the process, but I never cared too much about what he thought.

Putting my focus back on the present, I run the wiper blade just long enough to clear my view. And right on cue, the tall, moderately built silhouette of Taj comes around the corner, his body swaying as water flicks off the heels of his sneakers. The sound of passing cars over the wet pavement is the only sound I hear as I pull away from the curb and creep several feet behind him with my headlights off.

Every evening, like clockwork, he runs. Sometimes it's right after a lecture or dinner, but always before calling it a night. Some of those late-night jogs happen after he's finished fucking someone who isn't Siân. My suspicions about the two of them were spot-on, and I didn't need to see Kyla sneaking out of his place before dawn to prove it. It was written all over her face that day in their living room. The day I let my anger get the best of me. Not to mention the cuff link I found under her bed, an object I've been holding on to. At some point, it'll come in handy, but I'm not sure when yet.

Taj doesn't notice me right away, not with his hearing impaired by the earphones he's wearing. But the farther we get down the street, something alerts him of my presence, and he peers over his shoulder. The movement is quick at first, then he does a double take, almost as if he doesn't notice the old beat-up Chevy rolling slowly behind him the first time. When he picks up speed, I realize he's spotted me.

He's smart, though, keeping his pace even so as not to give himself away. We reach the end of the very long block, and when he rounds the neatly trimmed bushes at the corner, he peeks once more. A million thoughts are probably running through his mind, wondering if it's all in his head or if I am indeed following him. He gets his answer the moment I hit the curve, and then he pivots down a side street, still glancing behind him as he does.

I follow suit, stopping in the center of the street. Taj halts his run, his chest heaving as the light hits him at an angle. The rain has picked up; the droplets falling against my windshield with a vengeance. He's staring in my direction and maneuvering his head to get a better look at the vehicle. I sit still for a moment, a grin tugging at the corners of my mouth. I rev the engine, shift the gears, and spin the tires, causing the loud roar of the car to scream through the neighborhood. Taj flinches, but he's frozen in place.

This is what I live for. Even though I'm several yards away, I can still see the fear building in his chest. The colorless stare he gives as his brain tries desperately to catch up with his body. What should he do? Run or wait it out?

My grin grows wider, and I shift back into drive. Almost as if he can read my mind, Taj shuffles on his feet and takes several steps back. His feet move faster than his brain can register, and he falls flat on his ass. With his eyes wide, he crawls backward on his hands, then shifts and crawl-walks on all fours until he's upright again. He nearly loses his balance but somehow pulls it together long enough to take off into a full sprint down the street, glancing over his shoulder every few seconds.

Only one problem, though, he lives in the opposite direction.

He cuts across into the street, racing against the horsepower of the old Chevy I borrowed from a junkie. It's close—too close. I slam on the brakes, missing him by a hair. Taj freezes for a beat, staring into the car, his chest heaving and eyes full of trepidation. If not for the dark shades and hood I wear, he'd know who's behind the wheel. And the dread that creeps across his features when he realizes he still hasn't a clue who I am settles deep in my gut, making me feel—*full.*

He blinks, and all the sense seems to return to him as he scrambles backward and takes off east toward his home. A chuckle leaves me, and I quickly back a U-turn to follow him down another side street. He's running for his life, his legs moving faster than his body can stand. Taj trips again, but he keeps himself upright. Then he shoots down an alleyway, and I come to a screeching halt. He takes off, the evidence of his days as a track star ringing loud and clear.

Once he's out of sight, I flip on the headlights, a smile pulling on my face for a job well done. I didn't want to hurt him tonight, only scare him, and by the looks of things, I've done just that. Taj disappears into a neighbor's yard, and I pull off in the other direction. He got away for now, but I'm not nearly done with him yet.

Several hours later, I pull up in front of his brownstone, the old run-down car squeaking as I come to a stop. The rain has let up, but the ground is still slick from the downpour. Taj's blinds are open, and I can see straight inside. After being taunted and chased down by a car, one would think that you'd secure yourself inside, including making sure whoever the culprit is unable to watch you.

I huff. The people in this town are so lackadaisical with their safety.

I shut off the engine and glance around the neighborhood. It's quiet, but it's like this every night. Aside from Taj, most of the residents are small to mid-size families who are way too invested in their own lives to be worried about anyone else. The couple next door with their brand-new baby spend more time arguing than watching their surroundings. And the family across the street has their hands full with extracurricular activities, with the mom running herself ragged escorting the kids to and from soccer and ballet while the dad is busy doing someone other than his wife.

You learn a lot about a person by the things they try so hard not to say out loud. And in the week that I've been watching Taj, I've seen enough to tell me that the people in this community are just as pitiful as the fake existence Siân's coined for herself.

Clearing my mind, I focus on Taj. He's on the phone, his face twisted up in a mixture of emotions. I really rattled him tonight. *Good.* He disappears somewhere in the house, and I hop out of the Chevy, being sure not to let the door close too hard.

I pull my hood down over my head, so low that the only part visible of my face is my mouth and chin. Unlike Siân, Taj has one of those doorbell cameras that records everything in front of it. Slipping around the side where his car is parked, I duck out of the way, hopping on the porch when the motion sensor light above his driveway flickers to life. Dressed in all black, I blend in with the darkness and press myself against the wall of the house. Peering into the window, I notice him peeking out of the side window, the phone still pressed firmly to his ear.

"No. No. It's okay. My side light just came on. Must have been a stray animal or something," he says to whoever is on the phone.

The window is cracked. Otherwise, I wouldn't be able to hear him. By the perplexed look on his face, my guess is he's been explaining the events of the night.

"No, Kyla. Don't you think if I knew who it was, I would have called the police by now?"

My blood boils at the mention of her name. "Motherfucker," I blurt out.

Taj snaps his gaze to the window, and I have to jerk my head away to keep from being seen. His shadow grows as he approaches and glares out into the night. I push myself deeper into the siding of the home, staying as still as possible, only catching the breath I hadn't realized I was holding until Taj finally retreats.

He's walking toward the back of his house when I peer through the window again, my rage still getting the best of me. Siân is at home, fighting with herself over what's been happening, and he's entertaining that slut. They have to go—both of them.

Siân deserves better than for the two people she cares about the most to be constantly betraying her. She's perfect, a goddess, and he's choosing trash over the queen that she is. Had it been a one-time thing, maybe I could have forgotten it. But it hasn't *only* been once. In fact, in the past two weeks alone, he's fucked that bitch Kyla more than he has Siân. Is that why he's shit when it comes to pleasing her? Is he so distracted with fucking her best friend that he's forgotten how to fuck her? And he has the fucking audacity to dictate who she's friends with—and by that, I mean me.

My phone buzzes in my pocket, and I remove it to see a message coming in through the cloning app.

Siân: *I think we need to talk...*

I pull my shoulders back and look through the window again. Taj is in the entryway of his kitchen, carrying a water bottle.

"Hold on," he says to Kyla and holds the device out in front of him, then brings the phone up to his mouth. "Siân's texting me." He sets the bottle on the dining table, then punches in a message.

I watch the three little dots dance across my screen before his note finally comes through.

Taj: *Hey, baby. Sorry I didn't call you after my run.*

Siân is typing.

Taj: *I've just got a lot going on. Can we talk tomorrow?*

After a brief pause, she responds.

Siân: *Yeah.*

Siân: *Why not.*

"Hello," Taj says into the phone. "Be here in fifteen minutes, or we'll have to wait until next week."

I seethe, my hands balled into fists at my side. What does she see in this motherfucker? I've barely been around a full month, and already I know he's not meant for her. The bitch doesn't even care about her safety. Sucking in a breath, I hold up my cell and open the chat with Siân and me.

Me: *Hey, beautiful. How badly have you missed me?*

A car passes, stealing my attention, but a split second later, my plan formulates in my mind. The entire purpose of tonight was to get under his skin, to teach him I'm always watching and show him just how easy it would be to get to him. My phone vibrates again, but I'm not thinking about that now. I shove the iPhone into my pocket and hop off the porch, kneeling and waiting to see if the motion sensor will grab his attention again.

When it doesn't, I remove my switchblade, the gears clicking into place as I step up to his shiny blue Lexus. Glancing over my shoulder and up into the window, I see the top of his head, but his conversation with Kyla seems to have ended. Instead, he's scrolling through his phone and throwing back the ice-cold water, flicking away the condensation before dropping out of view. My guess is he's sitting now.

With the tip of my blade, I carve large letters into the hood of his car, a smile tipping on my face when I'm done.

Lei è mia. Ti ucciderò. *She's mine. I'll kill you.*

Taking a step back, I admire the words scratched in my native language. It's a promise, one I'll be acting out very soon. With one final glance up at the window, I jab the knife into the driver's side front tire, then run the blade along the door, ruining the paint. I close the switchblade, stick it back in my pocket, and grip my pistol. Taking it by the barrel, I tighten my gloved hand around it and slam the butt of the gun into his back window.

The sound of glass shattering fills the air, followed by the blaring of his car alarm, which catches Taj's attention. He rushes to the window as I walk backward around the bushes at the end of his drive. By the time Taj makes it outside, I am back at the old Chevy I left running out of direct view of his camera or any of those belonging to his neighbors.

"Hey!" he yells and comes to a running stop at the sidewalk.

With my hood still pulled low, I speed off, being sure to glance in his direction. He recognizes the car from earlier. It's written all over his face.

"You fucking asshole!" he continues to scream at the rear of my car.

A grin plasters to my face, and I pull my glove off with my teeth while keeping the other hand on the wheel. I dig out my phone, finally reading the message that came through a moment ago.

Siân: *Cocky much?*

"Oh, mia topolina, non ne hai idea." *Oh, my topolina, you have no idea.* I say aloud to myself and pull off into the night.

VILLAIN

14

SIÂN

I run a hand down the front of my pencil skirt as I read over the syllabus I put together for today. Anxious butterflies have been fluttering around inside my belly all morning. Things with Taj aren't any better, and after the other night, I don't expect any resolution from talking to him. Still, I know I can't ignore his presence forever. We work together, and even with how angry and upset I've been with him, part of me refuses to let him go. My heart aches at the thought, even while knowing he doesn't care for me as he should.

My cell phone pings, and I grab it off the desk. My lips pull up at the sides as soon as I see Christian's name appear on the screen with a text from him.

CHRISTIAN: I miss you. When can I see you?

I KNOW I shouldn't be so happy over such a stupid little text, but Christian makes me feel alive. He makes me happy, and he cares about me. He genuinely cares about me. I text him back a quick reply, letting a little of my flirtatiousness seep through.

*ME: When do you want to see me again? *wink face**

I PRESS the send button and look up from my phone as the door to the classroom comes swinging open. Taj walks into the room with his messenger bag slung over one shoulder. His dress shirt is wrinkled and untucked from his dress pants. He looks messy and out of place, definitely not the Taj I know.

His dark gaze penetrates me, and I wait for the moment when that feeling in my gut explodes, and I go rushing toward him, wanting nothing more than to be as close to him as possible. But the moment never happens. In fact, the only thing I feel is nausea, afraid of what he wants to talk about because if it has anything to do with the other night, I already know it'll end in a fight.

As he gets closer, I see his eyebrows are drawn down, his eyes gleaming, a permanent dirty look etched into his features, and it's obvious now that he's upset.

Great! He tosses the bag on his desk and then pounces on me.

"We need to talk. I hate the way we ended things the other night, and I can't stand having you think I don't give a shit about you. It's just not true."

I try not to roll my eyes. I don't believe him, not by a long shot, but I don't say the words out loud. More than anything, I don't want to fight. Not here. When I don't respond right away, he grabs me by the arm and glances over his shoulder, checking his surroundings before pulling me into his office. I grimace at the pressure of his grip on my arm.

"What's going on?" I ask, my voice harsh.

"I thought you'd never ask." Sarcasm drips from his words. A snide comment sits on the tip of my tongue, but I hold back, waiting for him to continue. "Don't tell me you can't see it."

My brows furrow. "I don't understand, Taj. I really don't. Nothing is going on with Christian. We're just friends."

A vein in his forehead bulges. "Friends?" He puffs his chest. "You think this is about him being your friend." He shakes his head. "Of course, you would think it's about me being jealous of him."

I pull my arm from his grasp and cross my arms over my chest. "Your reaction the other night seemed like jealousy."

"It's not jealousy, Siân. It's..." Frustration is a permanent fixture on his face. "It's that everything was fine, and then he appears out of nowhere. Suddenly, notes are being left for both of us, and someone carved words I don't understand into the hood of my car. You can't tell me that's a coincidence?" He pauses, and my defenses go up immediately.

"If you're trying to say Christian did this..."

"Look at me, Siân. Look at me and tell me it doesn't add up. He was fighting with me. He wants you, and he wants me gone. Can't you see that?" The anguish in his voice bleeds through me. I hear every word he's saying, but all I can see is jealousy. He's jealous, and that's shitty because I've given him no reason to be.

I shake my head and take a step back. "I honestly can't believe you're accusing him of property damage and attacking you because you're jealous."

Taj runs his fingers through his hair. He looks unhinged, and if I had to guess, he hasn't been sleeping well, probably because he's worried I'm talking to Christian or hanging out with him. My anger toward Taj mounts, and I want to escape this room and him.

"What will make you believe me?" he finally says, breaking the silence.

"Nothing, because I know Christian wouldn't do anything you're accusing him of doing. Plus, you have no proof to tie him to those events." I purse my lips and hiss, the anger inside me reaching new heights. During all of this, he only sees himself as a victim, and I can't handle it.

"I've been stalked for years, hiding from this person who is hell-bent on destroying my life. I need you to be supportive, to hold me and tell me everything is going to be okay, yet you're more worried about Christian. I understand that someone damaged your vehicle and left you a note, but now you know what it feels like to be me." I'm so angry I can't even stand to be in the same room as him right now.

"You aren't getting it, Siân," he growls, his voice rising.

My nose wrinkles, and I take a step back toward the door. "No, you aren't getting it, Taj, and that's half the problem here." I whirl around and escape the small office space before he can stop me. I grab my phone off the desk, noticing that I have a reply from Christian.

I'm too caught up in my emotions to respond, and thankfully, students filter into the classroom, making it impossible for Taj to start anything with me again. He would never make a scene or do something that would make him look bad. I watch as more and more students filter into the room, my anger slowly receding to a slow simmer.

When Taj finally comes out of his office, he appears a little more put together. I grit my teeth and ignore his presence, deciding I'll only talk to him when I must. As soon as class dismisses, I'm out of here.

~

WHEN I RUSH OUT into the courtyard, it's raining. It's a slow drizzle, but rain, nonetheless. *Dammit!* I peer over my shoulder. The idea of calling an Uber is tempting, but I'm only a few blocks away, and it's not like it's pouring rain. Knowing that Taj is going to be leaving soon sparks me forward. I don't want to talk to him right now. The wedge between us grows more and more every single day, and I don't know how to bring us back together.

I start on my trek home, knowing I have no other option than to walk since I left my car at home. As I walk, the sky gets darker, turning an angry gray by the time I'm off campus. I know it's only a matter of time before the clouds open and I get a shower.

Still, I move my legs faster, scolding myself for wearing a pencil skirt, white blouse, and heeled shoes, even if they're a small heel. The smart thing to do would've been to check the weather before leaving the house, at least without my car.

As I hustle, the rain comes down, slapping me with huge drops. The night sky makes it hard to see, and I nearly trip over my own feet. *Fuck!* I let out a ragged breath, barely catching myself.

It's when I nearly fall and catch myself on the exterior of a brick building that I hear the footfalls of someone behind me. Whirling around, I find a man less than twenty yards away, standing on the sidewalk. His hood covers his face, and he's wearing all black. It's hard to make out much more with the gloomy skies above.

Still, the hairs on the back of my neck stand on end, alerting me to danger. I'm not sure if he's following me or not, but I will not stick around to find out. As soon as I start again, this time moving a little faster, I hear the man's footsteps pick up as well.

Panic drives me to run, and my adrenaline spikes. I peer over my shoulder, my entire body lighting up when I find the man running behind me, only a short distance away. I turn down an alleyway, and then another, trying to break his trail, hopeful that he won't follow, only to be paralyzed with fear when he appears around the next corner.

My hands are shaking, and I'm soaked to the bone, but the fear of that mysterious man who could be my stalker following me spurs me forward. I'm only a block from the apartment, but it's a block too far. I hear him directly behind me, and a scream lodges itself in my throat.

Hope coats my insides when I spot the apartment ahead. I shove through my fear and race up the steps, barely getting the door open and closed. Twisting the lock into place, I open the blinds and peer outside to see if the man is standing there on the street, but there's nothing, just the streaks of rain on the window.

Letting the blinds fall closed, I turn, press my back against the door, and relax. I let out a breath that turns into a scream when Kyla comes walking around the corner from the kitchen.

Her face is a mask of confusion. "Are you okay?"

All I can do is nod as the blood in my veins becomes ice. I'm not sure what the hell is going on, but I know I'm not okay. Nothing is okay, and I don't know if it will ever be.

15

CHRISTIAN

I shouldn't like torturing her as much as I do. Something about the fear that rips through every fiber of her being calls to me. Knowing that I can hunt and claim her whenever I feel like it makes the chase even more fun. She can run to the ends of the earth, and I'll still be waiting in the shadows for her, reminding her she's mine.

Siân—so pure and demure. A woman lost in a sea of chaos, a world of darkness. A woman due to be fucked properly. I can't wait to break her, to introduce her to the world her father thought he was saving her from. I told her once that fate is the only thing that matters. Marco should have known he could never truly keep her safe. He may not have agreed to the deal his beloved made with my father behind his back, but it was still a deal.

People would call me sick for dragging this out. For taunting her and causing her to have to look over her shoulder at every turn. Fuck those people. We all have a vice, and terrorizing Siân only to be the person she runs to afterward fuels me. It speaks to the deepest part of my soul, the part I've been trying to keep at bay while in her presence.

I let it out three nights ago when I followed her home from school. The rain kept everyone indoors, making it possible for me to go unnoticed by everyone except her. Previously, when I watched, I kept my distance, only letting her know I was near with brief notes left in places I knew she'd find them. But this time around, I crave more. With each passing day, I need to be closer to her, but at the same time, I need to feed the evil beast. It's fun, and now the obsession is blooming.

I need to smell her, touch her, feel her against me again. The only problem is, I can't quite be myself with her yet. When she's near, the Christian she knows doesn't include the dark, sadistic parts of me. The pieces of my being that'll give her nightmares. The version that'll scare her in the opposite direction. I can't have that.

So far, she's only met my representative. The handsome, charming, mysterious man with a horribly fake American accent. I almost gave myself away that night in her house when I recited my note back to her. She didn't seem to notice, though. With everything that was going on around her and all the police everywhere, my slipup went right over her head with a measly explanation.

Thinking about that now pisses me off. She can't be so easily persuaded. Not someone of her stature, even if she doesn't remember her family legacy. But she is, and I don't like it. Of course, it benefits me and the plans I have laid out, but that's beside the point. If she stood up for herself, demanded more, and held the people around her accountable, there would be no way anyone could hurt her. Not without a fight first. Instead, she shies into herself and plays the role of this helpless girl, who'd rather suffocate in a minuscule existence than make any kind of noise.

Noise would mean people would see her, people would *hear* her. It would be the opposite of who she's decided to be. *Safe*. The word plays back in my head, just like it did three days ago when I taunted her and chased her back to her house, disappearing the moment she stepped foot inside. And just like I knew it would, it sent her right to me. Siân called me once she'd calmed down, though she skirted around the topic, pretending her only reason for calling was to hear my voice.

My plan is working, and with that in mind, I pick up my phone from the island in the kitchen of the penthouse loft I'm renting. It's the middle of the day, but I toss back the last of my whiskey and scroll through my contacts until I find her number.

"Hello?" Her sweet voice comes out in a hushed whisper. It's low, breathy, and shoots straight to my dick.

I stand, adjusting the crotch of my black slacks, and set the now empty tumbler down on the surface.

"Christian, you there?" Siân asks when I don't respond.

This fucking woman's voice alone drives me just a little closer over the edge. I shake off the wave of arousal and roll my shoulders.

"Time to cash in on that rain check, beautiful."

The line goes silent for a beat. The only sound emulating is the chatter of those in the background.

"Cat got your tongue?" I tease.

"Um. No. Sorry. I'm in class."

"Forever the student," I let out.

"What does that mean?"

Shit, I mutter when I realize I said that out loud in remembrance of the fact when I found her five years ago, she was also in school. And based on the information Tony gathered on her, I know she's studying for her master's this time around.

"Just that you seem to always be focused on school. Do you ever get out and have fun? And before you tell me yes, I don't mean hitting up some hole-in-the-wall bar that you'd rather not be at."

Siân sighs, and I swear I can hear a smile form on her lips. "Can I help you, Christian?"

"Yeah. Be outside of campus in twenty minutes."

"What? No."

"Yes. You owe me a rain check, remember?"

More silence. This time I can hear who I assume to be her professor—a soft female voice spewing about inequality in the workplace for women. Typical feminist crap and honestly, I'm surprised Siân's interested in a class like that. Everything she's exhibited doesn't fit the picture I have in mind of a woman who is truly a feminist. Now, it makes me wonder if it's all a front. Deep down, is there more to her persona than she's let on? I wouldn't be surprised since she is the daughter of Marco Giuliani.

Siân lets out a huff. "I can't do that."

"Why not?" Crossing the large space that is my living room, I step into the master and over to the walk-in closet for my Ferragamo Angiolo oxfords. More chatter fills the dead air around our call.

"I'm in the middle of class," she whispers, but this time, I'm certain a smile tugs at her lips.

"So leave." I sink down on the California king mattress and slip my feet into the shoes.

"Christian. I..." She pauses for a beat. "I shouldn't."

Dryness coats my mouth, causing me to wet my lips as I stand. "Not good enough."

"Huh?"

"I'm leaving my place now."

"Christian?" she says my name as more of a question—rhetorical, but a question.

"Aren't you tired of being safe all the time? Do something that's out of character. Live a little."

"Are we interrupting you, Ms. Danforth?" the professor deadpans, and the rest of the room falls still.

"Sorry." There's shuffling on the other end.

She's leaving class. I grin at the thought and lock the door behind me.

"Excuse me." The words are barely audible. Then a second later, all I hear is her. No teachers, not students, just her voice echoing through the hall. "Okay. I'll be in front of the business hall."

"Atta girl. Be there in fifteen."

"See you then."

She ends the call, and I make my way to the elevator and down thirteen flights to the garage where my Ferrari is parked.

When I arrive on campus, Siân is standing at the curve of the circular drive, in front of the business hall, just like she said she would be. She's nervous. Her posture is rigid, and she's holding her books to her chest while her gaze darts around. But the thing I wonder is whether she's searching for me or checking to be sure she isn't seen. It is the middle of the day, and based on my last account of the situation, she's still technically another man's woman.

But she's here in broad daylight, waiting for me to pick her up. Maybe she isn't so innocent after all. Maybe she is indeed tired of the lifeless existence she's been living.

I whip the 458 Italica in front of her and roll down the passenger side window. She huddles forward, her books still pushed to her chest, and the tiniest bit of cleavage peeks out through the top of her blouse.

"Very flashy," she points out without moving.

"What can I say? I like nice things. Get in."

Siân zips her spine straight and draws in a breath, her shoulders bunching up tight around her ears. I'm about to throw the car into park and join her on the sidewalk, but then she swallows whatever fear she has and takes a step down with one final glance behind her before climbing in next to me. She keeps her head forward, but her eyes dart in my direction every so often. And as I reach out and place my palm over the back of her hand, she gasps and finally gives me her attention.

"I'm not going to kill you," I say playfully.

A smile paints her lips, and something weird happens in my chest. A warmness spreads through me, and I couldn't even begin to explain why. I don't feel things, nothing close to this shit, but with her, I do. It was the same that day on her porch when I held her close to me.

"That's still up in the air," she throws back at me, and I notice her already relaxing.

"Trust me, you're safe with me," I promise, and shift gears.

"How do I know that?" She smiles again.

I chuckle. "If you weren't, you'd be dead already."

She gulps and settles into her seat, her grin quickly turning into a wavering frown. A smile of my own builds across my features, and I press on the gas, peeling away from campus and heading toward the highway.

For the entire ride, Siân relaxes a bit more with each passing minute. Neither of us speaks for the two hours it takes us to reach our destination. The goal is to get her to trust me, to force her to open up and accept that she wants more out of life. The simplest way to do that is to give her an outlet to be free and go a little crazy. Today, I give her a taste of what life is like in my world, a reality where hanging from the edge is often better than any other form of pleasure—well, just as good.

She's staring out the window as we approach the tall barbed wire fencing. Siân sits up, and with her brows furrowed, she glances at me. "Where are we?" she asks, while looking between me and the scene up ahead.

"Racing strip." The automatic gate slides open, and I slowly drive past the entrance. "Sit tight. I'll be right back."

After pulling over to the side, I exit the car, adjust my slacks at the waist, and stroll over to the ticket counter. A short, stocky Latino man steps out to meet me. I called ahead to be sure the lot was empty, and you better believe it's costing me. But where Siân is concerned, money matters none.

"Listen, man," he starts, his accent thick, "I could get in a lot of trouble if my boss knew."

I tune him out and dig my wallet out from my back pocket. From my peripheral, I see his eyes glaze over as I peel several large bills from the stack of cash.

He stops short, his words caught in his throat. The man reaches out a hand, the gesture tentatively hanging in the air as if he's unsure if he can take the money or not. He licks his lips and sucks in a breath, then meets my gaze again.

"The whole strip. Three hours max." I hold the bills between my fingers in his direction.

He's salivating at the sight of the cash, and doesn't hesitate to claim it. "Yeah. Yeah, man. You got it. I just need your ID to put on file," he adds without looking up at me.

I drop my shoulders and glance behind me to find Siân watching me from the car. Then I peel another two hundred from the wad and hand it to him. "Identification."

My eyes trail his frame, taking in his appearance. He's middle-aged, and based on his accent, I'd say he's new to the country. The dirt under his nails and bags under his eyes tells me he's overworked, and the decay on his teeth tells the tale of a man struggling to make it. Then I observe his name badge.

"Take the cash, Bruno," I order, my fake accent faltering, my Italian tongue rearing its head.

Bruno claims the money and provides me with all the necessary instructions. He offers me a rental, but I decline, opting to hit the track in the Ferrari. Once we're done, I walk back to the car, the warm Florida air swallowing me whole. It's not raining today. Thank fuck for that. But it's also one of the nicer days as far as temperature goes.

I make eye contact with Siân, who jerks her head straight to keep me from being caught watching me. *Too late, topolina.* The car screams when I open the driver's side door and sink back behind the wheel.

"Ready to take a risk?" I ask, but don't really expect her to answer. I already know the answer.

No. Even though she's dying to break out of her suffocating shell.

"What was all that about back there?" she asks instead of answering me. "All that money you gave him."

"I rented the strip for the day," I deadpan.

Siân's eyes grow wide. "Christian."

"Siân, let's settle something right now. Never question how I spend my money. You're worth every fucking penny."

She swallows, a smile teetering on her lips. Siân drops her gaze, and she fights to hide that she's flattered. My guess is she's never had a man treat her this way because Taj sure as fuck isn't doing it.

Shifting gears, I pull off, maneuvering my way across the large expanse of field until we reach the tracks. There's padding all along the sidewalls for added security. Because we're the only people here today, the track is empty except for a single worker that I can see in the announcement booth. From here, it looks as if we are the furthest from his mind as he appears knocked out cold with his chin to his chest.

I stop the car, place it in park, and reach over to undo her seat belt. Siân grabs my hand, stopping me, confusion riddled in her expression.

"What are you doing?"

I lean in. "Undoing your seat belt."

"Why?"

"You ask a lot of questions, beautiful." My eyes drop to her lips, and I notice her shallow breaths. She's more than nervous. She's afraid, unsure, and if I had to guess, a little bit intrigued.

"Well, that's because I'm not always in the habit of leaving town with strange men I've known for only a month."

I'm quiet for a beat but continue to unhook her seat belt. She doesn't stop me this time, but she doesn't release her hold on me either. In fact, her pinky finger moves along the veins on the back of my hand.

"Out," I say once I've succeeded in my task.

Her head moves in rapid succession, the fear of the unknown creeping its way on her face. "No. Why?"

"Because you're going to drive."

She stares at me as if I'm crazy, and her back falls into the seat. I could sit here and wait for her to wrap her mind around the idea, but I've never really been that patient. This month has been the longest I've ever gone without taking what I want.

"What are you afraid of?"

"Uh... dying," she deadpans with raised brows.

My jaw tics, and I exit the vehicle, leisurely making my way to the other side. I can see her watching me, her eyes raking over my frame as her mind and body betray each other. Wide-eyed, lips parted, she peers up at me. Her sultry green eyes carry a silent plea to me, and the pout of her full lips taunt me.

She looks so fucking beautiful from this angle, a mixture of trepidation and desire blending on her face. She leans forward a little, and I don't even think she realizes it. My dick twitches at the thought of having her on her knees with my cock shoved down her tight little throat. From the imagery alone, I'm already thickening behind the fabric of my slacks.

I don't give in to my need just yet because when I do, I want her to beg me for it. Only then will I fuck her like the beast I am.

Reaching out, I brush a strand of hair behind her ear, and her skin grows flush, her cheeks and neck visibly heating. The moment, as brief as it is, is firm and intense. Not once do we break eye contact, and I force myself not to yank out of that car and bend her over right here.

Siân stands without instructions, her body brushing up against mine ever so softly. And when she tries to wedge even an inch of space between us, I'm quick to wrap an arm around her thin waist. My fingers ache to feel her skin, and I don't even try to stop myself. But neither does she.

Siân's head falls back slightly, her mouth open as I cup her face between my palms. My hold is aggressive with my fingers digging into the nape of her neck while I rub my right thumb over her cheek. I skate my gaze over her, observing the change in her breathing again, and the lust building behind her eyes. A part of me expects her to break away, but she doesn't. Despite how tight my grip is or how hard I pull her against my chest, she takes it, almost as if she likes it.

And when I tilt her head back and bring my mouth to her neck, she releases a soft moan of anticipation. She wants my lips on her.

Pointing my sights past her shoulders at the open field, I smirk and whisper into her ear, "Time to have some fun. Get behind the wheel." I step away, pride filling my chest when she pushes out a disappointed rush of air.

"What? Christian."

Grabbing her by the hand, I guide her to the driver's side, put her behind the wheel, and kneel between her legs. The skirt she's wearing rises up her thigh just a little, and when I place my palms on her bare skin, she nearly gasps. I knead her flesh, the primal urge to bury my face in her heat tugging at my control. And if I let that happen, I'll ruin her, but now isn't the time for that. Soon enough, I'll know what the inside of her body feels like. I'll know how she feels when she comes on my cock. Eventually, she'll taste my name on her tongue as I fuck her body like it's the last thing I'll ever do.

"What have we said about taking risks?"

"I'm not driving this thing." She points at the car.

"Yes, you are." With one final squeeze of her thighs, I slide her legs into place and fasten her seat belt for her. "You can handle this," I reassure her.

Siân's shoulders slump, and she pushes out a breath. Back on my feet, I stroll to the passenger side and climb in next to her.

"I'm going to kill us," she says, wrapping her trembling fingers around the steering wheel.

Her hands are shaking, so I reach out and place mine over hers. "Relax. This car has the best safety features, and the track is loaded with all sorts of precautions."

Siân stares at me for a moment, but instead of protesting like I expect her to, she nods. "Okay. What do I need to do?"

A smile threatens to escape me, but I hold it in. "Adjust the seat. Do all your usual checks: mirrors, familiarize yourself with the gears."

She swallows, adjusting her seat while doing everything I've suggested. "Okay." She looks at me, uncertainty playing on her expression.

I take her by the hand, guiding her palm to the gearshift. Siân takes a breath and waits for me to instruct her. I watch her closely, enjoying the change in her demeanor. A second ago, she was scared, but it seems the moment she wraps her hand around the stick shift, she morphs into someone else.

With my palm firmly against the back of hers, I shift the gear. "Press the gas."

Siân floors it, and we take off, our necks snapping back, pressing firmly into the seat. She hits the runway, whipping the Ferrari as if she's been driving a stick shift her entire life. With little instruction, she hits the curve, the car drifting as she does. I snap my gaze to her, finding myself highly impressed.

The once scared and nervous girl is replaced with one who's handled a car like this before. *Interesting.* I guess I shouldn't be surprised, considering who her father is. If she was raised anywhere close to the manner I was, then Marco would have taught her how to handle a stick shift.

Siân screams as we come upon the next turn.

"Gentle," I coax. "That's it. Loosen on the wheel."

She takes instruction well, missing the padded railing by a hair. "Oh my God, Christian."

My chest heaves at the mention of my name on her tongue. I stare at her, fighting every urge I have to claim her.

"That's it, beautiful. Whip it."

She makes it around the track three times. "Shit. Shit. Christian. I'm going too fast," she yells over the roar of the engine.

"Let up, baby. Don't slam on the brakes. Just release the gas."

The car slows, but Siân grips the wheel tight.

"Don't choke the wheel. Just let it guide you. You're doing great."

She loosens her hold on the steering wheel and becomes one with the car. As the speed becomes more manageable, she gets a better grasp of the vehicle.

"There you go. Don't let it get away from you."

Siân presses the brake, maneuvering the Ferrari off to the side. Her breathing is out of control, and her hands are trembling from the adrenaline rush. "Oh, my God." She huffs out a breath. "That was crazy. I can't stop shaking."

I smile and reach for her hands, cupping them between my palms and bringing them to my lips. Finally, her nerves seem to settle, but her chest continues to heave. And when I plant a kiss on each of her knuckles, her breath catches, becoming more labored than it was a second ago.

"You did good," I praise, the recognition pulling a subtle grin from her. "Just try to breathe. It feels good, doesn't it? Letting go and doing something reckless."

Siân doesn't speak as she fights to get control of herself; her breaths, her mind, her emotions. They've gone haywire, and I can see the shell cracking, the slight hint of enjoyment that she's working double-time to keep at bay. But then something changes. There's a glint in her eyes, and her breaths are no longer heretic but labored—painfully slow and lustfully charged.

And in an instant, she's leaning over the seat, ignoring the tug of the seat belt to get to me. Siân crashes her lips on mine, her body melding against me, her mouth and hands hungry for my touch. But no sooner than our lips lock does she pull away, her eyes wide and her shoulders rigid with panic and regret.

"I-I shouldn't have done that." She sits with her back against the door and her hands out in front of her.

I blank.

Pure, adulterated thoughts flood my consciousness, and all I can think about is claiming her and leaving her dirty and ruined. At this moment, it's a challenge to remember why I'm here, why I haven't taken her yet.

Trust.

It's all in the name of gaining her trust. It's for that reason and that reason alone that I've stifled my darkest desires. When what I want to do, what I've *been* wanting to do is fuck her.

Hard.

Raw.

And fast.

Fuck, I'm hard just thinking about it—about her. The way she smells, the way she tastes. Does she whine when her pussy is sucked? Does she cream when fucked? Will she cry or beg for more as I bury my dick so deep she'll taste my cum?

I got a glimpse of her pleasure the night I watched her as she lay there unsatisfied by that bitch of a man, Taj. Oh, but she knows what she likes. My cock thickens against the underside of my boxers, throbbing and begging for a taste.

Just one.

That's all I need for now.

A lick, a suck, a stroke, anything to curb the desperation that's presented itself around having her. But she's not ready yet. No, she needs more time—I need more time. If I'm going to get her to come willingly, though, I'm not above forcing her. In fact, I'd enjoy making her do as I say when I say, to include coming on my dick until she can't see straight.

I want to ravish her pretty little pussy. My pussy. Pussy that has been promised to me since before she ever thought about being stroked and petted. Pussy that lacked the proper care, attention, and worship.

And despite everything I've just told myself, I reach across the space and drag her to me, holding her in place with a hand at the nape of her neck. A heaviness builds in my chest, warmth spreading to my dick like a wildfire. He's hungry for her, and I mentally promise that his time will come. He'll get his taste, and we'll destroy her for any other man.

Tonight, though, it's about her and fulfilling my selfish need to watch her come undone. Siân pushes against my chest when I shove my tongue down her throat, but my hold never wavers. I fumble blindly until I find the latch of her seat belt and release it, forcing her into my lap in one swift motion.

"Mm," she mutters against my mouth. "Christian," she breathes out.

Her skirt flares from the quick movement, teasing me with a glimpse of her black lace panties. My cock pulses as her sweet heat seeps through the fabric of my slacks. The head is already hard and pressing against the special place.

Reaching between us, I fondle her breast through her blouse and pull my lips away from hers only long enough to see her eyes glaze over. Her face is twisted in an array of emotions; arousal, fear, regret—need. And as I lean in and roughly suckle her collarbone, a soft groan escapes her. So soft that I wouldn't notice it if I wasn't paying attention.

With a shiver, she tentatively brings her palm to the back of my head. She doesn't touch. She's too afraid to, afraid that if she does, she'll lose herself. And goddammit, I want her to. I want her to let go and let me in—in her mind, in her body, and down to her fucking soul. I want her to taste the ghost of my name on her tongue and feel the phantom sensations of my touch. I want to break her and bring her over to the dark side where love is painful and sex is immobilizing.

"I—we shouldn't," she huffs with her eyelids squeezed tight.

I ignore her and force her crop top up around her neck. Braless.

"Fuck," I groan, my mouth agape as I struggle to control my breathing.

She knew what she was doing walking out of the house like this, her tight little buds easily on display. All it would take is a quick brush or flick, and her pretty pink nipples would bead. Just like they are now, swollen and begging to be sucked.

I wet my lips, and I don't miss the way her eyes trace the path of my tongue. Siân arches her back, a direct contradiction to the words she miserably failed to get out. Her mouth is telling me no, that we can't do this, but her body—her body wants it, *craves* it.

"Please. Christian. Mm," she stumbles and grinds against my erection when I take her tight little bud into my mouth, releasing it with a loud plop.

"Doesn't sound like you really want me to stop, beautiful," I breathe, my fake accent nearly faltering, but I catch myself. I flick the tip of my tongue over her right breast, then the left, and then I squeeze and pinch.

"I-I can't have sex with you," she professes around a moan. "I'm still with Taj."

A wave of anger takes over me, and before I know what I'm doing, my hand is around her throat, my fingers digging into her pressure points. "Don't you dare say his fucking name," I grit out.

Siân's eyes grow wide, and I quickly realize that I let my emotions get away from me. Immediately, I soften my touch, going from aggressive and angry to firm and gentle. Her skin, so delicate and tender, is already bruised and marked with the evidence of my rage, as short-lived as it was. The sight of my mark on her flesh sends a painful ache to my shaft. Siân relaxes, but uncertainty is still etched in her features.

Siân breathes deeply while making eye contact with me, her head falling back when I massage her neck and chest. Her body writhes in my lap, hesitation and need ripping through her. One moment she's into this. She wants to enjoy it, but the good girl in her, the cautious side of her, is telling her to stop me.

"Chris—"

I silence her with a kiss. "I don't give a fuck about him. Right now, I just want to make your pussy feel good."

"I can't have sex with you."

"Who said anything about me fucking you?" I twirl her nipple between my thumb and index finger.

With her eyes hooded and mouth agape, she asks, "You're—?"

"One day, you're going to beg me to fuck you. But today, I just want to see you come."

She swallows.

"You want it too, don't you? You want me to make this tight little pussy purr. I bet you've even dreamed about it." I trail my fingers past her navel, over the bunched-up fabric of her skirt, until I find her hardened clit. A shudder runs through her when I press my thumb against it. "Don't you? You picture me when you're fucking him?"

Her hips raise a bit, the meaty flesh of her ass running over my dick. The barrier between us pisses me off.

"Don't tense up on me now. I'm not going to fuck you today, but I am going to play with your cunt. And when you're on the brink of climax, I want you to remember this moment. Remember the risk. And then I want you to leave him."

I slip her panties to the side, my calloused finger finally touching her naked clit. She gasps, and we both stare down at her pulsing sex. So wet and swollen. So hungry and needy. It takes all the strength I have not to toss her into the driver's seat and bury my face between her thighs and feast on her. To lick and suck and blow on her angry red bundle of nerves until she's bucking and spewing profanities at the top of her fucking lungs.

Siân meets my stroke as I run my finger from clit to slit and back up, and when I rub circles around her nub, she lets go. All inhibitions and doubts become a thing of the past as she allows me to touch her.

Her pussy clenches around my finger when I breach her hole. I don't enter her fully, only teasing her entrance, slipping a little deeper with each push inside. In and out, I play until Siân is riding forward, forcing my finger into her dripping pussy. Wet sticky sounds fill the cab, and my gut clenches with anticipation.

Inserting a second finger, I reach around her and let the chair back at the same time, her tits jiggling in the process. She's so fucking perfect, sitting on my lap, completely overtaken by her desires. It's not fair, really, using her secret fantasies against her—fantasies she doesn't know I'm aware of.

"Oh my," she cries out. "That feels so good," Siân mutters.

"Is this how you touch yourself? Hm? When you're alone in the shower and you reach between your legs to find your sex hard and hungry, is this how you tease your cunt?" I ask, reminiscing back to the night I watched and beat off in her closet. Her walls constrict around my fingers. "There you go, baby. Grip my fingers with that pussy. Take what you need." She does so again, her slit growing slipperier by the second.

"Play with your clit for me. Show me what you do when no one is watching."

Siân is hesitant, so I force her hand to her clit, guiding tight rubs on her clit. The combination of stimulation to her bud and my fingers hooked against her G-spot promotes a flood between the valley of her thighs.

"Just look at that sweet little pussy. So fucking wet and needy," I say and grab her neck to kiss me again.

This time, Siân doesn't hesitate, not one fucking bit, and I love this shit. I love corrupting her and bringing her closer to my side. She's mine. Her body is mine.

"Your cunt is mine, beautiful," I say with venom on my tongue, my words and her breaths blending. "You fucking hear me?"

She's quiet, so I press our foreheads together and quicken my fingers, hitting her G-spot faster, harder, and not giving a damn about the pain-soaked pleasure that builds on her face. Mouth wide open, breath and words caught in her throat, eyes closed, and hips bucking wide, Siân fucks my hand, taking what she needs from me.

"Oh, God. Oh, God. I'm-I'm going to come, Christian."

"Look at me," I demand, with our heads still connected. "You like being my dirty little slut, don't you? You love the feel of my fingers deep in your pussy."

She moans. "Ahh."

"Say it." I pound into her and grind against her ass, my shaft searching for the friction. "Tell me you're my dirty little slut, or I'll stop right now. I'll leave your pussy hungry." My hips move faster as pressure builds in my gut, traveling its way to my balls.

Shit, she's so fucking hot sitting in my lap, her legs spread wide with my fingers in her cunt. I can come from the image alone, but then add the scent of her arousal and the sweet massage of my slack-clad cock under her ass? It's going to send me over the edge, and I'll be left with cum in my pants for the entire two hours it'll take to return her to campus.

But I don't give a shit. I want to come as badly as she does, even if I have to wait to feel her release around my shaft.

"I want to be your dirty little slut. Oh, fuckkkkk. Shit. Shit. Shit," Siân cries between heavy breaths.

"Your orgasms belong to me." I stroke her spot and replace her hand with my free thumb.

Strumming her clit and fucking her slit, I watch as she comes apart, her body quaking from the wave of her release. She arches into me, her ass lifting off my lap, and I have to force her back down from immediately missing her warmth. I dry hump her ass as she fucks my fingers, and I know I'm going to blow.

"Come for me, baby. Spill your honey all over my lap."

"I'm... Christian, I'm coming." Her words are low and hoarse.

"I feel you, beautiful. Fuck, I feel you. Gah," I groan. "You're mine," I whisper into her ear. "You're fucking mine."

Siân wraps her arms around my neck, nearly suffocating me against her chest, but I don't care. I'd die a thousand deaths if that means I do so with her climaxing around my fingers. She rides the wave with a tight grip on me, not letting go, even when she's done and completely spent.

Siân sucks air into her lungs, her body relaxing in my hold. We make eye contact while she continues to hold my neck. The moment is intense, the way we're staring at each other as if we can see into each other's soul. I wonder if she sees how black my heart is because I can see the gray slowly building until I consume her. It's there, hanging in the balance, waiting for her walls to shatter.

After a moment, I push open the passenger side door and help her out of the car, pulling her skirt down over her perfect naked ass the moment the hot afternoon air touches us. A change happens in her, and regret replaces the look of lust from a second before. Pulling her close, I roughly hold her face so that she has no choice but to stare into my eyes.

Just as I'm about to open my mouth to speak, my phone buzzes in my pocket. With one hand still on her, I dig out the device with the other. My father's name flashes across the LED screen. Hitting the answer button, I bring the receiver to my ear.

"What?" I stare over her head and out into the large expanse of the track.

"Abbiamo un problema e devi gestirlo. Tony ha la posizione." *We have a problem, and you need to handle it. Tony has the location.*

I glance down at a curious Siân, remembering not to respond to my father in my native language or I'll give it all away. She'll know that meeting me wasn't a coincidence, and I can't have that.

"Who is it?" I say sternly.

He rambles off the name of the person he needs me to kill, but he doesn't stop with his demands. He's angry that I haven't returned to Italy like I was supposed to a month ago. Father continues to make demands, orders I refuse to accept. I'll return home with Siân in my arms and not a moment sooner. So, he'll have to get the fuck over it.

I end the call and peer down into her big green eyes. "Tomorrow, end it with him. You're mine now."

Siân doesn't respond, nor do I wait for her to. Instead, I help her into the passenger seat, then round the front of my Ferrari. Once inside, I rev the engine and peel out toward the exit.

16

SIÂN

Nervous butterflies fill my belly, making me feel nauseous. I stare down into the nearly full cup of coffee, thinking about last night and how exhilarating and free I felt. How only Christian can make me feel. I recall my feelings when he told me to break up with Taj. At first, I was shocked, but the longer I thought about it, the more it made sense. After last night, there was no way we could go back to what we used to be. It's not fair to Taj or me. I don't want to be that girl who cheats, and what I did last night with Christian was wrong while still being with Taj. Even so, I'd do it again and again, which is precisely why I must end this between us.

With how strange Taj has been acting lately, I figured ending things in a public place was the best thing to do. The door to the coffee shop opens, carrying a gust of wind with it, and I look up from my coffee to find Taj standing there, his gaze darting around the room.

My throat tightens, and my heart thunders in my chest. I have to remember this is for the best, not only for me, but for him as well. As soon as he spots me, he rushes over, his eyes almost wild. His bag is half slung over his shoulder, and his hair is disheveled.

His eyes that once made me feel so happy and loved but now only leave me cold and detached collide with mine.

"What's going on with you, Siân?" he asks, letting out a harsh breath.

Is there a certain way to break up with someone? An easy way to let them go? I don't think so. Heartache hurts, and no matter what I do, this is going to end badly.

"I think you should sit down." I gesture to the chair in front of me.

I don't want this to turn into a big scene, but I can already feel the eyes of the few coffee shop patrons watching us.

Taj's lips turn down into an ugly frown. "What's going on, baby? I tried to call you last night and didn't hear a word from you. Kyla said you didn't get home until late."

It takes everything in me not to roll my eyes. Instead, I decide to jump headfirst into the thick of it. "There's no point in me dragging this out, so I'm just going to come out and say it." I pause, letting out a rush of air from my lungs. "It's over."

Silence. Complete silence blankets the space, and I wait with bated breath for the other shoe to drop, for him to say something.

"W-What do you mean it's over?"

"I mean... I'm done. I'm breaking up with you. I don't want to do this anymore. I'm tired of pretending we're this perfect couple when we've been falling apart for a long time."

Shock fills his face, and his gaze widens. "Please, Siân, don't do this. I know you don't mean it. I know you love me." His voice cracks, and the desperate sound causes my chest to tighten.

I shove up from the chair, my movements so quick the chair clatters against the wall, drawing even more attention. I can feel my cheeks heating, and I need to get out of here, not only because others are watching us, but because I know what Taj is going to do, and I can't handle it. This is for the best for both of us.

I grab my purse and take a step forward. Taj steps in front of me, but I shake my head and put my hands up to stop him from touching me when he reaches for me.

"Stop! Don't make this harder than it has to be." My voice raises an octave, and the sound is enough for him to pause, giving me the chance to slip around him.

As soon as I'm out of his grasp, I rush to the door and out into the street. I turn right and start toward the house. Each step I take vibrates through me. I don't even realize I'm crying until I reach the second block and come to a stop.

My chest is heaving, and my cheeks are wet. I wipe at the wetness with the back of my hand. I feel so weak for crying even though I know it's inevitable. Taj was my first love and my first sexual partner. He was the first man to love me, and regardless of what happens in my life going forward, I'll treasure that.

After taking a moment to catch my breath, I walk again. I turn down another street, feeling a little better and no longer crying. It's when I peer over my shoulder while I'm stopped at the crosswalk that my emotions change drastically.

The fine hairs on the back of my neck stand on end, and I don't even think. I just run, darting across the street without checking for traffic. I look back over my shoulder, my fear mounting when I see the mysterious man, dressed from head to toe in black, following close behind. My stomach tightens, and fear clings to every inch of my body. Disoriented, I pause for a brief second. The wind whips around me, and I'm blinded by my thick locks for a moment.

Where am I? Where is he?

That's all the time my stalker needs. In an instant, he's got one hand over my mouth and a steel band of muscle wrapped around my middle. He picks me up like I weigh nothing, his huge frame towering above me while I struggle to break free of his grasp as he walks down the alleyway, my body pressed against his chest. I feel his hard penis against my ass, and as I force air into my lungs, the panic makes it hard to breathe. I catch a whiff of something spicy, cologne maybe? It's spicy, and deep in my mind, I know I've smelled the cologne somewhere? I'm too scared to think about it much longer. My entire body shakes like a leaf in autumn.

Then, as fast as it happens, it's ending. The masked stalker releases me, and I fall forward, my hands pressing into the cold concrete. Like a newborn calf, I scurry to my feet and stand on shaky legs. I whirl around to escape, only to find nothing but brick walls surrounding me.

Dead end. No, I won't die here. I didn't come this far to die in some alleyway.

Forcing myself to stand tall, I twirl back around and find the masked man standing in front of me, his head cocked to the side. There isn't a single thing about him I could use to tell the cops. He's covered from head to toe in black, and even his eyes, which glitter with mayhem, seem to be black.

"Look, I don't know what you want, but—"

He shakes his head and presses a finger to his lips. A shiver rushes down my spine, and every muscle in my body tightens when he takes a step toward me.

"Wait, please... don't hurt me. Please..." I beg and continue to blab away, doing and saying anything to save myself. "Please... don't do this. Just... tell me what you want... tell me, and I'll give it to you. Money? Or...." My throat clogs with unsaid words. I'm afraid to hear what he has to say and even more afraid of what will happen next.

Taking another step forward, merely a foot of space exists between us now, and as tempted as I am to take a step back, I don't want to give this person the satisfaction of knowing I'm even more afraid of them than I'm letting on.

"You." he rasps, his voice thick with an accent. I can't make it out right at that moment. My attention is solely focused on what he just confessed.

"Me?" The word trembles off my lips.

He nods and then says, "I want you broken, crying, tears running down your face, while your fear fills my lungs, threatening to suffocate me. I want to drown in you because knowing you're afraid of me is like stepping on a live wire. It makes me whole. Without it, I don't exist."

"I-I..." I don't know what to say or even how to react. It's fucked up and wrong, and I need to escape him, but I know if I try to run, it will only feed into his twisted fantasy even more.

"Run, and I will grab you, pin you to the dirty ground, and fuck your tight cunt until you're gushing around my cock, begging for me to stop fucking you while loving the release I give you all at the same time."

I must be fucked up because my nipples pebble at his admission. I don't know this man, and the fear churning in my gut tells me I am afraid, but I'm also slightly aroused, which confuses the hell out of me.

As if the bastard knows this, he leans into my face, and I swear I can feel his hot breath on my cheeks. "You want to do it, don't you, *topolina*?" The pet name doesn't go unnoticed and sparks a memory in my mind that I refuse to grasp onto. "Go ahead, run. See what happens. If you don't believe me, then surely you have nothing to worry about."

My insides twist, fire igniting in my gut. I clench my hands into tight fists, my feet ready to carry me forward when he speaks once more.

"There's another way, *bellissima*. That doesn't involve me sinking deep inside you and ruining you for any other man on this planet."

Beautiful. He just called me beautiful. I'm not sure how I know this, but I do, and I can't believe I'm even considering what this man is saying right now. I should scream, yell for help, or try to run, but I know deep down that I wouldn't get away.

I wouldn't escape, and I would only make matters worse for myself. There isn't a single bone in my body that doesn't believe every word he's said.

"What?" I ask, my voice low and meek. I swear he's smiling at me through the black mask, even though I can't see his lips.

"Be a good little *ragazza* and get on your knees for me. I want you to take my cock into your warm mouth and watch as you gag on my length, trying to breathe while I steal the air from your lungs with every shove inside your mouth, all while I lick the salty tears that slide down your cheeks."

As fucked up as it is, my core tightens at his words, and I find my body reacting before I can fully think the situation through. *What kind of person am I? What is wrong with me?* That's all I can think as the hard ground connects with my knees.

"*Bella* choice." He growls in broken English while he reaches for the belt on his pants. I can't tell you how many seconds pass, but it isn't long before he's got his jeans pushed down his muscular thighs and the mushroom head of his cock pressed against my lips. My entire body trembles, and I rest my hands on my thighs, needing something to hold. This ain't my first blow job, but it is my first time doing something with a stranger, much less a man who's been following me and has admitted that he wants to hurt me. I'm either insanely stupid or smart enough to get out of this alive.

"Open for me," he orders, his voice harsh.

I peer up at him and part my lips to take his cock into my mouth. He presses forward an inch, and the air surrounding us becomes charged. I can feel the shift in energy almost instantly, and before I can even gasp, his hands tangle in the strands of my hair. My scalp burns, and I let out a soft cry of pain as he tugs my head all the way back, making my neck ache. "If you bite me or even consider hurting me, I will hurt you in unimaginable ways. Do you understand?"

All I can do is nod. My entire body lit up with fear while a small niggling of arousal builds. "Open that pretty little mouth for me again," he demands, and I open my mouth in an instant.

With his hold on my hair still tight, I can't move. I'm a victim to his rage, madness, a puppet he controls.

"You're going to look so fucking pretty with my cock stuffed inside your throat."

I won't lie. I can't lie. My core tightens at his filthy words. His eyes twinkle with some unreadable emotion, and then he does something I never expected. Using his other hand, he grabs me by the throat. His grip is tight, and panic fills my eyes when the pressure on the sides of my throat intensifies.

Leaning above me, he spits directly into my mouth, and I watch in horror and awe as he does this. "Swallow it. Swallow my spit like you'll swallow my cum in a few minutes. Swallow it and say thank you like the little slut you are. My slut. My *topolina.*"

I'm shocked. The air in my lungs can't reach my brain, so I remain there staring at him, confused and turned on. That is until he squeezes my throat a little tighter and black dots appear in my vision, bringing me back to reality.

"Answer me, *topolina.* E 'questo quello che vuoi?" *Is that what you want?*

The pressure on my throat lessens, and I gasp for air. "I don't understand." I wheeze the words out, unsure of what language he is speaking. All I know is that it isn't English.

"Is that what you want?" he growls.

I have no other option but to say yes. It's yes, or something so much worse, so I choose the lesser of two evils.

"Yes," I whisper, and that's when all hell breaks loose. Something inside him snaps, and I find myself completely at his mercy. Like a wild animal, he's on me. With his hand still in my hair, he guides his thick cock back to my mouth.

There is no warning that follows his next move. With minimal effort, he presses into my mouth, forcing me to open wider for him as he moves inside. He hasn't made it very far before I gag on his massive length. He's huge, bigger than anything I've ever had before, and I can tell, feel it, as his balls come to rest against my chin while he holds himself at the back of my throat.

Panic stirs in my belly, and I claw at his thighs, trying to push away from him, but he just holds me in place longer. I can feel tears leaking from my eyes. My lungs ache and burn with the need for oxygen, and I try to swallow, but nothing elevates the thick rod in my throat.

The man lets out a groan that's half man, half animal. Right when I'm sure I can't take it anymore, he pulls back and does it all over again. Once, twice, three times. I lose count, the lack of oxygen making me dizzy.

"Look at me, look into my eyes while I fuck your mouth. I want to see your tears, the drool dripping down your chin. I want it all, *topolina*. I want us both to remember this night forever."

This strange connection passes between us as I look into his eyes. Their darkness calls to me, and I want him to see what he's doing to me. Because as terrified as I am of him and what will happen next, a part of me wants to please him, and that's the most fucked-up part of all.

17

CHRISTIAN

She swallows, her eyes brimming with tears, her chest falling in sharp thrusts as I continue to fuck her face. Hard, fast, and relentless.

She loves it, despite the gargled cries and her shoving at my thighs to push me away. Her actions plead with me to release her, not to violate her in such a way, and if I were a good man, I would let her go. But I'm not even close to being a halfway decent man. I do what I want, and I take what I want, and this moment, with her on her knees in front of me, is no different.

And the best part is—she fucking loves it.

Her susceptibility is clear, and in the morning, she's going to hate herself for it. She'll resent ever letting me see into her slutty little heart. She'll despise not only me for doing this to her, for forcing her to swallow my cock in the dead of night in a dark and filthy alley, but she'll also hate herself for liking it.

Siân claws at my legs to get me off her, but sucks me like she loves the taste of my cock. Painful cries leave her throat, only to be drowned out by the delicious hum of a moan at the pulse of my dick on her tongue.

And when I fist her throat, her eyes roll back, and she arches into me. It's subtle, and she probably doesn't even notice that she's doing it.

"Fuck," I groan, my voice blending in with the sound of passing cars and the chatter from stray cats, mice, and whatever vile creature has made this alley its home.

If heaven existed, this would be it.

A world where I get to push and test just how far I can take my sexy little mouse. A life filled with me bringing her closer to the edge of darkness and her enjoying every goddamn minute of it.

That's why I had to do this.

After claiming her orgasm as my own in the front seat of my Ferrari and watching her come apart in my lap—the soft moans, her kisses, and the feel of her mouth on mine—I had to. I needed to feel her lips around my cock, and I couldn't wait months for that to happen.

"Questo e' il, topolina," I grunt. *That's it, little mouse.* "Aprire." *Open up.* With a handful of her hair, I yank her head back and tug my mask above my lips.

Leaning forward with my dick dangling beneath her chin, I crash our mouths together, but she squeezes hers shut, groaning and twisting to get out of my hold. When I fist her throat with my free hand, she stops fighting and accepts my kiss. I snake my tongue past hers, a roar building in my chest at the taste of her and the mix of saltiness from my pre-cum.

"So fucking perfect," I whisper against her mouth.

Siân tries to push me again, this time nipping my tongue with her teeth.

"Agh," I blurt and jerk back, the metallic taste telling me she drew blood. "Uno esuberante." *Feisty one.* I grin and run my bloodstained tongue across her cheek. Her tears mix in with the blood, sending a pulsing to my shaft and down to my toes.

I tighten my grip on her hair and bring my other hand to her chin, forcing her to look at me. As she stares into my eyes, something flickers in hers, and a shudder rattles through her body. If it weren't so dark and if not for this mask, I would guess she senses the familiarity between us. The eyes always give it away.

"You're going to have to do a little better than that, little mouse," I taunt with my heavy Italian accent.

I stand upright but keep my hand on the back of her head. Siân stares up at me, her shoulders shaking as tears continue to stream down her cheeks. She looks so damn hot and helpless on her knees, completely at my mercy, and it isn't lost on me she isn't trying really hard to get away. In fact, she's never put up much of a fight. Not now and not in the past. Maybe she likes having me as her stalker. She's called the cops here and there, but she never pushed them to find the bastard who tormented her.

It's the same in this instance. After calling the police the night she found my note, it was never brought up again, not by her and not by the department. After a week, they stopped coming around, and if I had to guess, they closed the case. Not to mention that most people would take extra precautions to keep their attacker at bay. Yeah, Siân likes me watching her. Something deep down inside her is just as broken as it is with me. Which makes us so fucking perfect for each other.

The tip of my cock aches to be back inside her hot mouth, and I'm inclined to give it to him. Gripping myself at the base, I line the head with her face, running it along her lips.

"Please, stop," she whimpers.

I ignore her. "Open."

And like a hungry little vixen, she does.

"Gahh," I moan as I sink to the back of her throat.

Siân gags, her face and eyes turning red. I grab her by the throat, all while never letting go of her hair. She can't breathe. I can feel it from the short intakes of breath around my cock. Fuck, she's going to kill me.

So fucking perfect indeed.

The harder I thrust, the more she fights. Saliva seeps out around me, coating her chin and my balls. I can feel her racing pulse as I press against the pressure points on her neck. My dick pushes against the wall of her esophagus, and I can feel it against my palm. And the sadistic bastard in me only drives me to hurt her more. Her eyes bulge —bright, wide, and laced in fear—as I choke her with both my dick and fist.

"Swallow this cock," I order and pull back, only to slam forward again.

A tingle runs up my spine, my nuts draw tight, and white-hot passion blurs my vision. Siân claws at my thighs, her nails breaking skin, but I don't give a shit. The only thing that matters is her on her knees and the thick rope of cum that shoots down her throat.

"Ahhhh," I jerk myself with her mouth, then let my wet, now limp dick fall along her chin.

Siân huddles over with one hand on her neck and the other on the piss-riddled ground to support herself as she struggles to pull air into her lungs. She coughs, and when I try to help her up, she swats at my hands and stumbles back against the building. I stand here a minute, not wanting to just leave her like this, something unusual for me. I don't care about my actions or how they affect people, and I never feel remorse. But despite how fucking hard I just came, I don't like the idea of using her and leaving her.

I have to, though, so that I can come back to her as Christian. She's going to need him—she's going to need *me*.

Stuffing myself back into my jeans, I walk backward toward the edge of the alley. And with one last glance at Siân, I turn and check to be sure the coast is clear before turning the corner once and then one more time to tuck behind another building and yank the mask from my face. But I can't leave her. I won't leave her alone and exposed like that.

So instead of getting the hell out of Dodge, I wait just a few feet away, peeking around the old, red brick building until, finally, I see her leave the alley. Her hair is a mess, her clothes hang awkwardly on her body, and she hugs herself tightly. When she quickly looks around, I duck out of the way, peeking out again to find her disappearing around the corner toward her home.

Once she's out of sight, I step out onto the sidewalk and speed walk to catch up with her. Keeping my distance, I stay close to be sure no one bothers her—to keep her safe. And when she runs up the stairs to her front door and bursts inside, I wait across the street at my regular spot for her to call. I know she will—she always does.

18

SIÂN

I've never been that scared in all my life. Not when I found the note. Not any of the other times my stalker has announced himself. I was entirely at his mercy, unaware of what he'd want from me next.

And no matter how hard I fought him, it didn't matter. That was the worst of all, the terror of knowing there was nothing I could do to stop it. Nobody to help me. No mercy from him.

Nausea churns my stomach, gnawing at my insides. I barely make it to the kitchen, launching myself at the sink, leaning into it, and gagging hard enough to make my entire body seize painfully. Over and over, I gag, emptying what little was in my stomach and splashing it around the drain.

His cum must be in there. Oh, God. Nausea strong enough to cripple me rolls over my body, and I gag harder than ever. Now there's nothing to do but dry heave until the worst of it passes. Once I can take a breath without my stomach clenching, I turn on the tap and hold a glass under the flow with a shaking hand. I rinse my mouth carefully, afraid I might start gagging again at the sensation of having anything in my mouth. Even water.

What if he didn't really run off? What if he followed me home? He'd see the house is empty except for me. He could come in here and continue what he started. There'd be so many more opportunities to do all kinds of painful, shameful things to me. No chance of somebody walking past and hearing the noise. Not even any rodents running around.

Every little sound in the house makes me jump, though it's amazing I can hear anything over the thudding of my heart. My fight-or-flight response is still going strong. He could be anywhere. At the back door—my head snaps around in that direction like I'll find that hooded figure standing outside. Watching me fumble around at pulling myself together after he defiled me.

After he forced me.

After I sort of liked it.

My stomach tightens again, and I squeeze my eyes shut, like that will do anything to block out what just happened. I can't be alone right now. I can't drown in this, which is exactly what will happen if I allow myself to stew in it. Blaming myself for not fighting harder to stop him.

Hating myself for becoming aroused. My panties are soaked, plastered to my pussy lips. It's an uncomfortable sensation, and I know I should change if only to clean myself up, but a part of me wants to suffer. To punish myself for being filthy enough to enjoy what he was forcing me to do.

Fresh juices flow from me at the memory, and I cringe in disgust. Who am I? Why am I still aching and wet? I should be weeping, scrubbing myself clean in the shower, not getting more turned on every time I remember some new aspect of what just happened. Right?

My hands tremble as I reach into the pocket of my jacket and grab my cell phone. I need to talk to somebody. I can't keep this to myself. It'll shatter me—and I don't know if I'd be able to put myself back together.

Strange, but my thoughts immediately turn to Taj. The impulse to call him is a habit more than anything else. You don't forget two years of essentially making somebody your world in the blink of an eye. We might've ended badly, but it wasn't always like that. There was a time I really loved him and believed he loved me. When I gave my heart fully to him. Why wouldn't I reflexively search out his number in my contacts?

But no. I can't call him. I broke up with him only a few minutes before my stalker found me. I have to wonder whether Taj would even answer my call, considering the way I left him back at the coffee shop.

And if he did? What then? My throat threatens to close when I so much as imagine telling him what just happened. Having to go through everything, step by step. I don't have a single doubt Taj would want me to recount every filthy, embarrassing detail, either. Not to shame me and not to get off on it—he wouldn't be that cruel. I can't believe he would punish me for hurting him by making me relive every detail.

He'd do it because he still believes I'm his. I'll be the first to admit he's confused me lately with the way he's been so hot and cold with no warning, but I know certain things are true. He's not a sadist.

He is, however, possessive. He'd pull one of those big, chest-puffing alpha male moves and promise to kill whoever abused his woman. He'd expect me to melt against him and bury my head in his shoulder, and whimper for him to help me. He would see this as his opportunity to sweep in and make everything okay again. He might even look at the timing of the situation as proof that I shouldn't have dumped him. That I need him. After all, look what happened only minutes after we were apart.

Even now, consumed by fear and shame, the idea of him smothering me in an attempt to get us back together somehow disgusts me more. That's saying something since I want to die from the disgust I feel toward myself.

The disgust and the shame. I couldn't bring myself to admit what happened. I couldn't bear admitting what it did to me. Not to Taj, who should be the one person I'd pour my heart out to. I wouldn't want to tell him even if we didn't just break up.

Instead, I call the only other person I can think of. Somebody I hardly know, but now strikes me as the only one who'd understand, who wouldn't judge me or blame me for letting this happen.

Christian's voice soothes me the moment I hear it, and I know I made the right choice. "Beautiful, how did you know I was thinking about you?"

"I need you." The second the words tumble from my abused lips, I know it's the truth. I do need him. Desperately.

Not the way he assumes, though. Not right now.

"That's what I like to hear."

"I don't mean it that way." My breath hitches before I can help myself. "Something… bad happened…"

And his demeanor changes. "What happened? Where are you?" he growls.

"I'm at home. Alone. He found me. On the street."

"Who did?"

"The guy who's been stalking me." I don't realize until a tear hits my shirt that I'm crying. "I don't want to be alone right now. Can you come over?"

When he hesitates, I know I've made the wrong move. He's going to think I'm too needy. "It's okay," I murmur. "You don't have to if you're busy. I can't expect you to drop everything."

"No, you aren't asking too much." Though he hesitates again—and when he speaks, he does it slowly. Like he's choosing his words carefully. "You caught me at an inopportune time, is all. I wish I could be with you right now. You have no idea how much."

"I really do understand." I can't help but slump against the counter. Now that the worst of the panic is over, I'm more exhausted than I can remember being. "I'm dead beat from head to toe."

"It's the effect of lessening adrenaline." The way he sounds, he knows what he's talking about. "Now that you're no longer in fight-or-flight mode, now that you know you're safe, your overwrought system is adjusting. What happened, anyway?"

A noise from outside steals my breath away before I can respond. "Siân?" Christian demands in a tight voice. "What's wrong?"

"I heard something." I can barely even get out a whisper with my throat tightening and my heart racing. "Outside."

"Would it make you feel better if I stay on the phone with you while you check the doors and windows? To make sure they're securely locked?"

It would, and it does. I go from one window to the other, assuring myself they're locked up tight. And while I do, I tell Christian about what happened. I spare him some of the worst details because I still can't bring myself to say certain things out loud. Shame heats my face at the thought of it. How much worse would things get if I had to talk about it?

"He forced you into an alley?" It's difficult to make out what he's saying. Like his teeth are gritted so hard, he can barely speak. Like a ventriloquist, only one who hasn't practiced. "He put his hands on you?"

"I don't understand why he won't leave me alone. And he's... what's the word I'm looking for? He's ramping up. This is worse than anything he's ever pulled before. He took a big chance, coming after me on the street."

"Perhaps the fact that it's dark out gave him extra courage."

"I guess so." I peer out into the darkness, ready to find a hooded figure watching me. I only see the outlines of what's there in the daylight. "Isn't it funny how the same things we're afraid of in the dark are what we're used to seeing in the daytime?"

"What?"

"Nothing." He's really going to think I've lost it unless I get myself together. "My mind's wandering. Maybe because I don't want to think too much about what went down."

"I'm sorry I can't be there with you right now. You have no idea how much I want to hold you."

"And I wish you could be here." So, so badly. Not only because I don't want to be alone, either. I shouldn't feel so attached to somebody I hardly know, but it seems like my heart's been following an agenda of its own when I wasn't paying attention.

"What else happened? Did he threaten you?"

Now, I wish I had never told him. "You know what? I don't think I want to talk about it anymore."

He lets out what sounds like a grunt. Is he disappointed? For a second, I think he might be. Like he wants me to drag out my pain.

"It's not healthy to keep these things bottled up," he advises me, and I see how off-base I was only a moment ago. It's going to take a while for me to unlearn everything Taj taught me. I'm too used to being with a man who draped himself over me like a cloak that got a little heavier all the time. Pulling on me, dragging me down. Taj would've begged and cajoled me to open up.

Once he finally showed up. That caveat is one I can't allow myself to forget. I'd have to beg him to take my call first, then handle the fallout once he deigned to give me his time.

"I know. But it's still fresh and dragging it all up isn't going to help when I'm here all by myself. I don't even have Kyla to keep me company."

That's when it hits me. "Kyla. She's already mad enough at me."

"What about her?" Christian asks with an edge of impatience in his voice. "She's the last person whose feelings you need to worry about right now."

"She's upset that I never told her about my stalker. And she has every right to be." I feel like I have to add that before he gets annoyed again. "Wouldn't you want to know everything about the person you were moving in with? If their safety was in question? What if this maniac shows up here, and she's the only one who's home?"

"Then he wouldn't bother her because you're the one he's after."

"That isn't funny."

"I wasn't making a joke." He sighs. "But you're right. I shouldn't be flippant. And now that I think about it, I can see how you'd be concerned. You're a good friend for considering her at a time like this. Maybe a better friend than she deserves."

"What makes you say that?"

"I'm always going to be on your side," he explains, and his voice is rich with warmth. Like I imagined the coldness only a second ago. "So, forgive me if I don't take it well when others are unfair to you. And it is unfair to think only of herself when you're the one afraid of this person. You're the one in danger, but she can only think about herself."

"I can't hold it against her. I'd be upset if the tables were turned. She's in danger, too—we can't forget that."

"Because you said he threatened to kill her." I make an affirmative sort of sound, and he lets out a long breath. "Of course. You're right. She has to be considered in all this."

Finally, he's seeing the light. Christian doesn't strike me as being slow on the uptake—no, his brain moves at lightning speed to where he always seems to be a step or two ahead of me—so it's surprising it took so long for him to catch up.

"It would kill me if anything happened to her because of me."

"You're a good person."

If I were a good person, I would've told her about my safety concerns before we moved in. I won't bother sharing that self-admonishment with him, since I don't feel like bringing the whole argument up again.

"Have you considered moving out?" he ventures. "That way, she'd be in the clear. You wouldn't be together anymore."

I drop onto the couch and stare at the wall across from me. A wall I might not be looking at for much longer. Now that he said the words out loud, the answer is obvious. I can't believe I didn't think of this before. The only way to secure Kyla's safety—and maybe get us back to being friends again, back to before she resented me—is to get out of here. To take myself out of the equation.

"You're right," I decide, and I feel the truth of my words settling into my bones. "I should move. I guess I could live on campus."

"Could you? In the middle of the term? I'm not an expert on how these things work, but wouldn't that be the sort of thing that has to wait until the beginning of the next semester?"

I'm sure he's right. This isn't the same as reserving a hotel room.

"I have a friend I could stay with." I'm sure Cynthia wouldn't mind having me, especially considering why I'd be moving.

"Not that I'm trying to dissuade you, but wouldn't that put your friend in potential danger if he sees you living with her?"

"No. Not Cynthia. She knows everything there is to know about this person, whoever they are. She's prepared for whatever happens." And if I so much as hinted at what happened earlier, she would demand I come home. I have no doubt about that.

But I've already asked so much from her. We've moved around so many times thanks to me and this obsessive monster whose penis I evidently enjoy being forced to suck. *Don't think about that. You couldn't help the way your body reacted.* I wonder how many times I'll have to repeat that to myself before I believe it.

"You know, there's a simple solution to your problem."

"What's that?"

"You could move in with me. For the time being, of course. It wouldn't have to be a permanent arrangement. Just until you find a new place to live. In the meantime, you'll be safe. So will Kyla."

Move in with him? My heart skips a beat, though not entirely thanks to the pleasure of knowing Christian will take this step for my sake. What man in his right mind would invite a girl he hardly knows to stay with him? Especially one with the sort of baggage I'm bringing along?

I sweep away memories of the alley in favor of another memory. A memory of pleasure so intense I wasn't sure I'd stay in one piece, afraid I'd fall apart from the force. He knows how to touch me. He knows the right things to growl in my ear while he drives me to heights I never knew existed. Taj certainly never made me feel that good. Not even close.

I'd have to be out of my mind to ignore that in the face of his offer. There's no doubt in my mind we have something special between us—like fate brought us together—but at the end of the day, men are always going to think a certain way. What if he takes my agreement as a green light to go as far as he wants, whenever he wants?

Would that be so bad?

"I don't know," I murmur while chewing my lip. "I'd only end up putting you in harm's way. Would you even want to take that kind of risk?"

"Do I strike you as the type who shies away in the face of risk? Or have you already forgotten the way I encouraged you to fly around that track?"

Good point. It wouldn't have to be permanent, either. He said so. I could live with him for the rest of the semester, then make other arrangements for on-campus housing. Right?

"Are you sure you want me to do this?"

"Siân." Something about the way he says my name makes it sound like music, the melody rolling over my body. "I never make an offer I don't intend to make good on. Don't you know by now how important you are? How I would kill anybody who tried to hurt you? You're safe with me. You will always be safe with me."

He means it. I've never been so sure of anything. That certainty is what it takes to make up my mind. "Okay. Let's do it."

I wish I knew whether my heart was racing out of excitement or apprehension.

19

CHRISTIAN

I can hear them fighting from the sidewalk, Kyla's voice ringing the loudest. She's angry. Today Siân moves in with me, and by the high-pitched screams, I'd say Kyla isn't on board with this plan. But fuck her. Siân is mine, and she belongs with me.

The door is wide open, and a stack of boxes line the left side of the creaky porch. I shake my head, slightly repulsed by the condition of this house. On the inside, the girls did a decent job to make it as liveable as possible, but someone has clearly neglected the exterior over the years. I wonder if it's the owners who have failed to take care of the property or the lack of homemaking skills possessed by Kyla and Siân. I never noticed it before, not from this side of the house, anyway. When I snuck in through the back, it was obvious no one cared for the property, but the other times I was here, I guess I looked past just how run-down it is. This is even more reason to get her the hell out of this place. Any woman of mine deserves to live in the lap of luxury.

I take the stairs two at a time and broach the doorway. Just when I'm about to knock on the frame to alert them of my arrival, Kyla, who's standing at the entrance of the kitchen, turns in my direction. She lets out a huff, a grimace plastered to her face as she looks me up and down.

Her nostrils are flared, and it's no secret she doesn't like me. I noticed that fun fact the night the cops were here, and from the moment I met her, I knew I'd hate her guts. But it was learning about her betrayal of Siân that drove the nail in the coffin.

I haven't quite figured out what to do with that tidbit of information yet, so I've been holding on to the details, waiting for the perfect time to blow this shit up. It's my secret weapon of sorts, a card tucked snugly up my sleeve until the perfect time.

Kyla inches forward, stopping directly in front of the entrance. "She's not going with you," she snips and widens her stance with her arms folded across her chest.

It's funny, and I force the laughter that threatens to spill past my lips back down. Does she really think she can stop me from leaving here with what's mine? She can try, and I'll snap her fucking neck right where she stands. If I want in, I'll get in. If I want Siân with me, she will be with me. And no barely one-hundred-sixty-pound bitch will stop me.

Siân peeks her head out around the corner, her face lighting up at the sight of me. Something happens in my chest in reaction to her response to seeing me. A warmth, an entity so foreign, creeps through my veins and sends my heart racing. What is she doing to me?

"Seriously, Kyla. Let him in," Siân yells, then finally comes into view, carrying a small box.

I twist past Kyla and rush to Siân's aid, taking that box from her grasp. "Let me handle that for you. Did you want me to load this and what's on the porch on the bed of the rental truck?"

Siân smiles and rubs a hand over my bicep. "Yes, please. I have some things to bring down from my room, but most of my kitchen items and clothing are already boxed and outside."

I nod. "I told you we didn't need any of that. We can buy all new things."

She lets out a breath as her eyes lock with mine. "I know, and I told you I'm not going to let you buy me all new things."

I inch forward, the box bridging a gap between us. "And what have I told you about questioning how I spend my money?"

Her chest heaves, her eyes glossing over with appreciation. "That I'm worth every penny."

"Exactly. So, what do you say we leave all this shit here and start over—just me and you?"

Siân is quiet for a beat to contemplate my words. The truth is, we won't be staying in this piece of shit town. We both belong in Italy, so I'm taking her back the first chance I get. I hate this fucking country and have been here way longer than I intended.

"You've got to be fucking kidding me?" Kyla blurts out behind me, her voice laced in vehemence.

Siân nods and licks her dry lips. "Okay. But I at least want to donate my things."

"Whatever you want," I concede.

"Siân, you can't truly be falling for this. Are you so dickmatized that you can't see he's playing you?" Kyla bumps me, sending me back a bit to plant herself between us.

Siân rolls her eyes and turns away from her friend. It shouldn't feel this good, seeing the decline of their one-sided friendship before my very eyes, but it does. In a perfect world, with a man who actually cared, I wouldn't take this from her, but nothing about the lives we live is perfect. Bad things happen to good people, and bad people rule this fucking planet. We're the same in a way—Kyla, Taj, and every other self-centered person on this earth. We take and we hurt without thinking about the repercussions, or in my case, not giving two shits about the outcomes.

There are some differences, though. They are cowards who disrespect her right under her nose. Everything I've done has been with Siân in mind, even down to the watching. She's the only thing that matters, and I'll ensure our time together by any means necessary.

"Kyla, please. I'm not sure what your deal is. It wasn't too long ago when you were shoving Christian down my throat at the bar. And this is my choice. Plus, it's not going to be forever, just until we can figure out this whole stalking mess. And I won't stiff you with the rent. I'll continue to pay my part—"

"Bullshit. Don't try feeding me lies you don't believe yourself. I won't buy this for one damn minute."

"Kyla, this is the only way to keep you safe."

"So now this is about me? This man has gotten in your head because this is not like you, Siân."

"Or maybe you don't know her as well as you think you do. She certainly doesn't know you," I interject, my tone hard and cold.

"What the fuck is that supposed to mean?" Kyla spins back in my direction, only to face Siân again.

Siân sighs, and a deep, aggravated rumble comes from her small frame. "You don't understand, and that's okay. But it's not safe for me to stay here. I know we haven't seen eye to eye on things lately, and that's partly my fault for not telling you about my stalker. This is me making it right. I couldn't live with myself if something happened to you."

"Okay, you want me to be safe, and yeah, it upset me that you kept something like that from me. But this..." Kyla points at the floor and leans in so that Siân has no choice but to look her in the eye. "Him." She gestures over her shoulder at me. "Isn't the answer. You barely know anything about him."

"You don't know what I know about him."

"What's his last name?"

Siân opens her mouth, only to close it again. Somehow, I keep myself from interfering. I know that I'll only be proving Kyla's point if I do. Siân wants to be with me, and she'll need to make Kyla see that all by herself.

"Where is he from?"

Siân takes a step back.

"How about what he does for a living? How is he supposed to provide for this lavish life he's promising you?"

Siân shakes her head, and I can see her nerves cracking. Kyla's interrogation is sinking in, making her uncomfortable and planting a seed of doubt in her mind.

"Who are his parents?"

Finally, I set the box down on the rickety coffee table and calmly approach. Neither of them is looking in my direction, and it's probably for the best. I can feel the heat rising from my pores as anger settles in my gut. Bad things happen when I'm pissed. Armon would be proof of that.

"We should get going." I reach out to touch Siân, but Kyla slaps my hand away.

She spins and points at me. "I'm not letting her go anywhere with you," she argues.

Red flashes across my vision, and before I realize it, I'm stalking toward her, my hands balled into fists at my sides. Siân jumps in the middle, stopping me from wringing this little bitch's neck with a soft touch to my chest. I glance down at her palm where it's pressed against me, then drag my gaze to her face. The softness of her features as she silently pleads with me not to react settles me in a way.

It's weird and so unfamiliar, but I concede. I take a step back and refrain from hurting her best friend in front of her. But my word is my bond, and Kyla is out of chances with me. The next time she gets in my way, she's dead.

"Wait outside. I'm just going to get my phone so that I can call the donation center to let them know we are on the way," Siân directs, and I nod.

I straighten my shoulders and push my frustration to the back of my mind. Letting my anger get the best of me right now won't bode well in my favor. Siân loves the people in her life. It's the only reason she's even moving in with me. It's all in the name of protecting someone who's playing with her heart like it's a game of darts. The nerve of this woman to stand here, judging anything Siân decides when she's the one harboring secrets. Kyla is the person Siân should question, the person she doesn't truly know.

"Okay. I'll start loading the truck."

"Thank you," Siân whispers, then rises on her toes to plant a kiss on my lips.

The asshole in me takes over, and I wrap my arms around her waist, keeping her in place. As I continue to kiss her, I maneuver us so that I can watch Kyla from over Siân's shoulders. She locks eyes with me, and I'll give her props for trying to stand her ground and not look away, but in the end, my stare rattles her. Kyla can sense the threat in my gaze. I know because she falters and drops her chin to her chest while awkwardly rubbing at her wrist.

Finally, I release my hold on Siân and watch the sway of her plump ass on the way up the stairs. When she's out of sight, I step out onto the porch and load the stack of boxes onto the back of the rental. It doesn't take me long to get through that pile before I move back into the living room. And as I pass Kyla, who has yet to budge from her spot in the center of the room, she sucks her teeth in my direction. My jaw ticks, but for Siân's sake, I ignore the slut.

"I'm on to you," she claims.

I chuckle and continue toward the box I set on the coffee table a few seconds ago. The air around me changes, and I know it's because she's directly behind me.

"So, you get off on preying on innocent girls? Someone weak you can control?"

I take my time picking up the box, still choosing to keep quiet.

"I know what you're up to."

I chuckle, swipe my thumb over my nose, and slowly face her. "And what's that?"

"I'm not going to let you hurt my friend. I can't put my finger on it, but you're not who you've been claiming to be, and I'm going to find out what you're hiding. And when I do, I'm going to the cops."

"As if you can actually protect her. Tell me, Kyla, what's really bothering you?" I ask and inch forward, causing her to stumble backward. "Is it really Siân's safety that concerns you? Or is it that you want to fuck me for yourself?"

"What?" She frowns. "You're fucking crazy."

"That is your MO, right? Or was I imagining things when I saw the way you looked at Taj that night? The way your face lit up when he walked into the room, and how your heart broke when he went straight for Siân."

Kyla takes several steps away from me until her back is pressed into the wall. Trapped with nowhere to go, Kyla glares up at me with a breath caught in her throat. I can see the tightness in her chest as she tries to find words.

I could give it all away, call her bluff right here and now, but then I'd be giving away my position, and Siân will know that I've been stalking her all along. Stalking is such an ugly word. I wouldn't call it that at all, especially when all I've been doing is monitoring what's mine.

"You don't know what you're talking about." She sidesteps to get out from between me and the wall.

I stare at her for a second. "Then why are you so nervous?"

Kyla pushes me away, putting her hands on me for the second time today. I don't think, and the next thing I know, the box falls from my grip, something inside shattering the moment it contacts the dingy hardwood floors. My right hand is around her throat in the blink of an eye as I slam her into the wall. Kyla's lids flutter closed when her head smacks the hard surface. She wants to scream, but her voice is trapped under my vise-like grip.

"Watch your-fucking-self. You don't want to know the lengths I'll go. Stay in your place, or next time, fix your whore mouth to threaten me —" I squeeze even harder, my heart racing at the sight of the fear building on her face. Leaning in, I press my mouth to her ear. "I'll rip your tongue out and suffocate you with it."

A shudder rips through her body as she tries to get away. Kyla claws at my forearm, fighting to get free. It all happens over a few seconds, and now I'm enjoying watching the color drain from this skank's face. Serves her right and should teach her to never test my limits.

The sound of Siân's footsteps descending the stairs snaps me out of my anger-induced haze. "Did something just fall?" Siân asks when she reaches the landing, just as I let go of her friend with a jerk.

"Ah, yeah. Sorry, I lost my grip on the box from the kitchen," I say while bending down to pick it up. "I'm pretty sure something broke."

Siân's shoulders slump as she walks up next to me. "It's okay. Hopefully, not everything is ruined. We can check when we get there."

Siân glances over at Kyla, who's struggling to catch her breath with her hand on her neck. The girl looks at me, and I sense she wants to tell Siân about what just happened, but when I narrow my gaze at her, she rolls her shoulders, and I know she's decided to be a smart girl.

"Are you okay?" Siân pries.

Kyla nods. "Yeah. I just... swallowed wrong."

"Oh. That's no fun," Siân says. "Look, I know you don't agree, but I'm safe with Christian. He would never let anything happen to me, and as soon as we get to the bottom of things, I'll move back home."

Kyla doesn't respond.

"I'll call you once I'm settled in," Siân promises and takes my free hand when I offer it to her.

As we turn to leave, Siân stops abruptly, and I glance back to see what's holding her up to find Kyla holding on to her arm.

Kyla works hard not to look at me. "Just be careful, okay? And if you need anything, call me—or Taj, and we'll come get you."

My muscles tense at the mention of Taj's name. Siân ended things with him, just like I told her to. Kyla knows that because it's something else they argued about. Which is funny to me, considering Kyla has been fucking him for God knows how long. You'd think she'd be glad to have the motherfucker all to herself now.

Siân lets go of my hand and pulls Kyla into a hug. I watch intently as they embrace, their postures a stark contrast to one another. Siân's is soft and endearing while Kyla's is riddled with tension and panic.

"I'll be safe, I promise." Siân kisses her friend on the cheek, then grabs the bookbag and purse that sits next to the door.

With one final look around, Siân closes the door, leaving an afraid Kyla alone with my threat playing on repeat in her mind. While her back is to me, I retrieve the note I scribbled before I arrived from my pocket, and as Siân is turning in my direction again, I pretend to be pulling the folded piece of paper from the mailbox attached to the wall.

"What's this?" I frown and unfold the page.

Siân's brows furrow, and she takes it from me. We each stare down at the page as she unravels it painfully slowly. There is already a change in her breathing, the once calm exhales turning sharp and forceful. She knows who it's from without having read the message.

Her face turns a ghostly shade of white, and her limbs go weak, but she keeps from falling. We make eye contact, and the look on her face makes me almost regret my actions. But as I've said a hundred times over, it's all a part of the plan.

Stage three: keep her close.

"It's from him... the stalker." Her words are barely audible. She mouths the words written in Italian, but I don't need to hear them to know what they say.

Stavi così bene in ginocchio con il mio cazzo in bocca, non vedo l'ora che anche la tua figa sia mia. *You looked so good on your knees with my cock in your mouth, can't wait till your pussy is mine, too.*

20

SIÂN

"Wow." I'm convinced I've said that word more times in the past twenty minutes than I have in my entire life combined. Other words could more accurately describe the surprise of finding out Christian lives in one of the nicest—if not the most impressive—apartments I've ever seen. A great big loft at the top of a towering high-rise. The moment he opened the door, it afforded me a breathtaking view of the city stretched out beneath and around us.

"You're impressed?"

He's so eager to please. It's touching and incredibly sweet just to see him like this. Sure, on the outside, he's just as cool and calm as ever, the sort of man who commands attention and respect the moment he crosses a threshold.

But deep down inside, it's a different story. I can't imagine he would enjoy it if he knew what was going through my head right now, but I find it sort of adorable how he keeps checking in to see what I think about this showplace. If I didn't know better, I would think he picked it out with me in mind.

I have to stop thinking that way. Letting myself even toy with the idea of him making me part of his life is dangerous. If I'm not careful, one such thought will lead to another, then another, until an entire arrangement of dominos falls, and I'm hopelessly infatuated.

I made that mistake with Taj—and even though Christian is an entirely different man, that doesn't mean I can't get hurt.

"What's it like to live so far above the world?" Stepping up to the window, I gaze down at the buildings below. It's a little trippy, and I have to inch away from the glass after only peering down for a few seconds. "It's making me a little dizzy. I didn't think I had a problem with heights until now."

Christian chuckles, sliding up behind me. I shouldn't let him have this easy familiarity. Wouldn't it be better if I at least set some boundaries? I don't want to encourage him to believe my staying here gives him free rein to do whatever he wants with me.

I want to do the right thing. I can't go making the same mistakes I did with Taj.

But I can't deny how comforting it is, having him so close. How right it feels. Like two puzzle pieces fitting together.

"Don't worry." His breath stirs the hair on the back of my neck, causing a delicious shiver to run down my spine. "I'm always here for you to lean on. I won't let you fall."

"Thanks for that." I giggle softly while slipping away from him, heading for the enormous kitchen. "Please, tell me you use this for more than a place to store plates and silverware."

He rubs the back of his neck, wearing a rueful grin. "The culinary arts have never been my area of expertise." A nice way of saying he doesn't cook.

I run my hand over the marble counter, admiring the shining appliances. "It seems like a waste."

"You're right." He looks very serious when he joins me at the counter topping the wide island. "It is a shame for something beautiful to go unused. Then again, it's downright tragic when that beautiful thing is mishandled, too." Something in his voice makes me think he's talking about more than kitchen appliances, but a quick look in his direction reveals a blank face. I can't read him sometimes, no matter how much I want to.

"Come on." His eyes light up before he takes me by the hand. "Let me show you the rest of the place." I follow him through to the bathroom, my eyes glazing over at the sight of the enormous shower.

"You can design any kind of experience you want," he explains, showing me the controls. "There are six jets, plus the overhead fixture. Be careful. If you turn the jets up to full power, it's a lot like getting sandblasted."

"You sound like you're speaking from experience."

"Let's just say I've never felt cleaner." He winks, making me giggle, and I can't help but think this was an excellent idea. Life had gotten too tense with Kyla, anyway. It's no fun going home when you know the other person living there resents you. Feeling like you have to tiptoe around for fear of upsetting someone.

I think I could be happy here, or at least secure for a little while.

You looked so good on your knees with my cock in your mouth.

Christian notices the way I shudder when those ugly words flash across my consciousness. Of course he would. He always seems to pick up on the slightest change in me.

"What's the matter? Are you unhappy? What can we do about it?"

"No, I'm not unhappy. Just, you know..." I shake out my hands, grimacing. "A little weirded out."

"Because of the note?"

"And everything that goes along with it, yes."

He eliminates the space between us, standing toe-to-toe with me before running a hand over my hair. "Remember what I told you. I would kill anyone who tried to hurt you. You've never been as safe in your life as you are at this moment, here with me. There's a reason I chose this as my home. It's a safe place, well-kept and secure. And now that you're here, I know why I chose it. Somehow, I knew you would come into my life. I knew you would need somewhere you could feel protected and secure."

It all feels too good to be true, but I so desperately want it to be. I want to believe him. "Maybe I'm a little jaded," I suggest. "Every time I've ever felt safe, he's proved otherwise."

"That was before me, remember?" He places a soft kiss against my lips, and for one moment, I allow myself to melt into him. He's so strong, so sure of himself. I wish I had just a fraction of that confidence.

The next stop is the bedroom. I can't help but feel nervous when I take in the great big bed with its almost obscene number of pillows and what looks like soft, expensive silk bedding.

"I have to be honest," I admit with a faint giggle. "I didn't think men lived like this. I mean, when they live alone. Without a woman's touch or however you want to put it."

"The truth?" He hugs me from behind, chuckling against my ear. "I had some help with the decorating. From someone with a much better eye than mine."

An ex-girlfriend? I stiffen at the thought of another woman decorating this apartment. I don't know why. He's allowed to have a past. My past isn't even very distant, is it? But the idea of someone else putting their touch on the place before I came into the picture leaves a sour taste in my mouth, nonetheless. I never considered myself the jealous type, but maybe I don't know myself as well as I thought I did.

Before I can go too far down the rabbit hole of despair, he adds, "She more than earned her fee. I would recommend her to anyone."

So, he paid somebody to help him. I wish I didn't feel so relieved at that, but I can't pretend I don't feel lighter and more comfortable now.

"It really is an amazing apartment. If I didn't know any better, I would think I woke up in a fairy tale."

He turns me in his arms until we're facing each other, then tightens his hold on me until our bodies are flush. My heart flutters at the closeness. "Allow yourself to enjoy this. Allow yourself to become comfortable with the idea of being safe and taken care of. Because that's what you are now. You are safe. I'm going to protect you."

Can it be this easy? This simple? Well, why not? Maybe I've already been through enough. Maybe fate decided to let up on me for once, to allow me to be happy. Would that be so unthinkable? Don't I deserve this after so many years of looking over my shoulder, always doubting, always wondering if somebody was waiting in the shadows?

"This is very new to me," I admit, allowing my hands to rest against his impressive chest. "I'm sorry if I seem ungrateful. Trust me, nothing could be further from the truth."

"I understand. You don't have to explain." His lips brush the tip of my nose, and when he pulls back, he's smiling. "All I ask is that you give yourself a chance. Allow yourself to accept good things coming into your life. Trust me, I'll make sure you don't regret it."

Trust him. It's easy to say, isn't it? And maybe I can trust him, fully and completely. He's never given me any reason not to. Not like Taj, whose red flags I was intent on ignoring for so long. His hot-and-cold demeanor, the way he'd keep me waiting endlessly, then show up with a million apologies. I turned a blind eye for so long.

Christian is nothing like that. He's never let me down. And now, he's welcoming me into his inner sanctum. That alone should be proof of his seriousness, his good intentions.

Although... My attention drifts over toward the bed, the only one in the apartment. "How are we going to do this? I mean, which side do you sleep on?"

His eyes narrow a split second before widening, understanding dawning on his handsome face. "No, no, it won't be like that. You'll take the bed. I'll sleep on the couch."

"No! This is your home. If anybody should take the couch, it should be me."

"And what kind of man would I be if I made you sleep out there in the living room?" His chest puffs out like I offended his masculinity.

I tip my head to the side, brows knitting together. "A man who pays a lot of money for this apartment and deserves to sleep in his own bed."

"You will sleep in this bed." He jerks a thumb toward the doorway and the living room beyond. "I'll sleep out there. End of discussion."

There doesn't seem to be much I can say in the face of his certainty, so the best I can do is thank him. It doesn't seem like those two words are enough, and I know I have to find other ways to show my gratitude. Maybe I'll make us a nice dinner or offer to do the housework to earn my keep. Anything, so long as it feels like I'm not taking advantage.

"It's been a long day already." He rolls his head on his shoulders, then stretches his arms. It isn't easy to ignore how the muscles bunch and flex under his skin. "Why don't you get settled in and get cleaned up? There are plenty of clean towels in the bathroom. Do you know where your toiletries and such are?"

I do since I packed them separately to keep them close at hand before I knew I'd be donating so much of the rest of my stuff.

It doesn't take long before I realize he was right about the shower. After a little experimentation, I find a delightful combination of settings where the jets on the walls don't hit me with something that feels like it's coming from a firehose. Once I'm able to settle in and enjoy the setup, the hot water massages my aching muscles—he was right, it's been a long day of hauling boxes up and down stairs—and before long, I'm enveloped in fragrant steam thanks to my body wash and shampoo. It's luxurious, like being at a spa. I can hardly believe I've ended up in this amazing place with this amazing man.

An amazing man who might be in danger, thanks to me.

It seems like even the shower isn't enough to wash away my anxiety. Now, it's Christian I'm concerned for rather than Kyla. I still don't know why she was so upset with me for leaving. I figure she'd be glad to see me go, glad to know there's no longer a target painted on her back. But there she was, arguing, fighting me. She'll see this was for the best. I'm sure she will. But that still leaves me worrying about Christian. No matter what he says, he doesn't know who we're dealing with. He's not the one who's had to run from this psycho all these years.

And he has no idea how far this guy will go. He wasn't there in that alley. He doesn't know how depraved this person is. How vile.

Right. Maybe if you tell yourself that, you'll eventually believe it. Even now, there was a stirring in my core at the thought of being on my knees and at his mercy...

I can only hope Christian makes good on his promise of keeping me safe. Otherwise, I'm at risk of getting hurt again.

And of liking it again, too.

"No!"

My eyes fly open, and for a split second, I don't know where I am. My heart is pounding in my ears, hammering hard enough to make me sick. I'm disoriented, sweating, shaking.

I was back in that alley. I could even smell the urine, the garbage left to rot in the shadows. I could feel the ground under my knees and the thighs of my attacker under my hands as he forced me—as he made me...

Rolling onto my back, I get an even bigger surprise. A man is standing at the foot of the bed, watching me. Maybe it's that I'm still half asleep, still stuck in that nightmare, but I scramble as close to the headboard as possible, hugging the padded surface.

He takes a step forward, and a beam of moonlight illuminates his familiar face. "It's only me."

Right. I'm with Christian. This is Christian's bed, Christian's room, Christian's apartment. I'm miles and miles away from that alley, somewhere safe and comfortable. I have nothing to be afraid of.

Still, when the pounding in my ears turns to more of a dull roar, and I can hear myself think again, one question demands to be voiced. "Why were you standing there? You scared me."

"I'm so sorry," he murmurs, his expression shifting into one of regret. "That's not what I intended. You called out for me when you were dreaming."

"I did?" I touch a hand to the side of my head, my mind still in a bit of a fog. The tangled mass of hair tells me I must have been tossing and turning, too. Now seems like the last time I should be worried about my appearance, but I can't help wanting to smooth it down. What girl wants a man to see her looking like something out of a horror movie?

Especially a man who looks the way he does—his magnificent physique displayed thanks to the fact that he sleeps wearing only a pair of boxer briefs. His body is extraordinary, chiseled, practically begging for me to run my fingers along the rippling abs and the V-shaped cut of his muscles as they trailed down, down, beneath his waistband.

Even now, still gripped with terror, I can't ignore the intensity of our chemistry.

"I'm okay," I murmur, finally loosening up a little, no longer clinging to the headboard. I force myself into a more neutral position and try to offer a reassuring smile. "Really. Thank you for coming in to check on me."

Instead of leaving me alone, which I half expect him to do, he sits on the corner of the bed near my feet, giving me my space rather than invading it. Just one more thing to appreciate about him. "Before long, you won't have any reason for these nightmares. Once you're accustomed to feeling safe and cared for, there won't be any reason for them."

"I hope you're right."

"I know I am." His eyes meet mine in the near darkness. They shouldn't glitter the way they do, practically blazing as they hold mine. I can barely breathe. He's so overwhelming. Not in a bad way, though. I don't feel threatened.

Instead, I feel... almost cherished. It's a funny word, one I'm not exactly comfortable using. I guess that's because I've never felt cherished before, not in this way. Certainly not by Taj, who's the only man I can compare him to.

I called his name, and he came on the run. He might've been fast asleep, but he didn't waste any time checking on me.

He goes to the kitchen, returning with a glass of water. "Here you go. In case you need it." He sets it on the nightstand, hesitating, and I wonder if he's as reluctant to leave me as I am to let him do it.

"Would you stay with me? Just for a little while?" There I go again, being needy, but he doesn't seem to mind. In fact, he wastes no time pulling back the blankets. I scoot over, rolling onto my left side so my back is to him when he settles in. The arm he drapes around me is like magic, easing whatever little bit of fear is left in me.

And now I am intensely aware of his nearness. Of having his body so close to mine, with only my thin nightshirt and shorts between us. It would be one thing if I didn't have the memory of his touch weighing on my mind, my nerves tingling at the possibility of knowing that sort of pleasure again. It would be one thing if I had nothing but fantasies of what it might be like to have his hands on me. If I could only imagine whether he'd know just how to work my body into a frenzy.

Now I know. It could be a subconscious craving for nearness, intimacy, something to lose myself in, but the reason behind a slow unfurling of awareness deep in my core doesn't matter. The result is the same, either way. I want him. I want him to take me away. To make me forget everything for a little while and sink into deep, delicious pleasure.

My body takes over for me, my ass wiggling a little against him in a way I know is bound to wake up what's under those briefs. I felt it against me in the car. How hard he was. How big he is.

He lets out a strangled choking sound. "What are you doing?"

"What do you think I'm doing?" I whisper, my heart in my throat and my ass against his dick.

"You don't have to do that." His hand is on my thigh, though, but his touch isn't sexual. I can't help but feel a little disappointed. This is not the way he's supposed to react.

"But I want to." It's easy to say it when my back is to him, when he can't see the growing embarrassment written on my face. Was this a complete mistake? I don't want to think it was, but he's making me wonder.

Instead of his hand creeping farther up my thigh, he pats my leg before wrapping his arm around me again. "Someday soon, we will. But not now."

"Why not?" I hate the disappointment in my voice, but I can't help it.

"Because you aren't ready yet." When I draw a breath, prepared to ask exactly what that's supposed to mean, he makes a shushing sound like he's quieting a child. "I would never take advantage of you, beautiful. And that's what I would do now if I gave in to what we both want. Our time is coming, though. Make no mistake about that." He presses a kiss against my ear, my jaw, the side of my neck. "For now, sleep. You need rest more than anything."

Normally, I would ask exactly who he thinks he is, telling me what I need. But he's right, unfortunately. I'm already fighting to keep my eyes open as it is.

Before I can thank him for being so understanding and considerate, I drift back off. This time, there are no nightmares. There's no anything. Just deep, solid sleep.

And when I wake to sunlight streaming through the window, I'm the only one in the bed.

21

CHRISTIAN

This is the most nervous I've ever been in my life. In fact, I can't recall a time when anything ever got under my skin. I'm not easily rattled, and the things that make most people squirm do nothing to me. I mean, how could it when you literally feel nothing—only pain, darkness, and destruction.

Yet, here I am, my insides turning flips as I drive Siân's old Chevy down the highway. Tonight, she's introducing me to the woman she calls her caretaker and insisted we take her car and not mine. Something about it being too flashy and wanting the woman to like me. Honestly, I can't care less. I'm taking her away from here soon, so getting to know this woman—whoever she is, matters none to me. But until that time comes, I'll go along with Siân's plan.

"Relax," she says from the passenger seat. Siân reaches for my hand and gives it a reassuring squeeze.

I glance between her and the road. "I'm relaxed."

Siân chuckles, though the gesture is so subtle I barely notice it. "Tell that to your face."

Wetting dry lips, I smile. "Why don't you help me calm down, then?" I throw my gaze in her direction again, catching sight of the blush creeping across her features.

"Christian," she squeals.

"What? You're the one worried about my nerves. It's only right you help settle them."

She stares at me as if she's waiting to see if I'm serious or not. When I don't say anything else, she rolls her eyes and shakes her head.

"I'm not giving you a happy ending while we're going seventy miles an hour down the highway," she finally lets out.

"And here I was thinking we'd agreed on taking risks," I challenge.

She's quiet for a second, and when I take another peek at her, I notice the hard swallow she takes. A grin threatens to form across my face because I know she's contemplating it. For the past two weeks, I've accepted every opportunity to encourage her to break out of her shell. And it's worked, mostly. We'd do small things here and there—tiny little bets around the loft, but nothing like what I'm suggesting. I've purposely been the perfect gentleman, sleeping on the couch every night except the first.

She's still a little shaken up from the blow job in the alley and the last note I left, so I've been pacing things with her. Getting her to trust me and making sure she's comfortable is imperative. So, I never push her too hard, and oftentimes, I give a little to keep things fair.

For instance, I've agreed to sit across a dining table like some big happy fucking family tonight. Now don't get me wrong, dinners were a big deal growing up. Except in the Russo household, there was nothing familiar about them. They were always a means to an end for my father, a transaction for whatever business was coming down the pipeline. I can't recall the last time we just ate and enjoyed each other's company. But these past couple of weeks with Siân have been precisely like that.

Every night, she cooks and sets place settings at the large dining table I haven't used since Jennifer furnished the place. Most of my meals are on the go, but with Siân around, I've even gained a few pounds. It's been a nice change, but meeting her proverbial parent isn't something I have in mind.

"I'm messing with you," I admit, even though I'd love nothing more than to feel her hands all over me. But it's fine because soon, she'll be mine completely.

We cross the county line into a small town an hour outside the city. It's a vast difference from where we've been staying. All the homes are spaced out, some with properties large enough to house animals. It's dark out, so I can't really see my surroundings, but as our headlights flash across the different yards, I get a glimpse of the type of place she's taking me to. It's rural, quaint, and I imagine everyone knows everyone.

"Why does...?" I pause, trying to remember the caretaker's name.

"Cynthia," she finishes for me.

"Yeah. Why does Cynthia live out here and not in the city?"

Siân sighs and settles into her seat with her eyes focused on the road ahead. "At the stop sign, make a left."

I nod and follow her instructions.

"We used to live out here together, actually. We moved around a lot when I was younger, but it's always been just Cynthia and me."

"She doesn't have any kids of her own?" I already know the answer to this because I know everything there is to know about Siân's life. It may have taken me a while to find her, but when I did, I learned as much as I could.

Siân shakes her head and drops her chin to her chest, while fiddling with her fingers. "No." She takes a breath. "Just she and I since I was ten."

"And your parents?" I ask softly.

Siân swallows again, and this time when she stares up at me, sadness is written in the lines above her brow. "Cynthia's my parent. Well, the closest I'll get to one."

"What happened?"

I can see the level of unease ripping its way through her body, but I ask her anyway. Getting her to talk about what happened means she can heal from it, and if she can heal, no one can use it against her—including me.

"They died. Well, they were killed when I was ten. Three more blocks and it'll be at the end of the circle."

"Sorry to hear that. Do they know who did it?"

She shakes her head. "It happened in Italy." She pauses, then looks at me. "Yeah, fun fact," she teases gingerly. "Hence the letters being left in Italian. I'm pretty sure whoever's been stalking me all these years knew my family. I don't remember anything, but from what Cynthia has told me, my father knew the man who killed him. He would have killed me, too, had she not gotten me out of there. After they killed him, they set my home on fire."

"What do you mean, you don't remember anything?"

"I was in bed when it happened. Cynthia woke me up, and we snuck out through a hidden passageway in my room. Apparently, dear ole dad was into some bad shit. I would have never guessed it because he'd been so good at keeping that from me. All I knew was that I was a girl who loved her father, and he loved me."

"And your mom?"

We make it to the end of the cul-de-sac, and I frown. Throwing my gaze around, confused and conflicted, I slow to a halt and turn toward Siân. Before I can ask her anything, she points straight ahead. It takes me a second to recognize the driveway and mailbox, but all that's behind it is a slit between rows of trees.

"Keep straight."

I press the gas, and the car rocks over the uneven payment.

"My mom was there, but we weren't close. She never really spoke to me or played with me. But I had Cynthia. She's been in my life since the day I was born and, in a way, took the place of my absentee mother."

"Um," I mutter.

"Anyway, Cynthia snuck me away and brought me to America, and we've lived here since. There have been different places and cities over the years, but this time around, we settled in here."

"Why here?" I continue to follow the pathway for what feels like forever. It has to be a mile long at least, and just when I'm about to ask how much farther, a mid-sized home comes into view.

"It had been quite a while. The stalker had seemed to disappear, and I finally felt like I could start a life. It took some convincing, but since I'm twenty-five now and getting my master's, I pled with Cynthia to let me live in the city. The drive to and from school every day was taxing, so it made sense. After a while, she agreed as long as I got a roommate and come home twice a month for family dinner."

Pulling the car next to the black SUV, I kill the engine and peer through the window at the home. Every light is on that I can see, and a second later, the front screen door flies open. A moment after, the top of a woman's head pokes out above the row of bushes that lines the porch. This is more of what I would expect for a person on the run, unlike where Siân lived with Kyla. It's off the beaten path, and unless you know it's here, you'd miss it. The thick greenery along the front provides not just curb appeal but added privacy.

Cynthia reaches the top step, a smile plastered to her aging face. She waves at us, and I realize she looks exactly how I remember. I was only fourteen at the time, but this woman hasn't changed a bit. She's older, obviously, with gray streaks flowing through her long flowing hair, but she's still just as pretty as she was all those years ago.

"You two look alike," I mutter.

"Yeah. It's kind of crazy, really. I guess what they say about starting to look like the person you spend every day with is true. People always assume she's my mother." Siân stares at Cynthia for a second, and without turning back to me, she adds, "You know, I've never told anyone any of that. Not even Kyla."

I reach for her hand and bring it to my mouth. "Thanks for trusting me with your story."

She gives me a soft, tight-lipped smile. "Come on, let's get inside. I'm starving."

I release her, and we climb out of the car at the same time.

"You made it," Cynthia beams.

Siân runs up the stairs to meet her, wrapping her into a tight hug. "We did. I've missed you."

The woman plants a kiss on Siân's cheek while squeezing her tight. "I've missed you, too." Cynthia takes Siân's hands and steps back to observe her ward. "Let me get a look at you," she chimes.

Siân spins, and the two laugh. Their bond is wholesome, something I've never experienced before, and a part of me is grateful Siân had that growing up. The only world I know is mayhem, but to see that she's lived differently warms me. And it almost makes me second-guess my plans—*almost*.

"Who do we have here?" Cynthia asks and cranes her neck to get a look at me. It's dark everywhere but on the porch, so it's not until I step up on the porch does she see what I look like. No sooner than her eyes land on me, her face turns pale, and her breath catches in her throat. Cynthia stumbles backward, but Siân's hold on her waist keeps her still.

"Cynthia, this is Christian, my new boyfriend." Siân beams with an arm outstretched toward me.

I force a grin on my face, keeping my eyes locked on Cynthia. She remembers me after all. The wide eyes and now ghostly complexion give it all away. I hold out a hand, and she accepts it.

"Nice to finally meet. I've heard so many great things," I add, gripping her hand tightly, silently daring her to say anything.

She's smart, and instead of screaming bloody murder at the top of her lungs, she sucks in a breath and puts on the best fucking performance I've seen in my life. "Boy, you're handsome. Good job, Siân." Cynthia swats at Siân. "Come on in before the food gets cold." She spins on her heels and stalks inside her home.

Even though her back is to us, I can see the tension and nerves working their way to the surface. Cynthia awkwardly glances around, but Siân doesn't seem to notice the change in her caregiver's demeanor. I watch her closely because the last thing I need is for her to blow my cover and ruin everything I've been working toward with Siân. All this time, I refrained from questioning her about her life before now. One, I already know everything, and two, she needed to be comfortable enough to share on her own.

"You have a beautiful home," I say, despite not giving a damn about the décor.

"Thanks," she snips.

We enter the dining room, and Siân takes her place at the small table, patting the seat next to her for me. I settle in beside her, scooting close and rubbing Siân's arm for appearance's sake. Cynthia disappears into the kitchen and returns a bit later with a large bowl of spaghetti in one hand and a salad in the other. She sets them in the center of the table and returns to the kitchen for a basket of breadsticks and a frosty, cold bottle of wine.

"Here, allow me." I hop to my feet, taking the cork from between her fingers and snagging the wine.

Cynthia flops into her seat, her gaze darting to Siân, whose attention is focused on me.

Once I get the cork out, I pour wine into a glass for each of us. Whiskey is more my speed, but when in Rome, right?

"Thank you," Cynthia says in a near whisper and downs the drink before I can return to my seat. "Let's eat, shall we?"

Siân wastes no time loading both of our plates with food, and I must admit, it all looks great. It's been too long since I've had authentic Italian food. Every cockamamie place here is nothing but knock-offs.

"Do you make your sauce from scratch?" I question and use my spoon to stir a helping of pasta onto my fork.

"The noodles, too."

"Perfect," is all I let out before stuffing my face. "Mm," I moan with a tilt of my head.

"Good, yeah?" Siân says with her mouth full.

"I haven't had good pasta in forever," I admit, this time out loud.

"Cynthia is the best cook. I swear she needs to open a restaurant." Siân bites into a breadstick.

Cynthia smiles, her posture finally settling just a bit. She's still on guard and I sense she's trying not to alarm Siân. If she indeed remembers me, which I suspect she does, then she knows what I'm capable of. I may have been a boy when she knew me, but she's well aware of my father and the way he raised me. It would be unwise to cause a scene when there is no one here to protect her.

"And as I keep telling you, my dear, it takes money to start a business."

That and the fact that they're living in this country under aliases, and if I had to guess, Cynthia never bothered with obtaining any kind of legitimate citizenship. She couldn't have, not without alerting my father that Siân didn't perish in that fire.

"I'll invest if this is something you really want." I spin another serving and devour it.

Cynthia stares at me, my proposal catching her off guard. "Th-thank you, but it's unnecessary. I'm way too old to be trying to start a new career at my age."

"Nonsense. There is no age limit to building a better future. You taught me that," she interjects.

"I did?"

They laugh.

"So, Christian, is that an accent I hear? Where are you from?" Cynthia bounces her gaze between her plate and me.

She definitely remembers me.

"All over. I work for my father's company and sometimes spend months, if not years, in one location. I guess I've picked up different accents over time." I consume another bite.

Cynthia nods. "That's nice."

"Eh. It can be exhausting if I'm honest."

"I imagine it could be. How did you meet my girl?"

Siân reaches for her wine. "Near campus. I was at the bar with Kyla, and he approached me."

"Oh, so, you're a student as well?"

I shake my head and swallow the food in my mouth. "No. I was new to town and just stopped by the first bar I came across."

"And it just so happened to be the bar near the university?"

I press my back into the chair and narrow my eyes at her. "A beautiful coincidence, I'd say."

"It is." Cynthia's tone is suggestive, and for the first time tonight, Siân seems to notice the tension in the air.

How could she not? The shit is so thick, you can cut it with a knife.

"I have something to tell you," Siân cuts in. "We have something to tell you." She places her small palm over the back of my hand.

Cynthia stops all movement, even down to breathing. Silent and pensive is how she waits for the announcement Siân is about to make.

"I've been staying with Christian."

Cynthia's eyes shoot open.

"And before you flip out, he's been letting me stay because I got another letter."

It isn't lost on me that she leaves out the part about being violated in the alley. I don't speak, though. I allow her to share this news in her own way.

"Even though the cops claim there have been no signs of forced entry, I know the stalker has been inside my home. It wasn't safe there for Kyla, and until we can get to the bottom of things or until I find a new place, I'll be living with him."

"Or you can move back here," Cynthia deadpans.

"I have school, and his apartment is only fifteen minutes from campus."

"Siân, I don't know about this." Cynthia shakes her head.

"It's okay. He's been a great host, and since I've been with him, there have been no other threats."

Cynthia makes eye contact with me, and I know she's thinking the same thing as me. There hasn't been another threat because I have her exactly where I want her.

"I see. Excuse me, I'm going to grab the water pitcher." Cynthia pushes away from the table and rushes into the kitchen.

Not even a second later, my phone buzzes in my pocket. I retrieve it and notice it's an alert from the cloning app I put on Siân's phone. With the device under the table, I open the software and skim over the text.

Cynthia: *Don't react. But as soon as you can, get up, go in my room, and get the gun from under my pillow. Christian isn't who he says he is.*

I inhale deeply, my nostrils flaring as I continue to read the message. My blood boils, and I manage to keep my cool. Cynthia's little warning would have worked if Siân hadn't left her phone in her purse in the car.

When Cynthia reenters the room carrying the water pitcher, I'm convinced is only a ploy. I excuse myself and claim to need to make a quick call. The ladies don't give me a rebuttal, and I slip out on the porch and jump over the five small steps. Unlocking the car, I snag Siân's purse from the floor of the passenger side and dig for her iPhone. Once I find it, I punch in her passcode and navigate to her message log. I find what I'm looking for and immediately delete Cynthia's alert.

Letting the door slam, I glance around the darkness, suck in another breath, then make my way back inside. I don't enter right away, needing a moment to calm myself down. The crisis has been averted, and I'll deal with Cynthia's sneakiness later. The women are quiet when I step foot into the room. Siân smiles at me while Cynthia sits uncomfortably on her end of the table.

"Is everything okay?" Siân asks after I'm seated with a hand on my shoulder.

I lick my lips, give her a soft smile, and lean in for a kiss. Siân melts into me, her tongue slipping past mine. Pressure builds in my gut, my body instantly waking at the taste of her. I drape an arm over the back of her chair, forcing her closer to me. It's as if I've forgotten the shit her caretaker just attempted, my anger and the blatant sabotage becoming an afterthought.

Cynthia clears her throat, interrupting our embrace. Siân and I stare at each other for a second, her eyes telling me a story her mouth has been too afraid to reveal. She's connected to me, and though it hasn't been very long at all, she's ready for me. Not that this is brand-new information. I've noticed the subtle hints and the barely there shorts she wears to bed.

Siân remembers how hard I made her come, just as much as I do, and if I had to guess, she's dying to come again. But after what I did to her in that alley and the confession she was ashamed to share with me about how much she liked being on her knees, I need to play this cool. She can like being violated all she wants, but the truth remains, I was a stranger to her at that moment. Christian can't claim her that way. Christian respects her body and her choice to do with it what she pleases. Christian has been patient, and the decision to take the next step needs to feel as if it's hers and hers alone.

"Sorry," Siân mutters, then picks up her fork.

Cynthia doesn't offer a response. She only glares at me while shoving a forkful of food into her mouth. With her elbows propped on the table between bites, she watches the two of us. I sense she's waiting for Siân to realize she's sent her a message.

Sorry to disappoint, mommy dearest.

We get through the next hour of dinner, and surprisingly, the rest of the night goes off without a hitch. Cynthia seems to open up to the idea of me, but I know it's all for Siân's sake. We're alike in that regard, both willing to put on a charade for the betterment of the one person who connects us.

Somewhere throughout the night, the conversation began to flow, and now we're helping her clear away the dishes.

Cynthia closes the refrigerator, then presses the lid on a Tupperware container. Holding it out to me, she says. "Enjoy."

"Oh no, I couldn't. You've already fed me so much." I wave a hand with the other pressed against my stomach.

"Nonsense. You said it yourself that you've missed good pasta, and there is no way I can eat all this alone."

I nod and accept the container. "Thank you. It'll be my late-night snack."

"All right, well, I guess you two should head back to the city."

Siân saunters up to Cynthia and wraps her into a hug. "Dinner was amazing, as always."

"It was. Thank you for having me."

Cynthia forces a smile. "It was a pleasure meeting you." She signals for the two of us to exit the kitchen.

I follow Siân toward the door, keeping an eye on Cynthia along the way. Knowing that the old bird is packing and is aware of who I am, I'd be a fool not to be cautious. With the way she snarled at me for half the night, it'll be just my luck for her to shoot me in the back. Her entire life has been devoted to protecting Siân, I don't see tonight being any different.

We step out onto the porch, down the steps, and over to the car. I open the door for Siân to enter, and once she's safely inside, I shut her in and walk to my side. Cynthia is still watching me, her eyes boring into my back. And when I make eye contact with her, a chill runs the length of my spine. Something tells me she doesn't fold easily, and it's something I can respect. Either way, though, I can't let her little warning slide.

I take my phone out of my pocket and search for Tony's number, dropping him a ping to my current location and a single text.

***Me**: Meet me here. Don't go in. Just wait.*

With one final wave, I bid Cynthia a goodbye, climb behind the wheel, and head back into the city.

~

After we returned home, I helped a tired Siân into bed. Tonight was good for her—for us. It helped her see this thing between us in a different light. From her vantage point, two people she cared about seemed to enjoy being around one another when, in reality, secrets were brewing right under her nose. Secrets that need to stay buried by any means necessary. The time will come when I tell my *topolina* everything, but now isn't it.

This bond of ours is still so fresh, and while her actions tonight, once we walked past the threshold of the loft we now share, tells me she wants more, all it would take is for Cynthia to divulge what she tried warning her about. If that happens, all of this will be for nothing. I can't have that. So as badly as I wanted to give in to what Siân wanted and fuck her tight little body to sleep, I can't—not now.

At the moment, I'm in my Ferrari, glad not to be in Siân's piece of shit Chevy. This is more up my alley—speed, horsepower, and style. My phone rings through the Bluetooth speaker as I turn down the familiar road.

"I'm here. Where are you?" Tony asks through the receiver.

"Almost there." I hit my lights and approach the long driveway that leads to the hidden property.

It's pitch black out now. The only light comes from the moon above us, though it's more than enough to illuminate the path for me. I inch over to the side behind where Tony is parked, just as I instructed him. Should Cynthia choose to leave her house at some point tonight, she won't immediately notice the cars, thanks to the secluded road and layers of thick trees.

Tony and I exit our respective vehicles simultaneously, both being careful not to slam the doors. Lurking in the dead of night isn't anything new for us. He knows the routine and doesn't wait for any instructions.

Dressed in all black, we make our way down the long, uneven driveway, coming out on the other end to more darkness. The moon is shining down on the house, so we at least have that going for us, but every light on the inside of the home is out. Considering how late it was when Siân and I left nearly three hours ago, it's probably safe to assume that Cynthia has climbed into bed herself.

But only a fool would assume anything in this life. Knowing that the woman is carrying, I have half a mind to bet she'll be up waiting for us. I'd never spoken to Cynthia in the past, but she's been under Marco's employ for as long as I can remember. The few times my father dragged me to their estate as a boy to handle whatever dealings they had going at the time, I'd see her tending to a then baby Siân. It's how I know her secret and how I know she is aware of mine.

The story is sad, really. All the lies, hidden truths—the murders. It could have all been avoided if people were just open about their demons. Instead, they hid behind the power they possessed, and now here we are—years later, living broken existences filled with deceit.

"Psst," I sound out to get Tony's attention.

He stops moving, his focus still on the house.

"No one's getting hurt tonight," I deadpan while pulling on my gloves, and he does the same.

"Figured as much, considering you asked for these." Tony holds up a capped syringe and several zip ties. "Though, I can't lie and say I'm not surprised."

"Yeah, well, so am I," I huff and take the vial of propofol.

"What's the plan?" he questions and shoves the zip ties back into his pocket.

"I'll take the front, and you sneak in through the back. If I have to guess, she's in there waiting for me."

"And you're certain she remembers you?"

"I'm positive." I spit off into the distance and move toward the front door.

From the corner of my eye, I notice Tony hunch low and scale the bushes that line the home until he finally disappears from view. Keeping close to the railing and out of direct view of the windows, I creep up onto the porch, peering through the tiny cutout above the door.

There doesn't seem to be any movement on the inside of the home, but I'm not stupid enough to take that at face value. This woman has spent the past fifteen years on the run from my family, and she recognized me almost immediately, not to mention her little warning to Siân. If it were me, I'd want it to seem as if I'm asleep and unaware, only to pounce when it's least expected.

I head for the door, checking the knob, even though I doubt it's unlocked. When I realize I'm correct, I remove my lock kit from my jeans and get to work. It takes me a second before I finally hear the click

I'm looking for. A smile stretches across my lips, and I slowly push the door open, staying low to the ground just to be safe.

The moment I get the door open, a loud gunshot ripples through the house, followed by the agonizing wail of my right-hand man. I rush forward, ducking around walls until I breach the kitchen entryway. Cynthia has her back to me with her weapon pointed at Tony's head. The light above the stove makes it easy for me to see what's going on, and I have to fight the urge to grin.

"Ugh. You old-ass bitch," Tony gargles.

"Who the fuck are you?" Cynthia demands to know, still unaware of my presence behind her.

I make quick work, grabbing her arms, forcing her gun toward the floor. "There, there, now."

"She fucking shot me," Tony announces, his voice strained. "No one's getting hurt, huh?" He throws my words back at me.

I tip my head. "Eh. *Almost* no one."

Snatching the pistol from Cynthia, I force her over to the breakfast table and push her down into the closest chair. She swings and kicks, but I hop out of her reach.

"You're feisty to be so tiny. I like it." I fold my arms over my chest. "Calm down."

"Calm down? You and your goon broke into my house to kill me."

I flick my thumb over my nose, then suck in a breath. "Okay, okay. I'll give you that. We broke in. But no one's dying tonight."

"Where's Siân?" she demands to know.

"At home sleeping, I tucked her in and everything. One moment." I hold up a finger and scan the room in search of the light switch. Finding it on the wall near where Tony still sits on the floor clutching his arm, I flip it on. "There, much better."

Cynthia squints from the sudden brightness, using her hand to shield her eyes. Once she's adjusted, she drops her arm and stares up at me. "What do you want?"

I cock a brow and pinch my lips together while snagging one of the empty chairs and positioning it directly in front of Cynthia. Her eyes narrow in on the Glock in my grasp, which causes her to shift awkwardly in her seat. I follow her gaze and then tuck the weapon behind me in the waistband of my jeans.

"Better?" I hold my hands up. "We just want to talk."

"So you break in with weapons drawn?"

"It's a good thing we did. Look what you did to my buddy here." I tilt my head to Tony.

She snarls. "I was aiming for his head."

"Ooo. You're a spitfire. I see why Marco kept you around," I tease.

Cynthia's eyes grow wide.

"Yeah. I know everything, but I'm guessing Siân doesn't. Am I right?"

"Please. Don't kill her, Christian. She shouldn't be held responsible for a deal that was made when she was a child."

"I'm not going to kill her. I just want to fuck her and give you a hundred evil little grandchildren."

"No." Her voice cracks. "Let her go, please."

I sigh and lean forward with my elbows resting on my knees. I toy with the syringe, weaving it through my fingers before finally removing the cap. Cynthia takes in the object in my hand. As panic creeps across her face, the color drains from her already pale white skin, and her breathing all but ceases.

"What are you going to do to me?" she asks, her words inaudible.

"You know, I came here with Siân tonight, hoping you wouldn't recognize me. You probably wouldn't believe me, but I care about Siân, and for her sake, I wanted for you and me to get along. But then you went and sent her that text. I know you think the worst of my family, and you're right to feel that way. We haven't really made things easy for you." I pause for a beat. "Actually, I'm a little thirsty. Do you mind if I get some water?"

Cynthia doesn't answer me, but I don't expect her to. I stand and walk over to the cabinet above the sink, checking each until I find the one with the cups. Then I open the fridge and remove the pitcher of water, pouring some into the cup.

Cynthia uses this moment to try to get away, except I expected her to make a move. Whipping the gun from behind my back, I aim it and shoot at the wall, purposely missing her head by a hair.

She freezes with her hands up in the air. "Okay. Okay."

"Sit the fuck down," I bark, my patience already slipping.

Cynthia shuffles back to her seat as I glance to my right to find Tony now up on his feet, blood dripping to the floor around him.

"You good?"

"Yeah. Through and through." He snatches the hand towel from the hook near the sink and wraps it tightly around his wounded arm.

I hand my gun to Tony, who takes it right away. Holding up the syringe, I squeeze a little of the medicine out and stalk toward her. Cynthia flinches and tries to retreat, but there is nowhere for her to go. She's quite literally stuck between a rock—*me*—and a hard place.

Up close and personal, I lean to her ear and say, "You've protected Siân, and for that, I'm grateful. I won't kill the only family she has left, but I can't have you telling her who I am. It's too early for her to know."

She nods in rapid succession. "I won't. Just let us go, and you'll never see us again."

I search her face. "She's mine now—*forever*."

A yelp slips out of Cynthia when I jam the needle into her neck, but she's instantly unconscious as I pump the drugs into her system. Over the next few minutes, we get rid of all signs that we were here, leaving nothing disturbed. When we're done, I lift her over my shoulder, then take her to the trunk of Tony's car.

We head our separate ways, him and Cynthia to a secluded location, and me back to my topolina.

VILLAIN

22

SIÂN

It isn't until everybody around me gets up and gathers their things that I realize class is over—and I sat here daydreaming through the entire thing. I don't think I paid attention to a word of the lecture. And I'm still so deep in the brain fog provided by my conflicting thoughts that I move a little slowly, stumbling slightly as I get up.

A quick glance toward the front of the room tells me the instructor isn't paying attention, chatting over something with his assistant. At least I have that going in my favor as I grab my things and hurry out of the hall with my head down. One thing I've always been dedicated to is my schoolwork, and my performance lately hasn't exactly made me proud.

Not that I'm failing or anything like that, but I'm not as on top of things as I could be. Mainly because my thoughts are always wandering. Most of the time, I wish I could be home—rather, Christian's apartment. It's so easy to think of that as my home, so tempting to imagine living there always. Over the past couple of weeks, everything's been just about perfect.

Which is where the reason for my distraction comes in. When I'm not wishing I could be home, I'm wondering why the people who are most important to me have drifted out of my life since he entered it. Kyla hasn't said a word to me since the awkwardness we shared the day I moved out. She must still be upset with Christian, though I can't imagine why. I know she thinks she's being a good friend, but I was hoping this would have blown over by now. That after a few days, she would stop ignoring my texts and at least try to talk to me. I could use an explanation, and I think I deserve one. Why is she so determined to hate him?

Plus, it would be nice to show her how great things are. She had nothing to be worried about in the first place. If I could talk to her, I could show her that. Maybe she could even come over for dinner some night, just to hang out. Just to ease her mind a little.

It's Cynthia who really surprises me. She seemed happy for us the night we had dinner at the house, yet when I called her the next morning hoping to get her true feelings—I want so much for her to like him, to like us together—all I got was her voicemail greeting. It's been that way ever since, too, for a few days now. She's never been like this before.

If this goes on much longer, I decide as I step out into the evening air, I'm going to drive out to the house and check on her. Only the fact that we're each other's emergency contact has kept me from doing that before now. If anything was wrong, I would've found out by now.

Is it childish of me to wonder if there will ever come a time when everything in my life will be good all at once? Is that too much to ask? I'm so happy to be with Christian now. I've never felt so good, so secure. So much like there's somebody who genuinely cares. When we're together, it feels so right. I don't have to ask myself what he's really thinking or why there are long stretches of time when I can't get ahold of him. After a while, that's all I ever went through with Taj. He made me question everything about myself, right down to wondering whether I was even worthy of him. That's something Christian hasn't put me through, something I doubt he ever will.

And I want to share that with somebody. Is that so wrong? Don't they want me to be happy? Especially Cynthia. Isn't that what a mother, even a mother figure, is supposed to want? Everything seemed so great during dinner, and the two of them got along so well. Was there something I missed? No, there couldn't have been, or else she would have told me about it. She would've wasted no time sharing her opinion, especially if it was a negative one.

Of course, I can't tell Christian about this. I feel he senses my unhappiness, but he doesn't push for answers. It might hurt him to know I'm feeling disconnected. I know he would blame himself for it, and that's the last thing I want. None of this is his fault. No, I should thank him for everything he's added to my life.

But that still isn't enough to make me feel secure when I'm alone, the way I am now as I cross the campus. No matter how much I wish it was.

It's been weeks since that last contact with the stalker, the day I moved in with Christian. But I know better than to think he's stepped out of my life—he's gone much longer than this without making contact. Probably trying to lull me into a false sense of security, waiting so he can catch me off guard. That's why I can never be off guard, not when I'm by myself.

My shoes slap against the sidewalk, my head on a swivel as I practically jog across campus to get to my car. Does he know he's doing this to me? Is he watching from somewhere, laughing to himself, knowing he's worked his way into my subconscious? In the end, maybe this is all he wants. To have power over me. Maybe it's enough to watch me run in the dark, always ready for him to jump out from behind a corner or to grab me from inside a car.

Or to force me into an alley. Bile rises in my throat, and I move faster, barely short of a run. I won't let that happen again. I can't. I'm so close to the car. Almost there...

The sight of paper stuck under the windshield wiper brings me to a stop. Well, my feet stop, at least. The top half of my body is still in motion, and I come within a hair's breadth of tumbling over before getting a hold of myself. My throat is so tight, my heart thudding sickeningly, blood rushing in my ears. My head snaps back and forth, eyes taking in everything around me. Where is he? Why won't he leave me alone?

With a trembling hand, I reach out and close my fingertips around one end of the paper and ease it out from under the wiper.

Then I bark out a laugh, one of surprise and relief. I might even laugh at myself a little as I figure out what was waiting for me. A damn parking ticket. All this over a parking ticket from campus police. The meter expired, and I didn't even think about it—I've been that distracted. "Siân, you need to get it together," I murmur to myself, still chuckling, relief now flooding my system to where I feel weak.

To think, I would normally mutter a few choice words at the sight of a parking ticket, but right now, it's like a gift. I tuck it into the glove box before starting off, shaking my head at how quick I was to jump to conclusions.

By the time I reach the high-rise, though, I have to remind myself that just because this incident turned out to be nothing doesn't mean I have nothing to worry about. Obviously, even living with Christian isn't enough to eradicate the fear that seems to have made itself part of my DNA. I wonder if that's possible—I've read studies and articles related to it in the past, more as a matter of curiosity than anything else. Is it possible for fear to make itself part of our very genetic material? Some researchers believe it is, citing multigenerational trauma that trickles down through the decades. Survivors of catastrophes, tragedies, and the effects on their grandchildren and beyond.

Did my parents' deaths set me up for this? Has this stalker left me unable to ever live without looking over my shoulder again?

I'm so upset by the time I reach the apartment that I'm barely able to fight back my tears. I have to do my best, though. I don't want Christian to worry.

"I'm home." I try to inject as much positivity into my voice as possible, even as I practically slump against the locked door once I've made sure it's secure. I'm safe now. Nobody can get to me here.

And when Christian comes to greet me, looking like a million bucks even in casual clothes, I do my best to put on a happy face. He deserves that. He deserves the best I can give him after everything he's given me.

But it isn't always possible to turn these things on and off at will, is it? As usual, he sees through me.

His smile hardens into more of a grimace before he takes my face in his hands. "What happened? What's wrong?" he murmurs, his calloused thumbs stroking my cheeks.

"Nothing. At least I don't think it was anything." I wish my voice wasn't shaking so much. I wish I could be stronger. "I felt like somebody was following me again. And there was a parking ticket on my car, but I thought it was from him." Now that I'm saying it out loud, I'm almost ashamed of how quickly I jumped to conclusions.

He continues stroking my cheeks, concern stamped across his features. "Did you have the Mace I gave you? What about the knife?"

"Of course. I never leave home without them." They're still in my jacket pockets, in fact. "I'm not used to having them, so it didn't occur to me to pull either of them out. I'm glad I didn't, or else I might have attacked an innocent person." Or macing myself, which would've made for a great story.

He leans in, brushing his lips against my forehead, a gesture that goes a long way toward soothing me. "You're safe. No one's going to hurt you."

"I know. Or I'm trying to know. I really am." I pull my head back to look him in the eye because it's important to me he understands this. "I don't want you to think all this effort you're putting into making me feel better is a waste. I promise it isn't. But when the police flat-out act like you're wasting their time when you're terrified, and you feel like even if something happened and you tried to get help, nobody would pay attention..."

He wraps his strong arms around me, letting me bury my face in his chest and inhale the familiar, comforting scent of his cologne. "You're safe. You have nothing to fear. And now, you're home. And I hope you don't mind, but I made dinner arrangements."

"Dinner arrangements?" I shouldn't be so surprised, but I'm normally the one who arranges these things. I like doing it since he's taking such good care of me, after all. It's the least I can do for him.

He takes me by the hand, leading me to the dining table. Sure, it's takeout—the containers are on the kitchen counter—but he took the time to plate everything up and even added candles to the table. "Aw, this is so nice." It must be the raging emotions I've run through tonight, but now I want to cry all over again. For a different reason, of course.

He cups my chin in one hand, just about knocking the air from my lungs when he smiles brilliantly. "Didn't I tell you everything would be okay? I'll always take care of you. And tonight, it seemed only fitting that we have an unofficial first date. After all, we sort of skipped that part, didn't we?"

I might laugh at the truth of that, but inside, I'm melting. He always knows just the right thing to do. Right now, any fears of a stalker might as well be a million miles away. We are on top of the world together and about to have a candlelit dinner.

A tasty one, too.

"My favorite." I sigh happily, sitting down to a plate of pasta with vodka sauce from a terrific little bistro in the city. I may or may not be addicted to it. And just like he usually does, Christian paid enough attention to know exactly what I would want most. There's a bowl of garlic bread on the table, salad, the works.

"I ordered some of their chocolate cheesecake, as well," he tells me, and my eyes just about roll back in my head.

Nothing could ruin this.

Nothing but a phone call halfway through the meal, when I'm only on my second piece of garlic bread, and there's still half a plate of pasta in front of me. Normally, I would ignore the call at least until dinner is over, but it's from the police department.

And right away, my blood turns to ice. Whose wouldn't? There are certain phone calls nobody wants to get. I highly doubt they're calling to ask for a donation.

"It's the police," I whisper, reaching for the phone with a trembling hand and imagining Kyla lying dead somewhere with a note addressed to me pinned to her blood-soaked clothes.

Christian watches silently while I answer. "Hello?"

"Is this Siân Danforth?"

"It is."

"Siân, my name is Officer Davis. I'm calling to inform you of a missing person's case we've opened. A friend of Cynthia's was scheduled to have dinner with her last night, and when she didn't show, they went to her house to see if there was a problem." His voice is professional, his words clipped. "The house was empty, and the number of newspapers on the front stoop tells us she's been away for a few days, but there were no signs of foul play inside. Has she contacted you at all?"

He might as well be speaking another language. All I hear are words, none of which make sense. Cynthia. Not Cynthia. Is this what he's been up to? Hurting her instead of me? Getting to me through the person who means more than just about anyone else?

I realize the cop is waiting for an answer, so I gasp out a single word. "No."

"You're unaware of anywhere she would run off to? Vacation home, a rental?"

"No, she's never had anything like that." I look across the table and meet Christian's gaze. He's staring at me with a look of concern. "She's never done anything like this before."

"That's what we've heard from everyone else we've spoken to. She's quiet, keeps to herself for the most part, but isn't the type to run off without telling anyone—especially if she made plans."

"Exactly. She's always conscientious." I'm only rambling out words now, hardly hearing myself over the pounding in my head.

"Please let us know as soon as you hear anything, and we'll keep you updated, too."

I appreciate his professionalism, even if it comes off a little brusque. At least it gives me a reason to get off the phone, which is good, considering I can hardly keep my hand from shaking long enough to maintain my grip on it.

"What is it?" Christian asks once I end the call.

I barely have the words to explain. "Cynthia's missing." It's all I can get out before my throat closes. I cover my face with my hands while Christian comes to me, taking me by the shoulders and pulling me to my feet.

I'm in his arms before I know it, and that's exactly where I need to be, because I'm not sure I can keep it together.

"I'm sure she's fine."

"You don't know that," I remind him in a weak whisper. "You don't."

"We can't assume the worst. She's a grown woman. I'm sure she has a life of her own you don't know about."

"That doesn't sound like her."

"You told me yourself you visit her twice a month, right?" He strokes my hair, his voice low and soothing. "Who's to say what she does the rest of the time? Everyone is entitled to a life of their own. She doesn't need to keep you updated on every little aspect, does she?"

"You're right." I wish I felt better, but I don't. My gut tells me something is terribly wrong. She would never run off anywhere without telling me where she was going and when she'd be back. Not after everything we've been through together. I couldn't possibly make Christian understand that since he wasn't there. He doesn't have that experience.

I can only tremble in his arms as fat, hot tears run slowly down my cheeks. "I feel so helpless. Like there's nothing I can do."

"The police know what they're doing. The best thing for you to do is wait to hear from them and be as hopeful as you can in the meantime. She wouldn't want you to collapse under the weight of your worry over her, would she?"

"No, that's true." Yet no matter how I try, I can't ease the pain in my heart. "She's all the family I have. I can't lose her."

"Hey." He lifts my head from his shoulder, his touch tender. "Have you forgotten? You have me now, too. And if need be, I'll be all the family you'll ever want or need. You're not alone, and you never will be again." His lips curve into a gentle, loving smile, and his eyes gleam with warmth. "I don't care how long it takes me to convince you. I'm prepared to spend the rest of my life making sure you understand."

"I'm pretty sure you're too good to me."

"Oh, beautiful girl, there's no such thing." He then casts a look toward the table, and his smile fades. "Something tells me dinner is over."

"I'm sorry. But it reheats well. I can always have it for lunch tomorrow."

"Of course, you can. Why don't you go into the bedroom and make yourself more comfortable, and by the time you come back, I'll have everything cleaned up? How about we take it easy with a movie?"

Right now, I can't imagine anything better—except a call from Cynthia, that is.

But the entire night passes without a call, without a text, without anything. I owe it to Christian to pay attention to the movie, to be present with him. He's doing everything he can to make me feel better, cuddling with me on the couch.

But my heart isn't in it. By the time the credits are rolling, I know just as much about what I witnessed in the past ninety minutes as I do about what happened in class earlier. In other words, my body might have been present, but my brain was miles away.

"I think I'll get ready for bed." I unfold my body before getting up and stretching after having spent the entire movie curled up next to Christian. Do I feel the least bit sleepy? Far from it. I doubt I'll get my brain to quiet down anytime soon. I might not sleep at all tonight.

The alternative is sitting around, making him uncomfortable with my nervousness. It'll be easier for both of us if I'm alone when I'm like this.

Something washes briefly across his face. Disappointment? It's gone before I can identify it, almost like I imagined it. "Of course. You get all the rest you need. I'm always here for you."

"Thank you."

I keep our kiss brief before going to the bathroom for a hot shower. I need to wash this day off my body, at least, if I can't get it out of my mind. Cynthia. My lifeline. Where could she be?

Showering doesn't help ease my tension. Neither does pacing the bedroom floor, chewing my lip, and wringing my hands. Why didn't it occur to me that something was wrong? Why did I assume she was ignoring me? I should've known better. I should've gone to the house and reached out to the police days ago. She could be home by now if I had been a little smarter.

I don't know how much time passes. An hour, maybe? More? Not that it matters. I don't feel any better after having walked what feels like a mile, at least, pacing the hardwood. My insides are in knots, my muscles tense as the panic threatens to rise and choke me. Worse, I might scream just to release some of it, and I'm sure that wouldn't go over well.

I was wrong earlier. I don't want to be alone. The longer I spend like this, the more inevitable it'll be that I go over the edge. I'm dangerously close as it is, teetering on the lip of a cliff.

I need... something. I need to forget. I need to lose myself in something bigger, just for a little while. Just to remind me there's more to existence than pain and loneliness.

Which is why I open the bedroom door.

Which is why I need to find Christian. Without him, I'm lost.

VILLAIN

23

CHRISTIAN

I'm standing in the kitchen. Everything is silent except for the sound of water hitting the tall glass. In the distance, I can hear my neighbor's music and their muffled voices. It's been a tough couple of days with trying to keep up appearances and running back and forth between the warehouse where we've been keeping Cynthia and being home when Siân's finished with school during the day.

I kept my word because hurting Cynthia isn't a part of the plan. Of all the people in Siân's life, that woman is the only person who's protected her, and she loves Siân, despite the secrets she's been keeping from her.

Tony doesn't get it, especially after the bitch shot him. And okay, *bitch* might be too harsh. But she's been the epitome of that, challenging us every step of the damn way. I respect her, though, because I've seen men much bigger and badder crack under lesser pressure. Yet this middle-aged woman has exuded more balls than some of the hardest of men.

Shaking off my thoughts, I suck in a breath and return the water pitcher to the refrigerator. As I bring the glass to my lips, Siân's soft footsteps against the hardwood floors grab my attention. With raised brows, I turn in time to witness her in those tiny little shorts she likes to wear to tease me. Her hair is a mess atop her head, and the collar of her oversized shirt hangs off her left shoulder.

Her eyes are wide, almost as if she's got something she wants to say but is a little too afraid to let it out. Siân glances around the room while running a nervous hand along the back of her neck. Then she takes a step forward and rests her palm on the island.

I lean against the counter, watching her over the rim of the glass. At this point, I'm not even drinking it, but I can see the nerves rattling through her. She definitely has something to say and looking me in the eye will make that harder for her. One thing I've learned about this woman is that she thrives without pressure. Just let her be. Allow her to be herself, and she'll show you exactly who she is or what she wants.

The urge to speak, to tell her to come and take what she needs, is loud, but I hold it in. Her desire is written all over her face and has been all night long. But instead of giving in, she battled with herself and the news of her missing caretaker, probably hating herself for having needs when the woman who's loved and protected her all these years is missing.

"What happened to that rest you were supposed to be getting?" I say after a beat and set the glass on the counter, resting both palms against the surface.

I wait for her to speak, to say or give me any sign of what's on her mind. Instead, she remains quiet and rushes toward me. In an instant, her mouth is on mine, much like it was that day in the front seat of the car. When she's too afraid to speak, to share her deepest thoughts, her body does it for her.

I've waited so long for this moment—for her to give herself to me—to want me, and I won't ever give it up. So I wrap my arms around her waist and turn us so that she's trapped between the counter and me.

I pull back to look at her, immediately recognizing the darkness in her gaze. This is more about her and what she needs to escape than it is about us, but the selfish asshole nature in me doesn't care. Her needs satisfy my wants, and though I know it's wrong, and in some way, I'm taking advantage of her vulnerability, I can't stop myself.

She's mine, and I am hers.

With my hands digging into her sides, I lift her and set her on the countertop. A shudder runs through her once her bare thighs connect with the cold surface. My girl is impatient, pushing the chill to the back of her mind as she cups my face and brings my mouth to hers again.

Her touch pales compared to her kiss. It's soft and that of a nervous woman, but her lips move hard and fast against mine. She's conflicted, unsure if she should give or take. I fight the urge to help and guide her and finally claim her body for myself. That's not what she needs, not tonight at least.

She needs to take charge of this moment and own whatever pleasure she seeks, the pleasure she's been missing out on. So, for tonight, I stifle the beast inside me, no matter how badly it wants to escape. This whole game has been about trust, and tonight, I'll give her that. I'll show her I am the only man she can truly let go with. Teach her the way a queen should be treated and introduce her to a world where what she says goes.

A deep rumble builds in my chest when she runs her nails along the underside of my earlobes. The touch is subtle, but that spot always drives me crazy. My mind races a mile a minute as I think about the things I want to do to her tight little body. And when I feel her pebbled nipples against my naked chest through the fabric of her shirt, I nearly lose my shit.

Even though I hate to put even the smallest of gaps between us, I break away and stare into her sated eyes. "What do you want, Siân?" I ask while skating my fingers over her thighs, enjoying the slight jerk of her leg muscles from my touch.

Siân wets her lips, her gaze darting over mine with confusion written in the lines that form above her brow. "You?" she says it as more of a question.

"No, baby. What do you *want*?" I lean in and trace circles just below her chin. "Do you want to come?" I ask against her flesh.

"Mm," she moans and reaches for my bicep. "Mm-hmm."

I suckle her neck, nibbling her skin and reveling in the soft cries that escape her. "Use your words. Tell me you want to come."

She swallows, her throat bobbing against my mouth, and I fight the smile that wants to make itself known.

"I-I want to come." She swallows again, her spine straightening as she does. "I want you to make me come."

"Good girl," I whisper, and she shudders.

"Say that again." Her voice rattles.

I grin and bring my lips to her ears, sucking the lobe before following her instructions. "Good girl."

She pushes a breath through her nose and squeezes her thighs together at my words, but I use my fist to force them apart.

"What else, baby? What do you want?"

Siân pauses for a moment, and when I look at her, I sense she's afraid to answer me. She looks away, but I grip her chin to keep her eyes trained on me.

"Never be afraid to demand what you need." I scan her face to be sure she understands. "Okay?"

She nods.

I shake my head. "Nuh-uh. Words, beautiful."

"Okay."

"Now?"

"I-I..." She swallows again. "I want your mouth down there." She tips her head toward her pussy, and I'm all too happy to oblige.

"Not good enough."

She squirms with a frown pulling at her brows. My sweet girl—I'm going to corrupt her if it's the last thing I do.

"Tell me you want me to eat your pussy." The deepness of my voice causes a chill to run the length of her spine.

"I want you to eat my pussy," she repeats this time with more conviction.

"Spread your legs then, baby."

She moves at a snail's pace, darting her gaze between my face and my hands on her legs. I help her along, pushing her thighs farther apart and scooting her closer to the edge of the counter. Her body jerks with the movement, and she leans back on her palms.

We both watch as I drag the tiny shorts from her body and toss them to the floor. When we make eye contact again, my breath catches in my throat.

"You're so fucking beautiful. You know that?"

She doesn't respond, but I don't expect her to. That was more for me than it was for her. I let out a hiss when I realize she was bare underneath those shorts. The scent of her arousal hits me in a wave, and it takes sheer willpower not to devour her. I want to savor this, take my time exploring every nook and fucking cranny of her being.

With my brows pulled tight in anticipation, I bring my face closer to her sex while running my thumb over her slit. I don't part her, yet. No, I save that for later. Right now, I want to see how she reacts when pleasure is only an inch away.

I stare into her light green eyes, watching the change of her features, and I continue to run my finger along her pussy. As eager as ever, she pushes her pussy toward me. My dick throbs against my pants, and I reach down to give it a quick squeeze. He'll get to play soon enough. Right now, it's all about her and *taking care* of her.

Siân falls back on her elbows, her sights still trained on me. We make eye contact for a beat before I put my focus between the valley of her thighs. Parting her lower lips, I lick my own with need and determination.

Her clit is already hard and swollen for me, and her sex is dripping. With the pad of my middle finger, I trail her heat from her entrance to her beading bud, coating it with her honey.

"Fuck," I groan. If she's this wet before I barely even touch her, I can only imagine what she'll feel like as she sheathes my cock. The tip of my dick aches at the thought, but I ignore the sensation. I don't know who wants this more—her or me. Hell, maybe we want each other the same.

Replacing my finger with my tongue, I follow the same path, enjoying the taste of her nectar. Sweet, just like her. So fucking perfect, so fucking special. I can't believe it's taking me this long to have her here with me like this. Marco feared for her, and rightfully so, but all I can think about is how much we missed out on. All the years we've had to be apart because her father sent her away, denying me what's mine—denying me her.

My hands swell over her thighs, and I grip her tight and bury my nose in her heat. I inhale the smell of her, locking it to memory. Siân lets out a loud moan when I suck her clit into my mouth, releasing it with a pop.

"God," she lets out. "Oh, my." Her hands find their way into my hair, and she holds me in place while slowly rotating her hips.

"Mm," I mutter. "You taste like heaven."

I spread her legs even farther apart and keep her folds open as I eat her, leaving nothing behind. Siân arches her back the moment I insert my tongue into her tight hole. Over and over, I enter her, all while teasing her clit with my thumb. Our eyes meet when I peek up to watch her reaction, and though brief, the connection feels intense, so much so I feel it down to my toes.

I return to sucking her clit and slip a finger into her pussy. Her walls clamp down around me, contracting as I curve my hand to stroke her G-spot. Siân's mouth gapes open, her head falls back, and her body seems to melt into the granite beneath her.

Rising to my full height, I continue to finger her cunt and plant kisses along her collarbone and neck. And when I finally reach her mouth, she's hungry to taste herself on my lips. Siân cups my face, losing her balance, but I'm quick to use my free hand to catch her and keep her upright.

I continue to finger-fuck her, waiting for her to balance herself before taking her pussy into my mouth again. Loud, sloppy wet sounds fill the kitchen, followed by her cries.

"Shit. Christian. That feels so good," she admits with her head back.

"Yeah? You like me sucking your cunt?"

She nods, then rubs at the back of my head, silently encouraging me to keep going. Luckily for her, I wouldn't have it any other way. Siân pants, and her legs tighten around my head, but I push them open and shove my tongue back into her hole.

Her body bucks, relaxing a second later, and I know it's because she's on the verge of coming. I return to licking her nub, then suck on it and stroke her G-spot at the same time. A part of me wants to stop and shove my dick inside her soaking pussy. If she's going to come, I want it to be with me buried deep. The night is still young, and now that I've gotten a taste, I'm not quitting that easily.

Siân arches into me, her hand still at the back of my neck, keeping me from moving. "Oh. Oh—Christian. Right there. Oh, God, please don't stop. Don't stop. Don't stop. Don't stop. Ohhhhh," she moans.

And I don't. I keep teasing her clit and stroking her spot until she explodes. Her cum pours out around my finger, spilling onto the counter as she clenches me with her pussy. My dick is hard as a rock now, the head throbbing so hard it hurts.

It's not until her breathing levels out that I pull my finger from inside her. I take to kissing all over her, and she's splayed out, completely spent, allowing me to do with her as I please.

"How do you feel?" I ask as I continue to plant kisses everywhere.

Siân stares at me for a moment, words lost to her as she tries to catch her breath. When she does, that dark gleam of desire that she had when she walked in here returns. "I want you to fuck me, Christian. Make me come on your dick."

Fuckkkkk, I groan inwardly.

Scooping her into my arms, I carry her into my bedroom, bumping into shit along the way. I'm so excited to finally be inside her. That girl, who only a few minutes ago was too shy to tell me what she wanted, commands me like a fucking goddess, and it's hot as hell.

I can't wait to be inside her, to feel her come apart around me, and call my name as she does. I want to dirty every single inch of her and brand my fucking name into her flesh. She's mine, and after tonight, the whole goddamn world will know it.

We're so close to living our new lives, and soon enough, no one will stand in the way. Not her fucking friends, not her life in this Podunk town—not even my father. I toss her on the bed, and she giggles while crawling back to the top of the bed. Siân looks on as I grip the waistband of my pajama pants and shove them down around my ankles, her eyes widening at my fully erect cock.

A smirk tugs at the corner of my mouth, and I stroke myself to taunt her. She's probably wondering how she'll take all of me, but I'll make it fit, even if it hurts her. Staring down at her still glistening pussy, her lips that are swollen from our kiss, and then her belly, my mind roams. I picture what she'd look like carrying my seed and make a mental note to get rid of her birth control first thing in the morning. Then I think about how I'll never stand for losing her again, adding another note to look into getting a transmitter. Barbaric, I know, but there are no lengths I won't go to keep her with me.

She will be mine no matter what, and the sooner I remove all other obstacles, nothing can stop us. I push the thoughts from my mind and climb into bed, the mattress sinking from my weight. Siân removes her shirt, and a second later, I'm nestled between her legs. Her velvet heat welcomes me, and my dick jerks as a thank-you.

Not bothering to reach for a condom, remembering the vow I made to knock her up only a second ago, I line my cock with her entrance. I press the head against her opening, but I don't dip inside. Instead, I coat myself in her juices, then rub it over her clit. We both stare between us, watching as I fuck her bundle of nerves to get her body nice and ready for me.

Once I'm sure she's wet enough, I meet her hole again, but she presses her hands on my chest, stopping me. "Wait," she says, out of breath. "We need a—"

Before she can finish, I thrust inside her so deep my balls are tucked against her soft ass.

"Condom." She trails off even though it's too late.

"I'll never use a condom when I fuck you. You're mine. Do you get that?" I pump in and out of her with my nails digging in her sides, and I bring her as close as I can.

I expect her to fight me on this, curse me for entering her without protection, but she doesn't. She gives herself to me, taking me inch by fucking inch. Tonight, I'm gentle with her, straining myself from pounding into her the way I've dreamed about for weeks now. She needs this—soft and subtle—lovemaking. But when the veil is down, I'll rip her apart with my cock, ruining her for any other man.

Siân wraps her legs around my waist, meeting my strokes and taking from me what she needs. Unlike the night I spied on her with her ex, she's falling apart at the seams, bliss written all over her features and frame. And when she grips my dick with her pussy, I know we're both going to get what we want—for her to come on my cock.

Siân tucks her arms under mine to hold me in place by my shoulders. I reach between us, spreading her cheeks apart to deepen my strokes, not stopping until she's convulsing under me.

"I'm coming again. Oh my. God, Christian, I love you."

I tense at her words, but it doesn't stop me from climaxing. My back buckles, and my nails bite into the flesh of her ass as I shoot my load deep into her sex. It takes a minute before either of us can move, and when we do, neither of us comments on the bomb she just dropped. A piece of me wonders if she even realizes she's said it, and the other half of me thinks about what that would look like. I've never been in love before, but maybe with Siân, I can have that. Maybe she can calm the beast that's constantly fighting to be freed.

24

SIÂN

I think I'm having a dirty dream. A dream where Christian is between my legs again, eating me like a starving man. Like he's feasting on me. Heat flares to life low in my belly, reminiscent of the scorching heat that almost consumed me last night, and I rock my hips in search of more friction. More pleasure.

"Mmm…" I moan, giving myself over to it.

There's vibration against my folds, and I realize Christian moaned in response. I reach down and run my fingers through his hair. The sensation is so strong, so real. Like the most vivid dream ever.

Only now do I understand this is no dream, that he's between my legs with his mouth covering my mound and his tongue doing unspeakable things to my sensitive folds. He eased me out of sleep by pleasuring me, pleasure he's still raining down with every lap of his tongue, with every insistent suck on my clit.

He releases it with a gentle popping sound. "I couldn't resist," he growls by way of explanation. "This sweet pussy was calling to me."

"Yes," I whisper back, tugging his hair a little in a silent attempt to make him start again. When I lift my hips, almost thrusting my sex into his face, he chuckles.

"Eager girl." He eases a finger into my channel, then follows it with a second. My back arches, a wordless cry tearing itself from my throat. "You're hungry for what you know only I can give you. Say it."

"Yes!" I cry out. "Yes, I'm hungry for you!" I'll say anything, so long as he never stops what he's doing, tormenting me with each long, sure stroke. Teasing my spot, massaging it, driving his knuckles against me when he goes deep.

"Show me what you want. Fuck my fingers, beautiful." I can only do as I'm told as my body takes over for my brain. Taking what it needs, working for it with every thrust of my hips. "Come on my fingers before I make you come on my cock again."

His filthy words are almost as exciting as what he's doing with his fingers—which only intensifies when he brushes the tip of his tongue over my clit. He works me like he was born to do it, so skilled there's no room for self-doubt or shyness. I don't have to hide from him. I don't want to.

The friction builds, my legs tensing as I lift my hips from the mattress and keep them that way, like my entire body is straining to prepare for my release. "Keep going," I whisper, my head rolling from side to side, fingers tangled in Christian's hair. "Please, baby... keep going..." I'm gasping for air, panting, fighting to reach the finish line. "I'm going to come!"

And when I do, it's with an explosion of sheer delight. "Yes!" I shout, my head snapping back, toes curled. Wave after wave of unspeakable bliss crashes over me, pulling me under where it's sweet and warm.

When I open my eyes, looking down the length of my body, I find him licking his fingers clean, his eyes half-closed in what looks like sheer pleasure. Like I'm some exquisite delicacy he's been craving for ages. Something about his greediness stirs the dying fire in my core to new life. It leaves me feeling sexy and sensual. Desired.

Our eyes meet, and I'd swear his look is darker than usual. Like there's something new behind them, something I've only ever caught flashes of before. It should scare me, that look, but it only makes me crave more. I want to know how far he'll take me.

"You've got my cock throbbing," he informs me in a deep, dangerous voice. As if to prove himself, he gets up on his knees and takes his shaft in hand. Pre-cum drips from the tip, the head dark and swollen. "I'm going to make you come on it again."

"Yes." It comes out before I know what I'm saying. "Make me come again. Fuck me, Christian."

"That's right." He's almost smiling, the expression holding a dangerous edge as he parts my thighs to make room for himself. "This pussy is mine. You already crave the way I feel inside you."

"I do," I admit, my chest rising and falling faster with every breath. Preparing for what's going to come next.

It isn't like the first time. He doesn't hesitate even a second before plunging in, parting my lips, and stretching my tunnel to the limit. That first thrust alone is enough to make my head fall back—he's so thick, driving me to the edge of pleasure and hinting at a little bit of pain, but I like it.

He must sense that, because he withdraws before slamming into me again. We crash together, and I can't help but gasp a little from the force.

"Mine," he growls before driving into me again, taking me by the hips and holding me in place. "Mine."

"Yours," I gasp out before he slams home. This isn't lovemaking. This is fucking—raw, dirty, and I could sob with joy because it's oh, so goddamn good.

"Only I will fuck you," he grunts, teeth clenched, his muscles contracting every time he thrusts into me. "Only me, beautiful. I'll make you fall to pieces on this cock. Screaming my name. Weeping from pleasure." His fingers dig into my hips, and it almost hurts, but I wouldn't make him stop for anything. I want to see how far we can go.

I reach out, my nails running down his chest until he sucks in a surprised breath and rewards me with sharper, harder thrusts that leave me squealing in time with the crashing together of our bodies. "And now that you're mine, you'll belong to me forever. Say it."

"Forever!"

"And one day, I'll take this ass." His fingers dig into me, making me gasp and grit my teeth against it. "I'm going to take all of your holes, Siân. Your entire body belongs to me." I only nod, tensing at the idea but brushing it off. Even now, I know he's saying it because he's half out of his mind with his dick doing the thinking.

My boobs bounce up and down from the force, and I hold them steady, squeezing them for his enjoyment. "Oh, yeah," he grunts. "Touch yourself. Play with them." I do, pinching the nipples the way I've only ever done when I'm alone. It's nasty, dirty, and it seems to drive us both even wilder.

I'm getting close, the familiar tightening coming up fast. "Come with me," I beg when the tension is too much to bear.

He responds by baring his teeth and pummeling me almost brutally until tears leak from the corners of my eyes, and there's nothing to do but scream his name the instant before I shatter, my heart ready to burst from the strain.

He drives himself home one last time, roaring his own release, but I'm too far gone to hear him. I'm floating in absolute bliss, my mind blown, every care and worry wiped away in favor of complete peace.

"Yes, *topolina*." He collapses partly on top of me, his body heavy and sweat-slicked, his breath coming in sharp gasps. "Yes, my Siân." I can only smile to show him I'm okay, still too weak and worn out to do much else.

But no matter how he's worn me out, I can't leave the world outside. Once I've caught my breath and gotten my wits about me, I look toward the phone on the nightstand. "Shit. I'm going to be late for class."

Christian is stretched out on his stomach. "I can't say I'm sorry," he replies, his voice muffled.

I place a kiss against the side of his neck, giggling as I scramble out of bed and hurry for the shower, feeling like a million bucks. Worshipped and adored and craved.

I shouldn't smile at the sight of his fingerprints on my hips while I'm washing up, should I? Why can't I help doing it then? He marked me. He made me his the way he said he wanted to.

And I like it. I liked it at the time, too. Liked the razor-thin edge between pain and pleasure he brought me to. The ferocity of him taking me, using me for his pleasure while giving me more than I thought I could handle. It's like having a sexy secret under my clothes, something only the two of us know about. I won't be able to stop smiling all day, I just know it. Will people wonder why? Let them. I have nothing to be ashamed of.

Though I'm going to be late as hell for class if I don't hurry. Morning sex is phenomenal, but it can put a crimp in a girl's schedule. Especially when she almost passes out from the intensity of her orgasm. Is it always going to be like this? I can't help but hope it is as I grab my jacket and run for the elevator.

Even if it means being moved to confess I love him before I probably should have.

I chew my lip once I'm in the elevator car, watching the numbers count down as I descend. I said it, loud and clear. He heard me. I know he did. Just because he was kind enough not to mention it afterward doesn't mean he's going to forget it, either.

It's not the fact that he didn't say it back that has me feeling nervous. It's the hope that I won't end up driving him away. Granted, his performance this morning wasn't what I'd expect from a guy who's scared to death now that the girl he's screwing is in love with him. Far from it.

But still. Once he has time to think it over today, is he going to feel the same?

I won't apologize. That much I decide while jogging to the car, checking the time on my phone as I do. I should have enough time to grab a coffee before heading in for class—and if I want to stay awake, I'd better. I'm not used to having sex late into the night. Taj was more of a wham-bam type of lover.

Could they be any more different? God, when I think back on how great I believed he was. No wonder he was so impressed with me being a virgin. He knew I wouldn't have anybody to compare him to. The man hit the lottery when he met me. I wish I could take back the time I wasted on him, but that's not how it works. I can only make smarter choices going forward, keeping in mind the pain I welcomed into my heart by overlooking one red flag after another.

Maybe that pain was all meant to prepare me for this new stage in my life. Taj had to happen in order for me to fully appreciate Christian and everything he wants to give me. His protectiveness, his strength, his respectfulness. He doesn't leave me hanging or keep me guessing. I always know where I stand with him.

Heat blooms on my cheeks when another thought hits me. Taj would never spend all the time Christian did to make sure I was satisfied. Please. I was lucky if he got me off at all, much less more than once. Christian pleasured me like he took pride in it. Like his only goal was to make me feel good.

The memory makes me bite my lip to stifle a smile while I'm waiting in line for an iced coffee. I might be a few minutes late at this point, but I can sneak in through the back door and take a seat without disturbing anybody. I've seen people do it all the time—and now I wonder if any of them were late for the same reason I am. Another smile teases its way across my lips.

Until I hear my name called, and not by the girl making the drinks. "Siân. So, you're still alive."

I know who it is before I turn around—her voice is familiar enough after all this time—though I don't know what she's talking about. "Kyla. You've got a lot of nerve saying that to me when I've been trying to get a word out of you for weeks."

Her nose wrinkles, her brows knitting together. "What are you talking about? I've texted you a bunch of times."

"I didn't get them."

"Oh, bullshit." So she's not in the mood to play nice. To think, I was actually in a good mood before this. "I think we both know the real problem, even if you aren't willing to admit there's a problem. It's him. He's the one doing this."

"Would you stop, please?" The back of my neck feels prickly, and I know it's because people are staring. "You're making a scene."

She ignores this. For all I know, she enjoys knowing she's attracting attention. "Sorry if I think it's more important to make sure my friend isn't being abused by some psycho."

"Okay, you've really lost it." I try to laugh it off, I really do, but the sound is hollow. "Things couldn't be better. I mean that. And if you were really my friend, you would know already. You wouldn't play these little games to screw with my head."

She touches a hand to her chest and puts on her most surprised expression. I've seen it before, usually when she knows she got caught lying and wants to fake innocence. She's good at that. "Me? I'm playing games when the psychopath you're living with is the one pitting you against everybody who cares about you?"

"You're the one who started a fight the day I moved out."

"And you know what he did as soon as you weren't there to see or hear us?" She pauses, eyes getting wider, her breath hitching like there's something big and emotional on its way out. "He barely stopped short of hurting me. He turned into a total maniac."

I've given her a lot of leeway over the years. I've let her talk me into things I didn't want to do because it was easier to give in than to argue. I've dismissed the many, many times she acted thoughtlessly, telling myself she was too good a friend for our relationship to suffer because I felt slighted.

But this? Now she's gone too far. "Admit you can't handle me being happy. Really, truly happy. Our friendship only works if you can push me around and tell me what to do. Now, I'm moving on, and you're threatened."

Her face goes dark red before her mouth twists in an ugly snarl. "I'm threatened because he threatened me. He scared the hell out of me, and I had to watch you leave with him, knowing what he's capable of. And no matter what you think, I've been trying to get ahold of you because I can't stop worrying."

"Well, you can stop for good. You don't have to worry about me again."

Her face falls, and for a second, I can almost believe she's genuinely hurt. "Don't say that."

"I'm saying it." My drink's waiting, so I make a grab for it before turning back to the girl who used to be my best friend. "If you can't handle me being happy, you're not a friend, and you never were. Don't bother trying to reach me again—if you ever did."

"You're being stupid right now."

"Yeah, well, considering I ever thought you were my friend, I guess this isn't the first time."

I ignore the outright stares of the other customers as I march past them with my head held high. Let them think what they want. They have no idea what I've been through.

And now I know for sure there's no hope of me paying attention in yet another class.

~

CHRISTIAN STARES at me like we've never seen each other before once I've finished giving him the recap of what went down at the coffee shop, and he's speechless with surprise.

Eventually, he finds his voice. "You know I would never do that. Right? I would never threaten a woman. Especially not your friend."

"Of course, I know that." I throw my hands in the air, feeling helpless. "But I had to tell somebody what happened, and you're the only person I can talk to right now." Since Cynthia's still MIA. I can only hope the police take her disappearance more seriously than they took my stalker case.

"I'll always be here for you to talk to." He pulls me into a tight embrace, sighing deeply once my cheek rests against his chest. Is it any wonder I feel the way I do about him when his touch is like magic?

"I thought she was my friend," I murmur, eyes closed. "How could I have been so wrong?"

"We don't always see what's right in front of us, especially when we don't want to see it." He sounds like a man who knows what he's talking about. Not for the first time do I remind myself how little I know about him. His feelings, his goodness, sure. But his past is a mystery. I don't have the first idea how many times he's been hurt or felt cheated by somebody he cared about. I hate thinking about him being in pain. Who in their right mind would ever hurt him?

He kisses the top of my head before pulling back, craning his neck to look down at me once I've lifted my head. "Have I ever hurt you?" he asks, eyes darting back and forth over my face.

I don't even have to think about it. "Not once."

"Do you feel safe when you're around me?"

"Always."

"So you know Kyla's full of shit? I mean, for real?"

"I already did. I promise." I touch the side of his face, the scruff on his cheeks rough but welcome under my palm. "I know she was making it up to, I don't know, get back at me for moving out. I've never been able to understand why she does the things she does."

She's not the only thing confusing me now. I wish I could put a finger on what's changed about Christian. He's stiff. Hard. When I smile, trying to assure him, his expression doesn't shift a bit. If anything, his nostrils flare a fraction, his breathing bringing to mind an angry bull. His eyes are darker now, the way they were this morning in bed. When the sense of being in danger only excited me more.

I want us to get back to that place. I need us to.

Which is why I take him by the hand, backing toward the bathroom. "Come on," I murmur. "It's been a long day, and I've gotten very dirty.

Why don't you help me get wet—I mean, clean?" I jerk my head in the bathroom's direction, giving him a suggestive grin.

One corner of his mouth quirks upward in a smirk as reality sinks in. "I think I can get you wet. I always do." The deep, carnal note in his voice pebbles my nipples and gets my juices flowing.

By the time I'm naked and stepping into the shower, my lips are slick and glistening with the promise of what's coming.

Christian wastes no time pushing me against the wall. Then he drapes my leg over his shoulder and buries his face in my pussy. As if all he needed was an invitation.

"Yes, baby," I coo, my head falling back against the wet glass. "Make me feel good."

Now, it feels like I'm the one in control. Like I'm the one inviting him to take me. And it's a powerful feeling, bringing him to his knees in front of me. When I bear down on him, grinding against his face, he groans like he loves it. All that does is make me wetter than ever, which makes him lick faster.

I'm so close to coming when he suddenly stops, removing my leg from his shoulder and standing in one fluid motion. "Turn around," he grunts, fisting his cock, his hand a blur. I do as I'm told, palms against the fogged-up glass, and he positions me before driving himself deep inside me.

"Oh, yes!" The angle is heaven, leaving his head stroking my G-spot with every upward thrust. "Fuck me, oh, God, Christian!"

"That's right," he pants against my neck, his tongue sweeping over my wet shoulder before his teeth nip just beyond the point of playfulness. "I'm going to take you in every way possible. Make you feel things you didn't think you were capable of." His hands slide up and down my body, stroking and fondling before cupping my breasts.

"Yes… do that," I beg, almost sobbing from the need to come.

He's got me so close, and now I'm hanging in limbo while he pumps in and out, his balls slapping my thighs every time we crash together.

I reach behind me, holding his thighs, the scar on one of them like a ripple under my fingers. A small imperfection that makes the rest more perfect. "Harder," I beg, so close to the edge I can almost taste it. "Please, let me come!"

One hand leaves my breasts in favor of sliding down my belly, eventually cupping my mound. He only has to stroke my clit a few times before I'm gone, leaning against him when my body convulses in that first deadly spasm before sweet release. He groans in my ear an instant before I feel his seed fill my sex, dripping out of me when he breaks our connection.

I'm still leaning against him, and I can feel his heart hammering the way mine is. "That was nice," I sigh, giggling softly at how quickly it all happened.

"Nothing like starting out the night with a quickie." He chuckles, and I know the night is far from over yet.

VILLAIN

25

CHRISTIAN

Motherfuckers.

I'll kill every single one of them. Every person who dares to stand in the way of what I want is a dead man—*or woman*—walking. I've been patient, biding my time until I can take Siân away from here. And in that time, I've kept from getting rid of her poor excuse for a best friend and her bitch of an ex. But my nerves are wearing thin. They're testing me and trying everything in their power to take Siân away from me.

I can't have that—I won't. Not after the past few nights—not *ever*. She's mine. I lost her once, but never again.

It took all the strength I could muster last night not to punch my fist through the wall when she told me the things Taj and Kyla said to her. And she knew it too, because she also knew exactly how to calm me down. She used her sweet pussy to snuff out my anger and push my thoughts to the back of my mind.

It worked only as long as it took for me to empty myself inside her. The moment we were done, the rage returned. I held my composure and fell asleep with her wrapped in my arms. But as I look over at her lounging on my couch in thigh-high socks and my button-up from last night, I remember the tears and sadness that invaded her beautiful face.

I can feel my muscles quivering under my skin, and I have to flex my hands to calm down. The need to hurt someone is rearing its ugly head, and for the first time in days, I realize just how long it's been since I've partaken in my usual form of release.

Pussy is great, and I love the taste and smell of my woman, but nothing gets my blood pumping like the blood of an enemy. And the longer I sit here thinking about everything, the need grows even more.

Siân—my topolina—is the only thing keeping me sane. Tony's words from the day we scouted out this loft come to mind, and I see now what he was getting at. His concern was the change he saw in me when it pertained to her. My decisions have been more rash than usual, and if I'm being honest with myself, I even move differently. For the longest time, I thought the obsession was enough. The taunting and teasing, the fear I provoked in her were all I needed. I was wrong, and never in a million years would I have been receptive to anything else.

Siân peels her eyes away from her textbook and peers up at me. My heart does somersaults when the thin line of her lips turns up into a smile. I swallow the lump that forms in my throat and push a heavy breath from my lungs. The air scrapes against my insides, a feeling I'm none too familiar with. My skin grows hot, and the quivering I once felt in my muscles has turned fiery at the thought of losing this—of losing her.

This is how it's supposed to be—the two of us against the world, and I'll be damned if another soul stands in the way of that. She told me she loved me, and at the time, I didn't have a response. What was I supposed to say? That I'd never been in love or believed in it. But that's not true. This thing I'm feeling, the nerves, the shortness of breath, the constant need to be near her—it's more than an obsession.

Love.

A fool's errand is how I always saw it. Love makes you weak. It blinds and changes you. Will Siân change me? Can I be the man she needs? Can she heal my black heart? Do I want her to?

The questions run on repeat in my head, and the lack of answers drives me wild. The only thing I'm certain of is that Siân belongs to me, and every other obstacle must go. Kyla, Taj, and anyone else who gets in my way—they *all* must go.

My phone rings, dragging me from my thoughts. Siân glances up at me again, a frown pulling at her brows. Ever since Cynthia went missing, and I promised to use my resources to help find her, Siân has stayed glued to my side, getting her hopes up only to have them crushed every time my phone rings. In the past, I'd enjoy being the one torturing her like this, but now that I've made her mine completely, body and soul, I resent the disappointment that washes over her every time.

Siân rises on her knees as I pick up my phone from the coffee table. She uses her eyes to follow my hand as I grip the device and bring it to my ear. She scoots closer, knocking her books to the floor. Papers scatter under the table, but she doesn't seem to care.

My father doesn't wait for me to greet him before he's throwing out orders. My jaw clenches at his commands, but I relax to keep from showing that side of myself to Siân. She still doesn't know this part of my life; the rage, the violence, the gore, or that I am the son of the man who ordered the hit on her family.

I rise to my full height, still feeling Siân's eyes on me. "This is my father. Give me a minute?"

Her shoulders slump, and she shifts from being on her knees to letting her feet dangle to the floor. *Soon, topolina. It'll all make sense soon enough.*

I step out onto the balcony, taking one quick glance behind me to be sure she isn't watching. Once the door is closed tight and I'm certain she can't hear me, I put my focus on the call.

"Christian, mi senti parlare con te?" *Christian, do you hear me talking to you?*

"Sì. Puoi smetterla di urlare, padre," I say, my tone laced in aggravation. *Yes. You can stop yelling.*

"È ora che tu torni. Abbiamo questioni di cui occuparci," he demands. *It's time for you to return. We have matters to attend to.*

"Sarò lì quando sarò—" *I'll be there when I'm—*

He cuts me short. "Ora. Non lo dirò di nuovo." *Now. I won't say it again.*

I swallow a breath. "Bene. Sarò in Italia tra due giorni." *Fine. I'll be in Italy in two days.*

My father, the bastard, hangs up without another word. I take a moment before reentering the living room. Clutching the phone in my hand, I squeeze it until I hear the screen crack. I was supposed to have more time. I *need* more time. What needs to be done can't be accomplished in a matter of hours. It will take days.

Shoving the device in my pocket, I grip the stone railing and look out at the city. I know how I'm going to do it because I've had it planned for so long, but I don't like being rushed. It leaves room for mistakes, makes me sloppy, and this can't come back to me. Not for the fact I fear the law, but because Siân can never know. She finally trusts me and isn't ready for the truth.

The sound of the sliding door opening behind me alerts me before I feel her presence at my back. She hasn't even touched me yet, but I know she's there, so close I can sense and smell her. It's funny how that works and just goes to show how much she belongs to me.

Her pheromones mix with the cool air, wrapping me like a calming blanket. "Is everything okay, Christian?" Her voice is low.

A sharp breath rips out of me as I slip the invisible mask I've been wearing for months—the one that represents the Christian she knows —back in place.

I face her and say, "Everything is fine." I reach out to touch her, my entire body coming to life when she rests her cheek against my palm. "I need to handle some things for my father, but I won't be long."

Her eyebrows knit together, and her lips press into a hard line. Siân reaches for my wrist to read the time on my watch. "This time of night? Have you heard anything about Cynthia?" She wraps her arms around herself, her eyes pleading for answers I will never give her.

Inching closer, I squeeze her shoulders. "I won't be long, I promise. And first thing in the morning, I'll get in touch with my contacts again. Nothing has turned up yet, but no sign can be a good sign."

The lie comes out way too easily, and unlike any other time in my life, I actually feel bad for lying to her. She's so trusting, and while it's something I love about her, I hate it just the same. It's the reason two people she cares about could disrespect her right under her nose—in her house and everywhere else. If I saw it, I don't know how she never did.

"How? Don't they say if you don't find a missing person during the first forty-eight hours, then you'll never find them?"

"Baby. Relax. You'll see Cynthia again. I swear that to you. I told you I will never let anyone hurt you. That goes for Cynthia too. I'll find a way to reunite you. Okay?"

Siân drops her chin to her chest, her body melting into me when I pull her close.

"I need to get going, but I'll come back to you."

She stares up at me with doe eyes. "Promise?"

"With my life. Let's get back inside. It's a little chilly tonight." I guide her into the living room, locking the balcony door behind us.

Once inside, I kiss her and turn on my heels for the exit, snatching my keys from the built-in bookshelf along the way.

"Christian. Can't you do whatever it is you need to do in the morning? I don't want to be alone."

I give her a soft smile and wrap my fingers around the knob. "Don't wait up." That's the only response I give her before stepping into the hall and locking her inside.

If I stick around and look at her, I'll be convinced to stay, and that isn't an option right now. My father just put a bigger damper on my plans, so shit needs to be handled tonight. The elevator feels like it's a mile away and the ride down to the garage seems even longer.

My footsteps echo through the vast space, bouncing around the concrete walls, and fill the silence with something other than my pounding heartbeat. Hitting my fob, I pop the trunk, then drag my duffel bag toward me. Tonight, I won't be driving. I need to be stealthy and smart. I remove the clothes I wear on these special occasions, along with the lone guitar string, Glock, and knife.

I drag my shirt over my head by the collar and toss it in the trunk, doing the same with my pants before slipping into the black sweatpants and hoodie I keep in my duffel. My car is parked at the back of the garage away from prying eyes, and at this time of night, most of the residents are locked safely inside their homes.

I pull the hood in place over my head, shove the guitar string and knife in the pocket, and tuck my Glock into the waist of my pants. Luckily, Taj is a creature of habit, so I know exactly where he'll be. Walking out of the parking garage, I start north. The direction of his favorite watering hole, the same place I first laid eyes on my Siân.

Every evening is almost the same. He gets off work, has a drink with his friends or coworkers, then heads home for his evening jog before calling it a night. This bar seems to be a place of comfort for all of them, him included. It's there where he feels safe—under the companionship of friends and the lone bartender who runs the joint—but tonight, he'll realize familiarity and comfort don't mean shit when someone wants you dead.

After trekking my way ten blocks, dodging traffic cams, and keeping my head down, I make it to the bar. I can see him through the window, shooting pool and laughing with his friends, and it makes me angry. I don't want his last moments to be happy or fun. I want him to be fearful and realize fucking with—and around on—Siân was a mistake.

I want to take my time and torture him. Filet his skin from every inch of muscle and bone. Maybe even pin his eyes open with needles as I slice off his dick so he sees it. But I don't have that kind of time tonight.

Crossing the street, I hit the back parking lot. When I spot his shiny blue Lexus, I take one last glance around, then pull out my knife. Shoving it between the weather stripping and metal of the door, I pop the lock with minimal damage. Not like it would matter if there were any. Taj is too fucking self-centered to notice.

Just like he couldn't even tell when *my* woman wasn't satisfied after throwing his sweaty body over hers and shoving his dick inside.

The thought alone has my anger brimming, but I don't fight it. Not this time. Away from Siân, I'm on familiar ground. I can fight, murder, and obsess without judgment—without scaring her.

When I open the door, the alarm sounds. Moving quickly, I pop the hood, then round the front and slice the horn's wires. Thankfully, the music and chatter inside are so overpowering, no one seems to notice.

Walking back to the front seat, I slip inside, close the door behind me, and lock it before crawling over the console and hiding in the back seat.

I wait for what seems like hours, my hot breath fogging the windows from the inside, and I'm worried it will put Taj on edge, but when the doors unlock automatically and he slides inside, I realize my earlier thought was spot-on.

"I know, baby. I miss you too. I'm about to leave now and head your way." He starts the car, letting his Bluetooth connect, then Kyla's voice flows through the speakers.

"Why are we still hiding, Taj?"

He slumps in his seat but holds his frustrations to himself. "We've talked about this, Kyla. Siân and I just ended things."

"Exactly. Sneaking around was fine at first, fun even. But she's obviously written us off. She's with that Christian character, so why not just tell her about us?"

"Because it's not the time. Yes, we're over, she and I, but I still don't trust this asshole. And telling her we've been fucking behind her back is only going to push her further away."

"Then what are we doing, Taj. Do you still want to be with Siân?"

He sighs and scrubs a hand over his face. "Kyla, can we not do this tonight? I just want to come over and be with you and get some rest before work tomorrow. Can we just have a calm night? Unless you want to cancel, at which point I'll head home now."

"No," she mutters.

"Hmm?"

He heard her loud and clear, but I see now he's just a manipulative bastard. Is this how he convinced Siân to put up with him for so long?

"I want to see you. We don't have to talk about it."

"Okay, I'll be there soon." Finally, he ends the call.

The plan was to wait—to take him to some secluded area so that his body wouldn't be found for months—but after hearing their conversation, I'm pissed. After all the bullshit they've tried to come between Siân and me, and he's still choosing this skank over her.

They have to go. I was going to spare Kyla, leave at least someone for Siân to have when we start our new life together, but this was the straw that broke the camel's back. Even her life is disposable at this moment.

My anger gets the best of me, and before he can drive away, I pull the wire from my pocket and rise behind him. I wrap the string around each hand, then quickly drape it over his head and cinch it around his neck.

Taj fights against me, his head instantly pushing back into the seat as he claws at my hands. It's a good thing I'm wearing gloves, something I never go without when I'm conducting business.

"Shhh," I mutter to get his attention. "The more you fight, the harder I pull, and you'll never make it out of this parking lot. There you go," I say when he relaxes a little, though he doesn't unhand the string that's now cutting into his flesh.

"What do you want?" He struggles to get out, his breaths labored and shortened.

"For you to stay quiet and drive."

At this moment, Taj glances at me through the rearview mirror. "Y-You."

"Surprise, motherfucker. Now drive," I bark.

Taj flinches and fumbles to reach the push to start button on his vehicle. The car hums to life, and with the tip of my chin, he places his hands on the wheel. "Please don't do this. She'll never forgive you."

I laugh. "That's where you're wrong. She's never going to find out." Placing the wire in one hand, I lean forward and hit the screen on his dash. Pulling up the GPS, I select the marked location I know as Kyla's. "Now drive."

Taj nervously switches gears, and I watch his face in the rearview mirror as he maneuvers out of the parking lot. He's smart. I'll give him that because he doesn't fight. It's disappointing because the fight is the best part, but right now, I'm fine with anything that will make this pass sooner.

We pull into the driveway of the house Siân once shared with Kyla. I order him to put the car in park and kill the ignition.

"I told you she was mine."

His eyes widen as we stare at each other through the mirror, and I tighten the string around his neck.

"I guess it doesn't matter since you've chosen that slut over a goddess. You really are a fucking idiot, huh? I should have known by the way you fucked her. You couldn't even be bothered to satisfy Siân before tucking your tiny dick and fucking another woman. That's right. I watched you, and I know all about your little rendezvous with Kyla in there. Well beyond just tonight. You fucked Kyla before showing up at the club that night, the evening I destroyed your car, and about a week ago on the sofa in this very house."

"It's not what—"

"Shut up," I bark, and he jumps in his seat.

"Please, man. You can have her. I'll never bother her again."

"I know you won't," I say before retrieving my blade and bringing it to his neck.

He tries to use the very moment when I released him for my knife to escape, but he's not fast enough. His throat bobs against my touch, his pulse racing with each passing second. If I had the time I wanted, I'd draw this out, taking my time as I carve him to pieces. Time isn't on my side, though. It has to be done so I can take my woman and return to Italy, where we belong.

"You're fucking sick," he gets out before I pin his head back with a hand on his forehead. Quickly, I run the blade across his throat, smiling as blood spurts from the wound and paints his windshield.

As his gags become nonexistent and his body stops twitching, I let go and slip out of the car. Glancing around, I find the neighborhood just as quiet and lifeless as it always is. Pitiful people, so oblivious to everything around them. The lights flicker on inside the house, and I hunch low to keep from being seen. A second later, Taj's phone rings from inside the car. When I ignore it and look up at the house, I notice Kyla's silhouette pacing the living room.

I stand upright, pull my shoulders back, and make my way to the rear of the house. Using the key I made months ago, I slip past the creaky porch, thankful Kyla is in the front room and unable to hear as I sneak in through the kitchen. Her back is to me as I inch through the foyer and past the table of pictures in the hall.

"Taj. What time are you planning on getting here?" she says to his voicemail.

"He's not coming." My deep voice startles her.

Kyla jumps, sending the phone to a shattering mess on the floor. "W-What? How did you get in here?" she breathes out, her eyes wide and chest heaving.

“I warned you not to test me,” I say, then lunge forward and wrap my hands around her neck.

26

SIÂN

I sort of wish Christian could've waited until morning to do whatever has to be done for his father, but whatever it is must be important if he hurried out of here the way he did. It's stupid to worry about being alone. I'm as safe as I'll ever be all the way up here. Even without him here.

Even so, the silence that spreads through the spacious loft unnerves me before long. The high ceilings and hard floors make for an acoustic miracle or nightmare, depending on a person's perspective. Right now, with every tiny noise echoing and reminding me how alone I am, I'm not a fan.

That's why I turn on the TV. It doesn't matter what's on—I only want the sound, the sense of not being so alone while paging through my textbook. Cynthia always wondered how I could study with the TV on.

The thought of her makes me lose my breath for a second. Why doesn't anybody know where she is? Even Christian, with all his resources, can't seem to find her. I eye my phone, wondering if I should text her again just in case she's been some place with no signal, but a breaking story steals my attention away from her for the time being.

"We have breaking news out of the downtown area," the news anchor announces in a grim voice. "Early reports point to the discovery of a dead body in an abandoned car parked behind what is rumored to be a drug den. The presence of the unidentified male was reported to police earlier in the hour, and by all indications, there was foul play involved. Police are currently gathering information from a witness who claims to have seen a dark-clad figure hurrying from the scene."

And Christian wonders why I don't want to be left alone? Now I wish I hadn't turned the TV on at all. I don't need to be reminded of how dangerous life can be, of how many people are out there just waiting to hurt somebody.

Rather than flipping the news off, I get up and go to the kitchen for a glass of water, then consider taking a shower while drinking the icy liquid. That way, when Christian gets home, I'll be fresh and clean and ready for whatever he has in mind. I can't help but smile a little to myself. He's turning me into a sex addict, but who could blame me when it's so good? Not to mention how natural it feels to be with him that way. Never once did I feel so connected to Taj.

I wish I could stop thinking about him. It feels unfair to my current relationship, constantly returning to the last one. Time will fix that, right? I hope so, since every time I so much as picture his face, I can't help but wince a little. What was I thinking?

Maybe it's the effect of wanting to push the past out of my mind, but all of a sudden, I need to be doing something. Anything. A little pampering might ease my nerves some. A face mask and new nail polish. Once it's dry, I'll take a shower and wash off the mask. Christian's bound to be back by then. I don't want to fall asleep alone.

My beauty products live in a pair of drawers in the bathroom vanity, which is where I head now that my mind's made up. Out of the handful of nail colors available, I choose a pale pink with a pearlescent swirl.

Normally, I'll grab a few Q-tips and a bottle of nail polish remover to clean up any little accidents, only there aren't any Q-tips available.

Christian might have some among his things. I make it a point not to pry into his personal items, but this is fairly innocent. It's not like I'm searching for banking information. What could I find in the bathroom? I open the top drawer and bend down, peering into the back.

Which is when I catch sight of something shiny among a few combs and squeeze bottles of hair product.

It's reflex, the way I reach back to grab onto the shiny object. Who wouldn't give in to their curiosity in a situation like this? Whatever it is, I'll put it back. It occurs to me as I close my fingers around the cold metal that I crave a deeper understanding of the man under Christian's beautiful exterior. I want to know him in all ways.

But this will not help me get any closer to him. Because I recognize the object from the drawer immediately, and it doesn't belong to him. It belongs to Taj. I turn it over in my hand, puzzled. His cuff link. I've seen it countless times, sitting with its mate on the dresser or on my nightstand. What's it doing here? Did Christian steal it? To what end?

I return it where I found it before, slamming the drawer shut. Lifting my gaze, I meet my own eyes in the mirror. This is one of those moments when everything hinges on a single decision. I can either pretend I never found the cuff link, or I can do a little more exploring if only to understand why Christian had it. Who is he? Does he have a habit of stealing things? I should know that if we're going to continue living together, right? The way Kyla deserved to know about the stalker.

That's what decides for me, what sets me in motion. The thing is, this apartment is almost comically clutter-free. No stuffed desk drawers, no mail left lying around. Still, there are places I haven't dared look through for fear of losing Christian's trust.

Starting with the nightstand in the bedroom. I know there are papers in there—I've heard them shift around while he's had the drawers open. With tomorrow's weather forecast echoing in my ears, I walk to the bedroom, my heart now fluttering like a hummingbird's. I'm not going to find anything wrong. I'm not going to find anything wrong.

On top of the pile is a lease agreement. The lease for this apartment. I pick it up, prepared to set it aside in favor of something more telling... except the date on the front page stops me short.

"A few weeks ago?" I whisper, staring at the date.

He didn't say anything about having only moved in a little while ago. He hasn't even lived here as long as we've known each other. It's not a lie, per se, but he hasn't been completely forthcoming with the truth. Is this a bad sign?

The last page is the signature page. *Do you know his last name?* Kyla's question bounces around the inside of my skull as I flip to the back. I'll know it soon enough. I can't wait to rub it in her face if I ever speak to her again.

There it is, written in black ink. Christian Russo.

Russo. Russo? Why does that name feel familiar? It's not unique, really, but there's something about it that makes the hair on the back of my neck stand straight up while goose bumps rise over my arms.

The name isn't the only thing that leaves me reacting that way. If it was, this might all be easily explained away. It's the handwriting that leaves me staring at the page, unblinking. Willing what I think I see before me to be an illusion.

I know that handwriting. I've seen it so many times, haven't I?

Now nothing could stop me from pulling documents from the drawer, flipping through them, my brain recoiling from what's right in front of it. It's the same handwriting on his car lease. The same on a sheet of legal paper that looks like he was writing out a list of things—only it's in Italian.

Italian.

"No. Oh, my God, no." But it's right here in front of me, along with a name I remember hearing Cynthia mention more than once. Russo. The Russo name was big back in Italy. I always had the sense of there being bad blood. I even suspected more than once that she blamed them for my parents' deaths.

But that can't be right. Christian didn't know anything about my family or my past. And if he was one of them, Cynthia would've recognized him right away.

What if she did? What if he—

"No." My voice doubles and triples on itself, echoing through the room. It's not possible. I won't believe it, even if the pieces are finally coming together and everything's making sense. We visited Cynthia, and now Cynthia's missing. He didn't seem very concerned, did he? No, he was quick to tell me he's the only family I need.

My stalker left a note the day I moved. How convenient. How perfectly timed, reminding me why it was a good thing to move out. It was his idea, wasn't it? When I called him after—

My stomach lurches, and I flee the bedroom, launching myself down the hall and into the bathroom once again. This time, I fall to my knees in front of the toilet and retch up everything left inside me. I can't help but remember that night, throwing up in the sink. How I clawed at my attacker's legs when he forced me to... and the scars under my fingers, scars Christian has on his legs...

The name he called me in the alley. Topolina. That's what Christian called me yesterday, in bed, while I was too busy being blissed out and almost unconscious to put it together. That's what he said; I can hear it now in my head. But I ignored it then. I've ignored so many things.

It's all so clear now, bent over the toilet bowl with the situation spreading out around me. The chance meetings that weren't so chance. The first note he left among the pictures. He couldn't come to me after the alley because he was probably wearing the same clothes and knew I'd recognize them—besides, his cologne would give him away. No wonder it smelled familiar when he grabbed me.

And Kyla. She said he threatened her, and I didn't believe her. I was so damn sure of myself. Now I see how he set this up, step by step. Alienating me from her. Silencing Cynthia before she could warn me I'm dating the son of my father's enemy.

My legs are shaking, but I somehow stand. The cold water from the sink doesn't do much to clear my head, but it rinses away the tears drying on my cheeks. I didn't realize I was crying, but it only makes sense.

How could I be so stupid? So blind? He set me up for this from the beginning.

For once, I don't freeze up in fear. I don't have that luxury now. He could come back any second, and there's no way I could pretend none of this happened. I can't go back to the clueless idiot I was five minutes ago.

He'd see right through me. And then...

I'm shoving my feet into shoes, shaking so hard my teeth are chattering, when the news anchor breaks in again. "In an update to the breaking story we brought you earlier, a make and model of the car discovered earlier this evening has been provided to investigators."

I look at the screen in time to see a car that looks a lot like Taj's appear. The car they found at the drug den was the same model as Taj's.

And there was foul play involved, right? Wasn't that what they said earlier?

"No, no," I whimper, tears filling my eyes again.

No, it can't be. This is all a coincidence.

But oh, God, what if it isn't? What if this was always the way things were going to end? And what if Kyla's warning to me at the coffee shop—the warning I told Christian about—means he'll go after her to keep her quiet?

Now I know where I have to go. We'll find someplace safe, the two of us, until I get this figured out. We'll be able to hide somewhere, won't we? No, I'll call the cops once we're barricaded in the house. No way can they brush me off this time.

On the way, driving as fast as I dare down streets that are fairly empty at this time of night, I try to get ahold of Kyla, but it's no use. Her phone goes straight to voicemail.

"Please, God," I call out in the car. "Please, don't let anything happen to her. Please." I don't know if God's listening or if there even is one, but I need all the help I can get.

The living room light is on, visible in the window when I screech to a stop out in front. That's a good sign. She's home. She might be completely unaware of all of this. I hope it doesn't take long to convince her we're in danger.

"Kyla?" The door's unlocked, and I burst through it at a run. "Kyla? Where are you?"

She doesn't answer. She doesn't need to. The sight of her splayed out on the living room floor is answer enough. There's a roaring in my head, and the room spins around Kyla's prone form. Her eyes are closed, and there are ugly bruises on her throat, and I don't know if she's breathing or not.

I would check. I want to—my body moves in her direction.

Until I register the presence behind me. Until a hand covers my mouth, a strong arm hauling me backward until I'm crushed against him with no hope of escape.

I know who it is. It was Christian all along, all of it, including this.

His breath is hot against my ear. "I didn't want you to find out this way."

To be continued...

Thank you for reading Perfect Villain.
This story will conclude in Beautiful Monster

About J.L. Beck

J.L. BECK IS A ***USA TODAY*** AND INTERNATIONAL BESTSELLING AUTHOR AND ONE HALF OF THE AUTHOR DUO BECK & HALLMAN.

WHEN SHE ISN'T WRITING YOU CAN FIND HER SITTING WITH A CUP OF COFFEE, IN A COMFY CHAIR, WITH A BOOK IN HAND. SHE'S A MOM (BOTH KIDS AND PUPS), WIFE, AND INTROVERT.

LEARN MORE ABOUT HER BOOKS ON HER WEBSITE

WWW.BLEEDINGHEARTROMANCE.COM

About S. Rena

S. RENA (SADE RENA) IS A ***USA TODAY*** BESTSELLING AUTHOR OF DARK CONTEMPORARY AND DARK PARANORMAL ROMANCE.

AS WITH HER CONTEMPORARY TITLES, SADE ENJOYS SPINNING TALES THAT ARE ANGSTY, EMOTIONAL, AND SEXY. BUT BECAUSE SHE LOVES A VILLAIN JUST AS MUCH AS SHE LOVES A HERO, SHE ALSO WRITES DARK, DIVERSE CHARACTERS WHO ARE FLAWED AND MORALLY GREY.

VISIT WWW.SADERENA.COM

Printed in Great Britain
by Amazon

13757185R00155